THE BOTULINUM PROJECT

ALAN S. BOYD, M.D.

The Botulinum Project
Copyright © 2020 by Alan S. Boyd

Requests for information should be sent via email to HIM Publications. Visit www.himpublications.com for contact information.

Any Internet addresses (websites, blogs, etc.) and telephone numbers in this book are offered as a resource. They are not intended in any way to be or imply an endorsement by HIM Publications; nor does HIM Publications vouch for the content of these sites and contact numbers for the life of this book.

All rights reserved. No part of this book, including icons and images, may be reproduced in any manner without prior written permission from copyright holder, except where noted in the text and in the case of brief quotations embodied in critical articles and reviews.

Revised edition.

Cover and interior design: Harrington Interactive Media

Printed in the United States of America

To my wife, Lori, for all her years of work, dedication, sacrifice, and support and without whom none of this would have been possible or worth doing. Her editorial assistance has made this book more readable.

To Taylor and Stuart: no parents have ever had better children, not ever.

To Jim Scruggs, father-in-law and man among men.

CHAPTER 1

The past 25 years had been a time of growth for the Florida panhandle. Places such as Destin and Fort Walton Beach had become small boom towns as visitors from all parts of the south flocked to the warm waters and tourist attractions. With Miami becoming increasingly dangerous and Orlando overcrowded, families were searching for out of the way areas to spend their vacation time and, more importantly, their money. The Redneck Riviera, as it had become known, provided both. Initially most of the visitor traffic gravitated to the western part of the panhandle but with its rising popularity the crowds became more problematic and people began to seek out less traveled venues.

Former sleepy little towns such as Mexico Beach and Apalachicola witnessed an exponential rise in tourists. While waterparks and amusement rides had yet to make their appearance, the handwriting was on the wall. The days of immunity to the problems of larger cities and towns were gone. Crime, particularly auto theft, public drunkenness and vagrancy rose commensurately. Restaurant and tavern owners now routinely dealt with problems heretofore largely unknown to them. Many had the local police department on speed dial as calls for assistance became routine.

Florida state highway 98 skirts the northern edge of the Gulf of Mexico and through Port St. Joe. Previously an unremarkable municipality with a stable flock of snowbirds, the increasing tourist trade had prompted new businesses to open, including a Texaco Mini-Mart near the town's eastern edge. Opened in late 1998, it had done a land office business selling gasoline, beer and the ever-popular lottery tickets.

There on opening day was a local boy, Paul Nobles, who weeks before had washed out of a nearby junior college after failing to post a single passing grade. His parents urged him to enter the military but its regimented lifestyle lacked appeal. In an effort to get them off his back, he found work. Initially, it was to be a temporary arrangement but one thing led to another, most notably marriage to his high school sweetheart, and ultimately he remained on the job. His protestations not withstanding, a return to the classroom appeared less likely with each passing season. With his tenure came more suitable working hours. He was now assigned the day shift during the week with nights and weekends off. Around 10:00 A.M. with a lull in business he stepped outside to grab a smoke.

Nobles was midway through his cigarette when he noticed a woman walking alongside the highway. She ambled slowly, which wasn't unusual. Paul had seen many such people during his employment. Most continued down the road but an occasional visitor would enter the store, often asking for a handout and smelling like road kill. Nobles' boss had instructed him in no uncertain terms to send such "customers" packing. If they refused to leave the premises he was to contact the authorities. Fortunately, that had only happened twice. Both times the police arrived in a timely fashion, escorted the person to the city limits and suggest they continue on their journey. Nobles knew he had been lucky. Acquaintances in similar jobs had seen fights break out and one had even been shot at. Realizing he was riding a string of good fortune, he had no interest in pushing the envelope.

As the woman began walking into the parking lot, Nobles crushed out his cigarette with his foot and folded his arms. He wasn't a large man, only 6 foot tall and 165 pounds but he assumed he could head this one off at the pass.

By the time the woman passed the gas pumps, Nobles could see she was a case. Her face, framed by hanging strands of dirty hair, was peppered with small mud drops kicked up by passing traffic. Dressed in an old bathrobe and fraying house slippers she looked almost comical. Protruding between her cracked lips was a dry and swollen tongue.

"Morning," he said flatly. "Something I can do for you?"

The woman continued her slow shuffle towards the front door without answering.

Nobles considered physically preventing the woman from entering the store but thought better of it. When dealing with potential troublemakers he had been cautioned never to touch them. It only gave them a reason to go off and besides, you never knew what you might catch.

He wedged his foot in front of the door. When she reached it she pulled on the handle with minimal effort.

"I'm afraid I can't let you go in there."

The woman turned to look at him. Her lifeless eyes were bloodshot and rimmed with the vague remains of her makeup. Her breath was stale and fetid.

"The lights," she said, her voice little more than a whisper.

"I'm sorry?" Nobles turned his head to hear better.

She shoved her hands into the pockets of her bathrobe as if searching for something.

"The lights."

"Light cigarettes?"

"The lights . . . they hurt."

Nobles had seen enough. Although conversing with some of the vagrants occasionally had it's amusing elements, it was more often a depressing experience. The entertainment factor with this drifter had played out.

"I saw you walking along the highway. Why don't you just keep following it out of town."

The woman took little notice of Nobles' words. She looked around the parking lot as if she were lost. Her lips moved intermittently but no sound emerged from between them.

"Did you hear me?"

Jerking her head in small semi-circular arcs, the visitor continued her surveillance of the convenience store grounds. "Water," she finally whispered.

Although Nobles would have liked to have taken the woman into the store and gotten her a bottle of water, this wasn't his first rodeo. He'd made that mistake in the past and had learned from it.

"If you're thirsty, there's a municipal park just down the road with a water fountain. There's even a covered picnic table where you can lie down and take a nap. It's got a nice view of the water and everything."

The woman gave no indication of having heard him. What little eye contact she made was fleeting, the vacant expression on her face suggesting considerable disorientation. Her conversation consisted of intermittently muttering the word "water." Nobles knew there was little point in continuing their interaction. Two cars had driven onto the parking lot which meant he'd soon be needed inside the store. It was time for Senorita Whackizoid to take it down the road. He gently grasped her bony shoulders, attempting to point her in the direction of the highway.

"Well, thanks for stopping by," Nobles said. An older man driving a new pickup was at the gas pumps staring at the two of them.

"It's been a thin slice of heaven," he continued.

The woman allowed him to redirect her posture but it was when he began to gently nudge her forward that she erupted.

"AAAAHHHHHYYYYAA!!!!!," she shrieked. Her feet moving in a slow backpedal, she turned to stare at Nobles as she slid away. The man at the gas pump flinched at the sound of her scream and stopped filling his tank. Another customer had been removing a toddler from his car seat when she heard the commotion. She instinctively clutched the child to her chest.

The woman's behavior jolted Nobles. He didn't think she possessed the energy to make such an uproar. The noise was unlike anything he'd ever heard and resembled the screams of a wounded animal. He recoiled slightly and steadied himself. She continued screeching at the top of her lungs, her eyes darting back and forth in no discernible pattern. The woman's face began to flush and her lower lip split open.

Nobles was about to step inside and phone the police when the woman collapsed. One second she was hollering at the top of her lungs the next she had fallen face first into the asphalt. His instincts told him to rush to the woman's aid. He glanced towards the man at the gas pumps. He looked equally confused.

"Is she okay?" the customer asked, walking hurriedly towards the scene.

Nobles decided to move the woman onto her back lest she inhale some dirt and suffocate. He was kneeling over her as the man approached.

"She looks to still be breathing," he replied.

"Check her for a pulse."

Nobles felt the woman's wrist and to his relief found that her heart was still pumping.

"Do you want me to call 911?" the man asked. He was already removing his cell phone from his pocket.

It didn't take Nobles long to answer.

"Yeah," he said as he stood. "I think you'd better."

My name is Justin Douglas. I attended medical school in Houston, a place known for its heat, humidity and generally low quality of life. It was quite different from my life in Rotan, Texas where I had grown up. I was a small town boy in the big city and it had taken some getting used to. My parents had been concerned about my living there. They had been to Houston twice and had no interest in their only son residing there. My attending college at nearby Abilene Christian University had met with their approval. In the first place, it is associated with the Church of Christ, the denomination our family had affiliated itself with since time immemorial. Secondly, it was close to home.

I could return whenever I wished and they were nearby if help was required.

ACU was fine with me. Many of the young people from my church had attended there and after talking with the school counselors I learned they had a very successful pre-med program. Most of their graduates had gotten into medical school. I enjoyed my time there but was glad to be getting on with what I wanted to do, namely become a physician.

Or so I thought. My introduction to medical school was unsettling. It wasn't the amount of studying that concerned me. I had always known it would be hard work achieving my dreams. It was the overtly secular environment in which it took place. I had always assumed, wrongly in retrospect, that mainstream society acknowledged the presence of God and His workings in the world around us. It seemed to make the most sense given the complexities and intricacies of the human body. Who would have better insight into these than the people studying them.

What I found, however, was at best an indifference to the notion there was a great creator whose handiwork we were just beginning to understand. In some instances, there was an outright antagonism to the thought God had anything to do with atoms, molecules, proteins and life processes. To be sure, some of my fellow students were believers and, rarely, committed Christians but most weren't and behaved as such. Drunkenness, promiscuity and lying, among other undesirable behaviors, were rampant. It seemed nearly everyone lived a worldly life and I was the odd ball. The professors, while probably more prone to sobriety, were as bad or worse when it came to their views of God.

He had no place in their scheme of things. Everything could be explained under the heading of evolutionary influences.

I wasn't dissuaded but I was cowed. I'd never had to defend my faith. Everyone I had grown up around held pretty much the same beliefs. After a few verbal skirmishes with fellow students on the merits of Christianity where I barely held my own, I shut up. There wasn't much point in entering a battle I'd likely lose. Besides, I was beginning to get a reputation as some sort of religious zealot. I would have to live with my classmates for 4 years and there was no point in making my life more difficult than it already would be. Shamelessly, I left my faith at the medical school doors. My attendance at worship services was scanty at best and as I gradually became disillusioned about the role God was playing in my life, it slipped away altogether. It wasn't my finest hour. I was glad my parents weren't around to see what was happening to me.

Somewhere in the middle of my third year of medical school I concluded my decision to become a physician might have been short sighted. The practice of medicine had a significant number of obvious shortcomings. First and foremost was the schedule. I was aware of the hours kept by the residents and interns in the hospital but had assumed such a workload would decrease upon entering private practice. I had assumed wrong. From my experience, about the only thing that changed was the size of the paycheck and that wasn't enough to balance the scales. At some point I expected to have a real life, not just snippets of it pieced around a call schedule. I needed to find a field of medicine that was both enjoyable and had a reasonable lifestyle.

One day at lunch, I attended a forum put on by the school's dermatology department. It was an introductory session on the specialty and how to pursue obtaining a residency position. I took away from it two important points. First, there were only about 250 positions available each year and with 16,000 graduates matriculating from medical school annually, the competition for them was and would continue to be fierce. The second was that I needed to cozy up to one or more of the department faculty and get involved in a research project. Not only would this allow me to place something of note on my curriculum vitae but would, presumably, result in a supportive letter of recommendation from that faculty member, a requirement for application to any residency program. While my grades were good, so would be those of all the other applicants in the pool. I decided to forge ahead full speed and make a play for a position. It was the sort of "throwing caution to the wind" attitude I was unfamiliar with. The only thing that scared me more was being stuck in a field of medicine I didn't really want to be in.

The next morning I called the Dermatology chairman's office and asked his secretary for an appointment. She informed me he had some time free just after lunch. I took it.

The department chairman, Dr. Alfred Jennings, was practically a fixture in the medical school. He had been there since the third year of the institution's existence and, as conventional wisdom went, had long since burned out. Nearing retirement and stuck in what amounted to a civil service job, he had decided to remain on staff until his pension was sufficient to allow him to do whatever it was he did with his free time. If Jennings had ever envisioned being promoted to a deanship or getting a better offer from a school back east, that ship had long since sailed. His career was over and he knew it.

I arrived at his office a few minutes early to give a good impression. His secretary had me wait in a chair adjacent to a filing cabinet. She said he was taking an important phone call but I heard no conversation through his cracked office door. When he eventually appeared and waved me inside his eyes were bloodshot and droopy leading me to suspect he had been taking a nap.

The room was dark with all of the shades pulled and only a single lamp on his desk providing illumination. On the office walls were numerous plaques and parchments attesting to Jennings' accomplishments. He had graduated from the University of Illinois back in the Stone Age and trained at the National Institutes of Health and Mayo Clinic. As a younger man he had investigated blood proteins found in the skin of persons with blistering diseases. It had revolutionized the diagnosis of such patients and had become a standard test within the discipline. Since that time, however, he'd done very little. I heard a rumor he'd been hospitalized for depression in the mid 1970's. If true, it would certainly explain his underwhelming performance in the ensuing years. Still, he was the chairman of the department and as such, held sway over who was ultimately selected to be a resident in his program. I needed his support.

I'd never been in this position before and didn't know what to expect. For some reason, I assumed he would want to know something about me. Where I was from. Why I wanted to become a dermatologist. That sort of thing. I was wrong. Though reasonably polite, he clearly wanted to get the appointment behind him and on to whatever would occupy his energies for the remainder of the day.

"So you were at the meeting yesterday?" he asked.

"Yes, sir."

"Well, there were quite a few people there so you'll forgive me if I don't recall seeing you."

"I understand."

"And you want to pursue a residency in dermatology?"

"Yes, sir."

"There's not much I have to add about the difficulty in obtaining one these days. Programs, ours included, have an abundance of exceptionally qualified applicants all with very good grades and board scores. What are yours like?"

I gave him a brief overview of my academic standing. Our medical school didn't rank students numerically but my marks would have placed me in the top 15% of the class. Jennings didn't seem very impressed.

"Okay, you should be able to make a decent run at a position then. If you were at the top of your class it might be a slam dunk. However, you aren't and you'll need something to bolster your chances. We encourage our student applicants to do a research project. It will allow you to see what the academic side of our profession is engaged in and it helps fortify your curriculum vitae. Without something like that in your application, frankly, I don't see you being invited to many interviews."

The man was forthright. I had to give him that. Jennings had a project he would toss my way if I were interested. He had made himself clear – declining wasn't an option. So I did what any other red blooded American medical student would have done. I gleefully accepted the work while proclaiming my undying interest in pushing back the frontiers of cutaneous ignorance.

Jennings had been contacted by a drug company 6 weeks earlier. Specifically, Omega Pharmaceuticals. They had been interviewing academic centers throughout the United States and Europe encouraging as many as possible to test and eventually bring to market a product which would make them shamelessly wealthy. The company was relatively young but had been seeking to dip its toes into the American cosmaceutical business. With other companies raking in billions selling facial peels, injectable collagen and various laser contraptions, Omega was eager to follow suit.

Jennings and some of the other faculty had been treated to a lavish dinner at Tony's, one of Houston's premier restaurants, while the company representatives made their pitch. It seemed to have worked. Jennings was certainly taken with the project but I suspected it had to do more with the financial windfall destined for the departmental coffers. He showed me a copy of the cover letter he had received with his packet of materials furnished at the dinner. At the bottom was a name, email address and cell phone number of the person to contact if the department chose to move forward - Jennifer Maddux. The chairman suggested I give her a call. But what was the material to be studied? What was the product they were so high on?

"You've heard of injectable botulinum toxin, I assume?" Jennings asked.

"Certainly," I responded. I failed to tell him I knew practically nothing about the stuff other than what I had read in the newspaper.

"Omega wants to market a topical formulation."

"A topical formulation?"

"An impregnated patch to be specific. Imagine the market for something that can relieve wrinkles without having to get a shot in the face. The return would be astronomical."

No doubt, I thought.

Jennifer Maddux suggested we meet for lunch which sounded good to me. I envisioned being taken to some trendy eatery while she tried to sell me on the project. However, she had numerous meetings during the week and wanted to grab something to go, meet in the downstairs lobby of the Medical School and eat outside on the park benches. It was disappointing but I figured I'd live. We met the next day.

I had some experience with drug detail people. They were often glad handing outside a meeting room as they provided lunch for the internal medicine or surgery residents. They were usually young, attractive and rarely over 40 years old. Maddux fit the bill.

"So, how much do you know about our proposed research?" she asked as we sat down.

"Well, just some of the basics," I said. I was lying. I had spent the evening studying for my upcoming pediatrics in-service examination and hadn't read any of the paperwork Jennings had given me. "It's something that's certain to be quite prominent in the future," I said with an air of importance.

"You got that right," she replied. "This product has the capacity to put injectable botulinum toxin on the back shelf."

"What's it going to cost?"

Maddux looked at me as if I were some grease stained tow truck driver.

"Probably a couple a hundred for a single series of treatments. All of it dispensed through physician's offices. The private practice boys will be lining up for miles to get on our provider list."

"Undoubtedly."

"Six months ago Omega purchased the initial animal model research from a group in Milan. That helped streamline things with the FDA who granted us a fast track waiver for human testing. Penn, Miami and UCLA have all signed on and are beginning to enroll patients. I was sent here to work with UT Houston and Baylor University, hopefully to get them on board as well." She took a big bite from her sandwich. "Which they will, of course."

I was impressed with Maddux. She couldn't have been more than 26 years old and already living life in the fast lane. We talked for about a half hour before she began glancing at her watch. I told her of my interest in applying to dermatology and that I would like to be involved in the research project.

"I was hoping you'd say that," she said with a smile. She reached into her briefcase and pulled out an official looking packet with the Omega Pharmaceuticals logo plastered on the front. It was every bit of 3 inches thick.

"Some of the papers are pretty dry but they should give you background on the drug's mechanism of action. The protocol is what's most important. It goes over in detail what each test site will be doing and what will be expected of them."

I thumbed through the material, noting it contained a mind numbing amount of basic science. I nodded appropriately trying to leave the impression I knew what I was looking at. Hopefully, no decision of any substance in the project would fall to me. I was better at being the gopher.

"Sounds good," I said. "So do you want me to call you?"

"No, just get in touch with Dr. Franklin, she's the point person at UT."

I swallowed hard. "Dr. Franklin?" I asked.

"Yes," Maddux answered. "Dr. Lillian Franklin. You do know her don't you?"

Oh, yeah. She had given some of the dermatology lectures to our class during the second year of medical school. A short, frumpy woman she had been married twice, or so the rumor went, and had buried both of her husbands. After the first ten minutes of her talks one could understand why. The poor fellows were probably thrilled to have passed on. She had caustically dressed down one of my classmates for asking what she considered a pointless question. No one bothered to raise their hand again. I would have rather done research with Joseph Mengele.

"Yeah, I know her," I said. "I mean, I've heard her speak before. She's the faculty sponsor for this research?"

"We were thrilled to get her considering her busy schedule. Rated really top notch in the field."

"Okay. I'll get in touch with her." What else was I going to say?

The remainder of the week was devoted to studying and preparing for various examinations looming on the horizon. When I had procrastinated as long as possible I walked up to the dermatology department secretary and asked if there was some free time on Dr. Franklin's schedule.

"What for?" the woman asked flatly. She'd obviously dealt with medical students before.

"I need to speak with her about the Omega research project. The rep for the company and I had lunch and asked me to . . ."

"Got it," she interrupted. She looked over a computer printout of Frau Franklin's schedule.

"She has some time now. You want it?"

"Right now?" I had been hoping to delay the inevitable a bit longer.

"Yes, right now," came her impatient response.

"Well, alright. Now would be great."

The secretary picked up the phone and punched in a series of numbers. I could hear the grating sound of Dr. Franklin's voice from the receiver. It could melt rock.

"She's expecting you," the woman said as she went back to her typing.

"Thanks," I said politely. Never get on the bad side of the department secretary I reminded myself. Or at least that's how the conventional wisdom went. I walked down the hall to Dr. Franklin's office and knocked on the closed door.

"Enter," said someone on the other side.

I opened the door half expecting to find her wearing a black cape hovering over a large metal cauldron.

"Dr. Franklin?" I asked.

"Yes," she answered without looking up. On her desk were piles of papers and medical journals. Actually, the whole office looked like a small hurricane had come through. I was at a loss as to how she ever found anything.

"I'm Justin Douglas, one of the third year medical students. Dr. Jennings suggested I . . ."

"Have a seat," she commanded, motioning to one of the chairs in front of her desk.

I did as I was instructed.

"Dr. Jennings told me you'd probably be stopping by. I'm just putting the finishing touches on this grant so if you'll give me just a minute I'll be right with you."

"That's okay. Take your time." After all, what else did I have to do today anyway?

Lillian Franklin had been in the department for over 15 years. Originally from Massachusetts, she had done her undergraduate work at Dartmouth and her medical training in Seattle. Known for her prodigious work ethic, she was one of the most published authors in dermatology circles over the past decade. With interests in at least half a dozen aspects of the field, she had been on the short list for several department chairmanships in the country. Until she interviewed there, that is. Apparently, her demeanor was as annoying to others as those at UT Houston. After being passed over at the University of Chicago she realized she had risen as far as she was going to and made peace with her fate. Dr. Jennings had promoted her to full professor with tenure as a gesture of goodwill and to keep her from bolting into private practice. She'd not been seriously looked at for another academic position in the past three years. The dermatology residents kept out of her way and tried to muddle through as best they could while in her clinics.

After about 10 minutes, she set the paperwork aside, removed her glasses and rubbed her eyes.

"How much do you know about this project?"

"I've looked over the packet Miss Maddux gave me," I answered with a smile.

"You met Barbie?" she asked caustically.

"We had lunch earlier this week."

"What an idiot," Franklin spat out. "Thinks she knows something about dermatology and basic science research because she attended a few company meetings. Still, the firm does have a lot to offer."

Meaning money I surmised.

"I went to Scottsdale for Omega's kickoff seminar about the product," she said as she cleaned her glasses with a tissue.

Lucky stiff.

"The prospectus looked acceptable. Not great, but good enough to get past the morons at the FDA. It would never have passed through the NIH, I can tell you that," she said gesturing to one of the stacks of paper on her desk.

Well, of course not.

"What the project needs is a scut monkey."

There it was. The time honored term used to describe someone occupying the lowest position on the totem pole. Designated to do all the grunt work and receive little, if any, credit.

"You up to it?" she asked.

"Absolutely," I responded brightly. "Sounds like a real opportunity."

Franklin stared at me blankly.

"Uh huh. Well, anyway, since no one else has applied for the job, I guess it's yours."

What a ringing endorsement.

"So when do I start?" I asked, almost afraid of the answer.

"Now," she said. "See that thing in the corner?"

I looked in the general direction she was pointing. Near the door was a large cardboard box with the name Omega Pharmaceuticals on it.

"That contains the files of about 25 people, mostly women, who answered an advertisement in the newspaper. Supposedly they are interested in being test subjects. Also in there is a list of exclusionary criteria. You need to contact each prospective subject and determine their qualifications. There is also a template for making notations about each phone conversation. It's pretty much cookbook so even a medical student can handle it."

Her warmth was giving me the vapors.

"As you might imagine, Omega is interested in getting this up and running like yesterday so you'll need to have gone through all the names by this time next week. Bring it back to me then," she said. "What rotation are you on?"

"Pediatrics," I answered.

"Well, then it shouldn't be too difficult for you to get it completed on time."

I got the feeling I could have said I was about to undergo a liver transplant and she'd have said the same thing. I walked to the box and picked it up. It was heavy. When on earth was I going to find the time to do all this?

"Next week then," Franklin said as she went back to working on her papers.

CHAPTER 2

In the ensuing 7 days I was on call in the hospital twice and too tired to carry on much of a conversation, hampering my efforts on the charts. I did manage to get out of the hospital early on Sunday and spent the rest of the day calling people on the list. Most were acceptable candidates, without the exclusionary conditions of any neurological problems, heart disease or diabetes. Still, slogging through the list of questions was drudgery. Some of the women recited in painfully exquisite detail their entire medical history replete with family dynamics and political commentary. By Tuesday, I had completed all but 5 so I brought them with me to the hospital hoping for a chance to call some prospects during the day. Before an afternoon conference, I found an empty hospital room on the cardiology floor and finished the job. Hopefully, meeting this deadline would gain me some points with Franklin.

On Wednesday, one week to the day, I knocked on Dr. Franklin's door, box in hand to tell her I had completed my mission.

"Did you get through them all?" she asked.

"Yes ma'am," I answered respectfully.

"Good. There's the next set," Franklin responded, pointing to an identical container in the same corner of her office.

I looked at the box and then back at her. "There's more?" I inquired.

Franklin looked over the top of her glasses at me. "Of course there's more! We have to enroll 75 patients. The first box only had 25 names and I'm assuming some of them didn't qualify. Am I correct?"

"Well, yeah," I said sheepishly.

"So, there's more to do, isn't there?"

"I guess there is," I said, trying not to let the disappointment show in my voice.

"See you next week then," Franklin said as she waved good-bye.

I set my box on the floor, picked up the new one and walked out the door.

Gary Page strode into the 5th floor boardroom of Omega Pharmaceuticals corporate headquarters in Miami. Fresh from a three day excursion in the Caribbean aboard his 48 foot cabin cruiser he was tanned and rested. Only 46 years old, he appeared younger than his age but then, he was a frequent visitor in his plastic surgeon's office. Page had grown up in Boston, Massachusetts. His father was an attorney in a large Boston firm with a reputation for both his legal acuity and extramarital affairs. Gary's mother lived the comfortable and pampered life on her husband's earnings either oblivious to his infidelities or too drunk to notice. The family owned homes in Boca Raton, Florida and Telluride, Colorado which she frequented in season for weeks at a time. Gary had been sent to boarding school in New Hampshire at Phillips Academy. His visits back home became less frequent over the years as there was little reason to return. His father was never around and even If his mother were at home, she was usually too inebriated or self absorbed for much interaction. Gary had seen the handwriting on the wall years earlier. His parents were more than adequate providers, but emotionally unavailable. He was on his own.

Not surprisingly, Gary fell into the typical traps, drug and alcohol abuse with a smattering of minor criminal offenses during his time at Phillips. He was on academic probation for much of his tenure and twice his father was summoned from Boston to speak with school administrators about impending suspension. Gary learned valuable lessons from his father during those visits, namely that throwing money at a problem could, in certain, cases, make them disappear.

Gary's parents had hoped he would attend an Ivy League school but his grades were so poor no amount of influence could make that happen. His father wanted him to enter the legal profession. By the time of Gary's graduation, he had such an ingrained enmity for the man that following in his footsteps was out of the question. The only course at Phillips which had interested him was chemistry. His parents bought him an upscale condominium in Boston while he attended a small college in Braintree.

Initially, he picked up his behaviors where he had left off. One Friday night during his first semester he and an acquaintance from across the hall had attended a party at an upscale condominium complex within walking distance. They had left separately but in similar conditions, namely bombed out of their minds. At 6 A.M. the next morning Gary was awakened by someone pounding on his door and screaming for him to get up. It turned out to be his neighbor's girlfriend who was unable to awaken her sleeping boyfriend. Page ran into the condo to find his friend cold and motionless in bed. An autopsy later revealed alcohol poisoning. It was a wakeup call he heeded. Page put his partying days behind him, focused on his studies and graduated on time with an overall B average.

But what next? Teaching was out of the question. Not only did he not have the patience for it, the compensation was unacceptable. Industry? That was a possibility. The money would be steady and the benefits good but it would mean pursuing additional degrees. At least another 8-10 years in the trenches and all of it in the laboratory. Not something he saw himself doing. Chemistry had been interesting but the prospect of becoming a "company man" didn't suit him. He may have left some of his more self-destructive behaviors behind him but it didn't mean he was ready for the suit and tie world.

Three days after graduation, Page was packing for a week-long vacation in the Cayman Islands when his phone rang. It was his mother. From the sound of her voice, she either had been drinking or crying or both, a not uncommon scenario with her phone calls. The night before, his father didn't return home from work. His mother assumed he was spending the night in the law firm's downtown apartment. When Gerald Page failed to appear in his office the next morning, his secretary became concerned and sent a security guard to the apartment. The law firm's managing partner was found face down on the floor, dead from a massive coronary. He was 54.

Gary cancelled his vacation and began the unpleasant task of making funeral arrangements. He and his father had never been close and his passing evoked little in the way of emotion.

Still, he was well respected in his profession, a fact attested to by the large turnout at his service and the deluge of condolence cards and flower arrangements which arrived at the Page home.

Three days after the funeral, the family's attorney came to the house to visit Gary and his mother. He knew better than to show up before 10 A.M. when Mrs. Page would still be sleeping or passed out from her nightly appointment with a vodka bottle. He arrived just before noon telling the maid Gary and his mother were expecting him.

The three met in the library, Mrs. Page wearing sunglasses despite the dark atmosphere of the room. The attorney, a long time family friend named Felton Whiteaker, kept the proceedings short. He asked them to sign a few papers and promptly got on with the reading of the will. It didn't take long. Mrs. Page received all the properties and a substantial annuity to cover upkeep on the family's homes and her day to day expenses. Whiteaker realized the woman had few outside interests aside from drinking and shopping but there would be sufficient income to allow her to continue those pursuits. It was hard to tell from her demeanor, but she seemed satisfied with what she had received. Besides, there was little reason to protest. Overall, she had been a marginal wife, her main contribution to the marriage being providing her husband with a son and allowing him to pursue his work and affairs of the heart. She had stayed out of the way and for that she was being handsomely compensated.

Gary Page knew next to nothing about his father's finances apart from the fact he was loaded. It turned out, he was more loaded than either he or his mother realized. Early in his career, Gerald employed the services of an accountant and tax attorney who funneled large sums of money into shrewd investments. Over the years, these had grown exponentially and fine tuned such that Gary Page was set to receive a lump sum of nearly 30 million dollars, most of it without any substantive tax liability.

Gary was stunned. He had always known his father was wealthy but had no idea he was worth that sort of money. While the scenario of new found riches bounced around in his brain, Whiteaker sagely counseled that the capital should be left where it was and not wasted in a spending frenzy. Gary agreed. He now had enough money to live comfortably for the rest of his life. The decision of what to do with his college degree seemed a distant memory. Thirty million dollars gave him the time to consider all possibilities.

Several weeks after his father's funeral, Gary had dinner with a classmate, John Pennington. Pennington had a cousin working on Wall Street who had told him about a startup biotechnology company he had heard of. The CEO was searching for people with biochemistry backgrounds and, more importantly, investors. Pennington's cousin knew his financial resources were limited but he might be interested in working in the laboratory. Pennington met with the CEO and was impressed. At dinner, he brought the subject up with Page. Having no other irons in the fire, Gary agreed to talk with him.

Pennington introduced the two over drinks at a local bar. The company's production plans were intriguing. One problem existed, however. Capital. Jerry Fields didn't have much of it and he was scrounging for investors. Page, on the other hand did. How much did Fields need? The man quoted him a figure. Page said he'd think about it.

The next day, Page contacted Felton Whiteaker about the proposal. He agreed to check into the matter. Within the week, he phoned Page with his findings. By nature, Whiteaker was a cautious man and not prone to recommend speculative investments haphazardly. However, nothing he found aroused his suspicions and the amount of money in question was only a modest fraction of Page's net worth. He cautioned him about the risks involved but essentially gave him the green light to proceed. Page called Fields that afternoon telling him he was in. Fields was delighted. As things turned out, it was a well timed investment. Page seemed to have his father's flair for schmoozing and with his background in chemistry, he was well suited to promote the company's products to larger pharmaceutical interests. He oversaw some of the research and development aspects of the operation but was largely responsible for field operations. The company grew steadily. After 15 years the company had developed and taken to market 7 different products, mostly chemotherapy agents. They were making serious money.

One day on his way to work Jerry Fields suffered a massive coronary. So widespread was the damage to his heart muscle, he was put on a transplant list. His days with the company were over. Page offered to buy him out. Fields readily accepted. A few months prior to his 40th birthday, Gary Page assumed the helm of Omega Pharmaceuticals.

"Good morning everyone," he announced, taking his seat at the head of the table. Perfunctory greetings were exchanged as the attendees ceased their conversations and began to pay attention. Page motioned to his assistant, Stephanie, who handed him a leather briefing folder. He opened it and glanced at the itinerary.

"Oh, yes. The patch study," he said with feigned surprise. "I'd almost forgotten."

Gentle chuckles arose from the meeting attendees. The new product in the corporate pipeline had been his consuming interest during the previous 6 months and it was no secret Page was placing a lot of stock in its success.

"So where do we stand?" He began rolling up his sleeves, an indication it was time to get down to work.

One of the young men at the end of the table spoke. "Well, the lab in Ireland is almost ready. The technicians are top notch. I've spoken with the site manager daily over the past few weeks. He assures me everything is on schedule. They're set to begin their preliminary cultures by week's end. Assuming everything goes as planned they should be ready for full scale production within 4 weeks."

"And the testing?" Page inquired.

"The protocol is in place and has been reviewed by 3 separate consulting firms", a woman on his right interjected. "With the names on the letterheads, getting it past the FDA shouldn't be too difficult."

"Ah, yes," Page said as he took a sip of his coffee. "The ever blessed oversight of the feds. I assume we have a good idea who's on the committee?"

"Yes, sir," came the response from another minion. "My understanding is that the panel overseeing our research is largely unchanged from the seating of 6 months ago."

"Have we 'contacted' them?"

The young man smiled. "We have. I'm arranging for sizeable donations to their universities. Endowed chairs, that sort of thing. I doubt we'll get a rubber stamp. They'll have to find something they don't like. However, any significant obstacles are unlikely. Ironing it out and resubmitting it will only be a matter of a few weeks. After that, we should be good to go."

Page was pleased with what he was hearing, although it wasn't anything he didn't already know. The botulinum patches would be a unique product on the market and one that would swell Omega's coffers. He had the best and brightest of his staff working on the project and they knew of his keen interest in their progress. The key, in part, would be pushing ahead as rapidly as possible. One thing Page had learned in this business was that although haste occasionally makes waste, it also makes money. His only concern was circumventing any obstacles in his way and pressing forward with all due speed, both of which he excelled at.

The end of my pediatrics rotation allowed me a week to devote to the second, and eventually the final box of patient applications. Using all my free time on such a project wasn't what I had in mind for my vacation but I assumed in the end it would be worth it. I took most of the paperwork to the medical school, using the dermatology library as my base of operations. It allowed me to focus on what I was doing without the distractions inherent to my apartment as well as raising my profile within the department. I ran into Dr. Franklin nearly each day informing her of my progress. She appeared largely nonplussed and offered no compliments on my diligence.

The task of interviewing the men and women in the dossiers wasn't all consuming allowing me ample opportunity to look into the background of the research itself. The library contained dermatology journals and textbooks which provided sufficient information. When a particular periodical wasn't available I walked to the medical center library and searched for what I needed. What I learned was actually quite interesting.

The botulinum toxin protein had been known about for decades if not centuries. A waste product of the bacteria *Clostridium botulinum,* it's typically found in spoiled foodstuffs, including canned vegetables and meats. Being tasteless and odorless, victims are usually unaware a problem exists until paralysis begins to set in. The muscles responsible for breathing are affected and death by suffocation follows shortly thereafter. Not pretty, but quite efficient.

In the early 1970's, experimentation with the molecule in animal models began. In exquisitely small doses it exerted a relaxing effect on the muscles into which it was injected. When combined with stabilizing compounds, a timed release formulation was obtained leading to sustained paralysis of the treated muscles. Initial testing in humans began in Europe. The results were spectacular. Despite the occasional side effects of temporary muscle paralysis, headaches and bruising, after fine tuning the dosing regimen, the use of botulinum toxin became wildly popular. Patients were willing to pay extravagant sums of money, all in cash of course, for a more youthful appearance. Market forces would eventually demand a topical delivery method, thereby eliminating the drawbacks of needle injection.

On Thursday, when I had completed the last of the paperwork, I knocked on Dr. Franklin's door.

"What?" she replied.

I didn't know whether to open the door and let myself in or yell through it. I opted for the latter.

"It's Justin Douglas, Dr. Franklin. I'm done with the last of the applications."

"Enter," Franklin yelled.

I set the box on the floor and turned the door handle. Franklin, as usual, was sitting at her desk surrounded by piles of papers.

"All done?" she asked without looking up.

"Yes, ma'am," I answered. "Do you want it with the others?"

"Yeah." Franklin removed her glasses and rubbed her eyes. "Did the secretary get in touch with you about Saturday's meeting?"

She hadn't but that wasn't surprising. After all, I was at the bottom of the food chain.

"No," I responded.

"Well, there is one. Jennifer Maddux wants to go over the paperwork you generated and get an idea of how many patients we'll have in the study. It's at 8:00 A.M. here in the department library. Shouldn't take more than the morning. I assume you can make it?"

Of course. After all, I have no other life. I live to serve others.

"Sure," I said as I removed myself from her office. "I'll see you then."

Omega Pharmaceuticals' laboratory in Dublin was situated in a small town 10 kilometers beyond the city limits. Housed in an old warehouse, it bore a nondescript placard above the front door identifying itself as a chemical company. Several years earlier, a laboratory in Munich under contract with Omega had been vandalized by an animal rights group. Nearly a million dollars of damage had been done and the company had learned an important lesson. Keep a low profile.

Within the building were two large rooms. The first was dedicated to growing the bacteria in large quantities. With it came its unique product, botulinum toxin, or btox as it was known on the shop floor. It was that protein to which the second room dedicated its efforts - extraction and purification.

Along one wall were work stations for infusing the protein into a gel-like matrix and assembly into patches.

In charge of the plant was a biochemist named Terry Mac-Gregor. Originally born in Scotland, he had attended the University of Edinburgh before obtaining his PhD at the University of Wisconsin. When the headhunters for Omega Pharmaceuticals began putting out feelers, MacGregor's name was mentioned more than once. With a downturn in Europe's pharmaceutical industry, MacGregor had taken a job near Manchester, England. It wasn't in his field, toxin biology, but it paid the bills. His wife, however, hated the place and made it known she would be more than happy to leave at a moment's notice. The thought of residing in sunny, southern Florida appealed to them both.

After reviewing the prospective applicants Page phoned MacGregor. Within 5 minutes he knew this was the man for the position and offered him the job. The Scotsman accepted on the spot. But there was a hitch. Page needed someone with know-how to get the plant in Dublin up and running. Before he could re-locate to the tropics, he would have to move to Ireland and oversee the startup. It wasn't exactly what he wanted to hear, but it was better than doing industrial inorganic chemistry. Either way, he was thrilled to be leaving Manchester.

MacGregor's expense account was seemingly limitless. He contacted Omega's accountants almost daily who rubber stamped his requests. Two weeks after taking charge of the project, equipment began arriving at the laboratory. Calibrating the machines went smoothly and MacGregor earned a small bonus when the job was finished ahead of schedule. All that remained was to obtain the starting materials and begin production.

The meeting on Saturday morning was an eye opener. Jennings, Franklin, Maddux and one of the third year residents were there. I had seen the resident around the department offices during my week spent at the library. His name was Galen Hart and he was from Chicago. He was also a self-absorbed narcissist. His father was a prominent dermatologist, having trained at U of C before going into private practice at a swanky office on the north shore. Somewhere along the way he had worked with Jennings and the two of them had kept in touch over the years. A marginal candidate at best, Galen called in every marker he could think of to land a residency. It worked. In return for his position, he agreed to do a year of research in the department following his internship. He got along reasonably well with the other residents but clearly no great love abounded for him. I was about to find out why.

The first order of business was Maddux giving an account of where the project stood. That took about 15 minutes and to her credit, she was succinct. When she was done Jennings thanked her.

"So where are we with the enrollments?" Maddux asked.

I knew better than to open my mouth. I was young but I wasn't stupid.

"We have 65 patients who have met the criteria," Franklin announced. "They've all been contacted and are ready to begin."

There was no mention of my part in the matter. Big surprise.

"Excellent," Maddux said as she wiped cream cheese from her mouth. "My understanding is that the drug will be ready for shipment in 2 weeks. You can begin dispensing it after our final site check. Where are you planning on doing the patient visits?"

"We have some rooms and a nurse specializing in drug studies already reserved. It will be in our clinic space across the street," Franklin responded. "Julie's experienced and very good with patients. I emailed you a copy of her CV last week."

"Right. Right. I remember seeing that," Maddux said. "She's certainly the sort of person we had in mind when we were looking for someone to bird dog this. I don't see any problem there. Who is going to do the grunt work?"

"We have Dr. Hart," Jennings said motioning towards the resident. "And a medical student, Justin Douglas who will be helping. I believe you've met them both."

I smiled and waved my hand slightly.

"I've looked over the protocol and it seems appropriate," Hart interjected. "I have a few suggestions about how we might tighten up the patient visits so that they don't disrupt the flow in clinic. Also, the proposed statistical analysis has some flaws which will need revision."

Maddux peered over her glasses at the resident. "Right," she said flatly. "I think we'll keep the protocol as it is." If the rebuke stung Hart didn't seem to show it. Probably not smart enough to know when he's been taken off at the knees, I assumed.

The meeting ground on for another hour, comprised mostly of technical talk about what to do if a patient became ill and the like. Just when I thought things were going to be drawing to a close and I might be able to salvage what was left of my Saturday, the chairman piped up with the question of the hour.

"Miss Maddux," Jennings said with a professorial tone to his voice. "Forgive me for broaching this subject . . ." The drug rep broke out into a huge grin. "But can you give us some idea of the reimbursement our department can anticipate? I realize you may not have all the figures at your disposal, however we are approaching the end of the fiscal year. Any additional monies will ultimately affect our final balance."

Maddux allowed Jennings to complete his question before answering. "When we initially spoke on this matter I threw out some preliminary figures given to me by the accounting department at Omega. Yesterday they emailed me the final numbers. I was planning to contact each of the sites with the good news but since we're all here, I'll tell you in person. Name universities with departmental status will receive a $35,000 honorarium for allowing Omega Pharmaceuticals to mention their institution as a test site. Obviously, UT Houston would qualify under that designation." Maddux was strolling back and forth in front of a portable lectern at the end of the table. "In addition, for each patient enrolled, the reimbursement is $2000 and if they complete the course of treatment that figure rises to $8,000."

Franklin's eyebrows lifted. It was the first time I had seen her genuinely impressed with something, presumably no easy task.

"So if we manage to get most of our patients through the study our department will receive over half a million dollars?"

Maddux feigned ignorance. "I haven't crunched the numbers but that would seem about right."

Jennings cleared his throat. "Well, that is certainly a substantial incentive for our participation. I think I can speak for the group in saying we are definitely interested in proceeding."

"Excellent," Maddux retorted. "Omega Pharmaceuticals is thrilled to have you on board."

The remainder of the meeting took only 20 minutes with Jennings and Franklin lavishing praise on the great work the drug company had done in putting the project together. When the group broke up Franklin pulled me aside.

"You heard what Jennifer said about the time frame for the study, didn't you?"

"That the drug would be ready in 2 weeks?" I asked.

"Right. That means we need all our ducks in a row. On Monday, I want you to get with Julie in the clinic and begin outlining who comes in when, etc. She'll coordinate all of this with Maddux." With that she turned to walk down the hall to her office. She had gone only a few paces when she whirled around. "By the way, are you still on Pediatrics?"

"No, ma'am. I finished last week. Monday I start on psychiatry."

"Where? Here?"

"I'm not really sure where I'll be doing my rotation. I requested St. Joseph's but you never know."

"And St. Joe's is less time intensive, I assume?"

"That's what I've heard."

Franklin thought for a moment. "Plan on being at St. Joe's. I'll talk with the Psych chairman and see that you're assigned there. I want you to have as much time as possible for the Omega study."

Patrick Murphy was in a bind. Not only was the market down for cattle futures but a particularly wet winter had ruined much of the hay set aside for his livestock. Making a living as a farmer and rancher had never been an easy lot. Little wonder so many of his friends and acquaintances had left the business. Now, however, things were approaching a crisis point.

Murphy worked the Irish farmland his father had left him 15 years earlier. Initially, there had been the typical cycle of good years and bad. Some seasons he was able to make enough money to actually go on vacation. Three years previous he had taken his wife and two sons to Euro Disney. But since then he and his brethren had experienced a string of bad luck. Falling crop prices had hurt him, not to mention the drought that had practically devastated the harvest 2 years ago. He was eventually forced to take a job in the nearby town of Duncan unloading freight cars to make ends meet and his bank was unwilling to extend him any more credit. Without a sufficient infusion of cash he would be unable to put in the new crop of potatoes. Sitting at his dining room table reading the agricultural reports in the paper wasn't improving his mood.

"Any good news?" his wife asked as she prepared lunch for herself and their two sons.

"Is there ever?" he responded sarcastically.

"That bad, is it?"

"Seemingly." Murphy downed the last of his coffee before placing the empty cup in the sink. "I spoke with the bank yesterday. They don't want to loan us any more money."

"You worry too much," she said. "You'll find a way to get the potatoes in. You always do."

His wife. Ever the eternal optimist.

"There's one other possibility. Selling the cattle."

Monica stopped her work. "All of them?"

"Yes," he answered. "We won't make much money but the feed is about played out. Even if I can get Sean to let me have more on credit it will just add to the overall cost and I'm not certain we can recoup that when it comes time to sell."

"But the farm has always raised cattle."

"I realize that, but something has to give. I'm not saying it's an absolute certainty but it appears to be the only viable means for getting the crop in the ground."

Monica was quiet for a few minutes. In the previous months, her husband's disposition had become increasingly sour.

"Anyway, I'm going to talk with the broker at the feedlot and see what he'll give me," Patrick said. "I don't see any other options."

CHAPTER 4

On Monday, I wandered into the Psychiatry department's lecture hall for the medical student orientation. As this was the final rotation of the academic year, we were all well acquainted with the process. At 8:00 A.M. Dr. Covington, one of the faculty members, strode to the lectern and announced how happy he was that all of us were going to be with them for the next 8 weeks. Several months earlier we had submitted our bid lists for preferred hospital campuses - Hermann Hospital in the Medical Center, LBJ Hospital near loop 610 or St. Joseph's Hospital downtown. I had done my Obstetrics rotation at St. Joe's the preceding fall. The drive wasn't too bad but parking was a hassle. We were relegated to a lot across the street. Sauntering past empty Colt 45 bottles and spent hypodermic needles before a 36 hour shift was depressing.

The psychiatry rotation, however, was another matter. We still had the same parking facilities but the starting time was better and, more importantly, the departure time was greatly improved.

While I held no animosity toward the mentally ill, I had little experience with the subject given the relative sanity of my own family. My father, decrying the lack of discipline and suitable work ethic as causative factors of such psychological conditions, had fostered a jaundiced influence on my opinion of the field. I didn't consider him an ignorant man but he was, after all, limited in his study of the subject. I, on the other hand, prided myself in being better educated. Shortly after beginning my hospital rotations, I came to realize my father's assertions were far closer to the mark than most professionals were willing to admit. His recommendations of a "good old fashioned butt kicking" might well have solved more problems on the wards than group therapy and vocational instruction. I had requested St. Joseph's since I had no interest in pursuing a career in psychiatry and wanted to make my passage through the required rotation as painless as possible. Unfortunately, that sentiment was shared by many of my classmates. There was always an oversupply of students listing St. Joe's as their first choice.

As Dr. Covington made his remarks, one of the department secretaries began passing out envelopes bearing the rotators names. Judging from their expressions as they opened their mailers, most of my cohorts seemed to be getting what they wanted. The box on my paper originally had the name Hermann Hospital printed in it. However, it had been crossed out and "Saint Joseph's Hospital" written in red ink. Franklin had been good to her word.

The individual rotations were to begin at 1:00 P.M giving me an opportunity to address a few items in my mailbox. Having wrapped them up by 10:30 I dropped by Dr. Franklin's office to inform her of my assignment. She would already know, of course, but touching base seemed a prudent thing to do. It bolstered my profile and made me look like I couldn't soak up enough of the dermatology experience.

Dr. Franklin wasn't in her office. I considered leaving a message but decided to inquire from the department secretary as to her whereabouts. Eva Braun was out of town and wouldn't be back until tomorrow. The thought of using the medical school weight room for a much postponed workout was appealing. It had been some time since I had engaged in any kind of serious exercise. My thoughts were interrupted by Galen Hart's arrival on the scene.

He was dressed to the nines per usual. Hart wore custom made shirts with his initials emblazoned across the front pocket and Armani ties. His leather loafers cost more than the furniture in my apartment. As much as it pained me, I had to admit he cut a dashing figure.

"Got all the paperwork set up for the study?" he asked as he walked down the hall leafing through his mail.

I was surprised he spoke to me. "Yeah, I think so," I responded. "I'm supposed to meet with Julie later today to finalize the initial patient visits."

Hart never looked up from his sorting. "Good. See that you get it squared away. I don't want to have too many rooms tied up. It slows down the clinic." His tone was as disdainful as it was condescending.

If he was trying to get under my skin, he'd been successful. I'd worked far harder on the project than he had.

"I'm sorry, I never got the chance to ask you at the meeting Saturday what your role was going to be in this study."

Hart ceased the perusal of his mail. "Mostly making sure you don't screw things up." A wry smile came across his face. I couldn't tell if he was trying to back pedal from his remarks or let me know where I stood in the pecking order. "You've never done clinical research before, have you?"

"Nope," I answered defiantly. "Not a lick." I considered mentioning that if a worm such as himself could do it, the process must not be too intellectually taxing. I decided against it. It was rumored in some residencies the house staff could preemptively strike a candidate from consideration if they felt working with them during the coming years would be problematic. For all I knew, such a policy was in place at UT Houston.

"Why am I not surprised," he said returning to his mail. "Well, it's more difficult than it appears. The drug companies lay out thousands of dollars to get their products evaluated with even more hanging in the balance should the data prove insufficient to the FDA. They don't tolerate sloppiness. Neither do I."

One thing had to be said for Dr. Hart. He possessed a keen sense of his own import.

"I'll do the best I can," I said.

Hart had already begun walking away. He stopped and turned. "Don't do the best you can. Give Omega what they want. Keep that in mind and you'll do fine. Don't and you'll find yourself lucky to get a Family Practice residency in Amarillo." That said, he continued his trek down the hall and, fortunately, away from me.

"What's the word Sean?" Murphy asked as he walked into the man's shop. Sean McMillan ran the local feed store in town. The Murphy clan had been trading with the McMillans since before the Great War. They were friends of a sort, at least enough to talk soccer scores and the occasional bit of politics over a pint at the pub down the street.

"Prices are down and rent is up," he remarked. McMillan had been using the same catch phrase since Murphy had known him. He wiped his feet on a large mat just inside the front door. A light rain had made the sidewalks a muddy mess. "Any word on the extension from the bank?" he asked.

McMillan already knew the answer.

"Last thing I heard was they weren't going to give me any more credit. Not much of a surprise," he said acidly. The only thing Patrick Murphy was beginning to dislike more than politicians and lawyers was bankers. "I could ask again but I doubt it will do any good."

The store owner went back to plunking the keys on his lap top computer. His fingers were thick as broom handles making single strokes a challenging task.

"What can I do for you today?"

"I'm thinking about selling the cows."

McMillan cut his eyes away from the computer screen. "All of them?"

"All of them." Murphy shook the water from the brim of his cap. "Any idea if I'll get any sort of a decent price for them?"

"Cattle futures have been steady for the past month but I don't know what the broker will give you. I've heard the same story from at least 3 others in the past week."

"So the market's going to get crowded."

"You could say that. If you're going to rid yourself of the beasts, I suggest you do it sooner rather than later."

"Sound advice, Sean. I'm going to need some more feed."

McMillan looked over the top of his glasses at his friend. "You're already up against the line here as is. Sure you want to do that?"

"Of course not," Murphy retorted. "But I'm out and the cows still have to eat. What do you have?"

"Nothing you'd want," McMillan said.

"Don't give me that. I'm in a bind here. Surely you have something out of date in the warehouse."

"Can't do it Patrick. The Inspector General gets wind of it and I'm out of business."

Murphy shook his head. "Look, I don't need much. Just a half dozen sacks."

McMillan looked into his friend's eyes, his desperation impossible to miss. It was becoming an all too frequent occurrence. Patrick Murphy was trying to retain his property and feed his family. The land had been in his family for generations. Finally , McMillan nodded slowly, his mouth twisted into an uncomfortable appearing contortion. He motioned for Murphy to approach the counter.

"I do have a small stock of feed I can't move," he said softly. "It's off the books."

Murphy thought for a minute. "Is it safe?"

"Probably."

"Probably?"

"It's a generic brand out of Cardiff. I haven't heard or read anything that would lead me to suspect otherwise. Still, it's not exactly kosher selling it after the expiration date. I can let you have it for what I paid for it. Cash. And no receipt."

The specter of breaking the law wasn't appealing to Patrick Murphy. He'd been brought up in a strict Catholic home where lying and dishonesty were among the most harshly penalized infractions. It was a practice he continued in his own household with his sons. Regardless, Murphy's disdain for the governing bodies constantly interfering with his life and livelihood galled him in the worst way. If it came down to obeying some arcane edict from the European Union and putting food on his table, it wasn't much of a decision.

"I'll take them."

Patrick Murphy reached into his wallet, extracting the appropriate amount of cash which he gave to McMillan. He drove his van around to the warehouse and loaded the half dozen bags of feed into the back before beginning his drive home.

I walked into St. Joseph's Hospital and made my way to one of the conference rooms for our orientation. I recognized nearly everyone present since we had rotated together on other services. We made small talk for a few minutes before the attending psychiatrist entered the room.

His name was Donald Macon and his substantial girth wasn't his only baggage. Rumor had it that at one point his medical license had been suspended following a battle with substance abuse, in his case Demerol, the physicians' drug of choice. The same drug would later claim the life of one of our classmates a month prior to graduation. As he strode past me I noticed the overwhelming fragrance of stale cigarette smoke. The man smelled like a walking ashtray.

"Okay people," he said. "Let's get down to business." During the next 15 minutes he outlined what would be expected of us on the psychiatry service. There were daily checkups on the in-patients as well as a morning group therapy session where we were to be seen and not heard. After that there would be an opportunity for us to ask any questions we might have as well as a 45 minute lecture on psychopharmacology. Since Macon had other responsibilities he released the group for the day. All except me.

"Is there a Justin Douglas here?" he asked. Several heads turned in my direction. I raised my hand.

"I need to see you for a few minutes. The rest of you may leave."

"Boy, you just can't seem to stay out of trouble, can you?" one of my classmates whispered over my shoulder.

As the others quickly vacated the room I stood and walked towards Dr. Macon.

"Yes, sir?" I said.

Macon flipped through some pages on a clipboard he carried. "You were a late add on to the St. Joseph's service."

"Is that a problem?" I asked.

"Not really. I don't much care who rotates where. But I was informed by the dean you were to be allowed as much time off as possible for some kind of research project."

"I wasn't aware of that," I responded. I was lying but the part about not knowing the dean had gotten involved was true.

Dr. Macon set the clipboard aside. "As you know, the psych rotation isn't as taxing as some of the others. However, there is a minimum amount of effort and learning required. With your extra duties I hope you know what you are getting yourself into.

The final in-service exam will comprise 50% of your grade. As such, we encourage the students to spend as much time as possible in preparatory reading for the test. Just keep that in mind."

Knowing I would be treated differently than others on the rotation left me feeling uneasy. Perhaps the amount of money flowing into the dermatology department made for a unique situation. I was beginning to wonder if all of this was a good idea.

The dermatology clinics were held on the 4th floor in a building across from the medical school. From Monday through Friday the dermatology residents, attendings, rotating students and house staff from other services saw patients in the offices. I had not been there previously but had no trouble finding it. At the front desk I asked for Julie, explaining who I was and why I was there. I was directed to the back where I met the research study nurse. Julie Bergstrom was a nurse practitioner who had been with the department for 5 years. She occasionally filled in as a traditional clinic nurse but for the most part her efforts were devoted to working on the various drug studies conducted at the clinic.

"You must be Dr. Douglas?" she said with a smile.

Despite the fact that I was far removed from graduation, like most medical students I enjoyed hearing their name proceeded with the word "doctor". It was also my experience when someone referred to me as such, they usually treated me more humanely. Of course, the opposite could be true as well.

"I'm Justin," I responded deferentially. "Are you Julie?"

"That's me." Julie was possessed of an openly bubbly personality, something I was to find out later neither faded with fatigue nor became unduly annoying. It was genuinely the way she looked at life. The glass was always half full and rising.

"I have been going through the boxes Dr. Franklin sent over," she began. "I can tell you spent a great deal of time and effort on them. They looked really good."

What was this? A compliment? From someone associated with the dermatology department?

"It wasn't too difficult. Just have to pay attention, that's all."

"That's an attitude that will carry you far in life. Drug studies certainly require attention to the details. In fact, sometimes that's about all they are. I spoke with Jennifer Maddux earlier today," Julie said, changing the subject. "She was quite pleased with your processing of the initial paperwork. She and her site inspection team will be here next week to look things over."

Julie was about to sit down at a nearby table when she suddenly asked, "Would you like to see the product we'll be using?"

"Sure, why not," I answered. It occurred to me that I'd never even seen the stuff.

Julie went to the refrigerator and opened the door. Inside were several dozen boxes with the Omega Pharmaceuticals logo emblazoned on the front. She removed one, closed the door and set it on the tabletop between us.

"Here you go," she said handing me one of the cellophane covered packets.

Inside the clear wrapping was a piece of malleable plastic about a sixteenth of an inch thick and half the size of an index card. On one side was a blue covering and on the other a piece of thin, wax paper. Beneath the latter was a sticky surface allowing the patch to adhere to the skin.

"Pretty cool, huh?" Julie asked. "Each of these boxes and patches is number coded so we can track them throughout the study. The patients are required to bring them back to us at their monthly visits. They receive either a placebo or the real deal. Since only a fraction of the toxin molecules pass through the skin when applied as a cream, occlusion therapy with these patches allows for a set amount of the drug to be absorbed. It operates on the same theory as the nicotine patch. Sort of a time release thing but designed for 8 hours instead of 24."

I had to admit, it was ingenious. If this were to work, it would revolutionize the administration of botulinum toxin. Without the discomfort, mess and potential danger of using needles, whichever drug company got this to market first would make a killing.

I was turning the item over in my hands, marveling at its simplicity when I heard a familiar voice behind me.

"What are you doing here?"

I turned to see Dr. Hart standing behind me, a steaming cup of coffee in his hand and a menacing scowl on his face.

"What does it look like he's doing here?" Julie shot back. Her voice was noticeably edgier.

I wasn't accustomed to being defended by women and felt compelled to shoulder the responsibility myself. Besides, I was still annoyed at Hart's attitude during our last encounter. As a third year medical student I wasn't allowed to express anger. Passive aggressiveness, however, was another matter.

"Just going over some of the paperwork and scheduling as per your suggestion," I said indifferently. The man was a toad.

"Is there something you can do for us?" Julie asked. Being someone he couldn't push around gave her a legitimate advantage. She clearly didn't like Hart and didn't much care how that sat with him.

Galen Hart emitted a snort-like laugh before taking a few sips of his coffee and slithering back down the hall.

Julie returned to her seat but declined to acknowledge what had just taken place. "So," she said gesturing at the patch still in my hand, "the patient applies that overnight for three consecutive days and when they're done, they're wrinkle free."

<u>Outstanding</u>, I said to myself.

CHAPTER 5

Patrick Murphy parked his van in front of the modest house he shared with his wife and 2 sons. As he made his way into the mud room, he called for the boys. They came running around the corner of the den, their shouts increasing with each step. He broke into a big smile, bent down on one knee and gave them a simultaneous bear hug.

"Okay, you two squirrels, get those feed bags out of the van and into the barn." Michael and Clayton grumbled but returned to their room to put on their shoes.

In the kitchen Monica was warming some water for tea as she put the finishing touches on the evening meal, in this case, soup with thick rye bread and canned fruit. She brushed her hands off on the apron around her waist before giving her husband his welcome home embrace. "How was work?" she asked.

"The usual," he responded.

"Did I hear you tell the boys to unload some bags?"

"Yeah, I stopped by McMillan's place after work. I got some feed for the cows."

"Did you put it on the account?"

"No. I paid cash. I didn't want to run the bill up any higher than it already was."

"Still planning on selling them?"

"Yeah."

Her husband sat at the kitchen table pouring some of the hot water into a tea cup with a bag in it. Monica could tell something was bothering him. She placed her paring knife on the counter and pulled up a chair next to him.

"What is it?" she asked.

Patrick could never keep anything from his wife. She could always tell when he was troubled and it was one of her most endearing qualities. He had learned years ago the easiest thing to do was simply level with her. She would continue to gently pester him until he did.

"I bought some of McMillan's feed he couldn't move. I got a good price on it."

"What do you mean he couldn't move'?"

"He has some bags of outdated feed he was having trouble selling."

Monica sat back in her chair and folded her arms. "You shouldn't have done that," she said softly.

Patrick stared at her with a tired expression on his face. "Well, it wasn't something I wanted to do. We have no feed for the animals. It will buy us some time until I can sell them to the broker in a few days."

"I hope you're right," Monica said.

The psychiatry rotation proceeded according to plan. There were rounds in the morning followed by a didactic lecture usually from Dr. Macon. The talks mostly dealt with medications used for depression, psychosis and mania. It was interesting enough since it was different from the one's we'd had on the surgery or internal medicine services. The best part, though, was that we were done by 11:30 and often earlier. I got in the habit of vacating the premises quickly putting me back at my apartment by noon with plenty of time to get to the dermatology clinics by 1:00.

In the hallway one day I found myself walking with Lisa Penning, one of the women in my class.

"Why are you always dashing out of here so quickly?" she asked.

Lisa was from Nebraska. Her father was an obstetrician at the University of Nebraska in Omaha and she had expressed an interest in following in his footsteps. I had always liked her. She had been an occasional attendee of a study group I participated in during our first year. Besides being easy to talk to and more than a little attractive, she seemed to have an ordered outlook on life, something I found uncommon in our classmates.

Once, when I was sitting on a bench outside eating my lunch and reading a copy of *Left Behind*, she had approached me and asked how I was enjoying my book. I had only rarely spoken with her in the past but she sat down and we chatted for the remainder of lunch. The conversation soon turned to matters theologic. Before long, I found myself confessing to her some of the struggles I was having with my own religious beliefs. After we had returned to class, it occurred to me how unusual it had been to spill out some of my angst to someone I barely knew. It wasn't like me to be so open. Lisa had listened carefully, asking few questions and interjecting none of her own points of view. I was surprised at how much better I felt and wondered if she, as Esther of the Old Testament had "attained your position for such a time as this." She had helped lighten my load and I was grateful. It was nice to see her again on the psych rotation.

"Oh, I have a project I'm doing with the dermatology department," I said. "The clinic starts at 1:00 so I have to hot foot it out of here."

"Are you headed back to the apartments?" she asked.

"Yeah. Do you need a ride?"

"Do you mind?"

"Don't you have a car here?"

"I took the bus this morning."

"Sure," I said. "No problem."

Once inside my truck we made small talk for a few minutes. She sat in the passenger side with her hands folded neatly in her lap. I was glad I didn't have my spit cup in the cab, a standard feature given my proclivity to dip snuff as I drove. I guess it wouldn't have mattered much. Growing up in Nebraska she surely had friends with the same bad habit as myself. Still, I didn't want to give her the impression I was some redneck from Dirtsville, Texas.

"So are you interested in dermatology?" she asked after a particularly long dry spell in the conversation.

"Yeah," I answered, nodding my head. "I think it's pretty interesting. It probably makes the most sense in the long term. Time for family and all."

"But you aren't married."

"No," I said smiling. "But I assume at some point, I will be. When kids come along I want to be able to go to their soccer games and hockey matches. That sort of thing."

"Oh, well that makes sense."

We continued to drive in silence for a few more minutes. I noticed she continually checked her seatbelt and made sure the door was locked.

"Is my driving that bad?" I asked.

"What?" Lisa asked as she turned to look at me. "Oh no, I just have this thing about car safety. My mother was killed in a wreck when I was nine. Ever since then I've been obsessive about wearing a seat belt."

"I'm sorry," I responded. "Did your dad remarry?"

No sooner were the words out of my mouth than I regretted uttering them. What a putz.

"No. No, he didn't," she said softly.

"I apologize. I didn't mean to pry. It's none of my business." I could feel the flush of embarrassment spreading over my cheeks.

"It's alright," she said. "I enjoy talking about my father. After my mother passed away, he left private practice and went on staff with U of N. He needed more regular hours since it was just the two of us. One time I asked him why he didn't remarry or even date for that matter. He said that until I was older his primary focus was on parenting, not his love life."

"Wow," I said arching my eyebrows. "That's an uncommon attitude."

Lisa had a wide smile on her face. Her father's nurturing and self denial had been a source of great comfort to her.

"He's a man of considerable integrity. I have enormous respect for him considering the sacrifices he made on my behalf."

"Yeah, I would think so."

We rode in silence for a while until Lisa decided to change the subject and asked about my research with the dermatology department.

"Well, it's not really all that spectacular," I said trying to sound modest. After all, I was little more than a glorified gopher. "The higher ups wrangled some sort of a contract with Omega Pharmaceuticals to test this topical formulation of botulinum toxin. I mostly just screen the patients and get them set up for their clinic visits. Julie, the drug study nurse for the department does the lion's share of the work."

"Still," Lisa responded. "I would imagine that would set you up pretty nicely in the future for a dermatology residency."

"Theoretically," I replied. "The competition for slots is wicked. There aren't but about 250 available positions in the US annually. You have to have some sort of research on your resume if you want your application to get any serious consideration."

"Your grades are good, aren't they?" she asked.

"Yeah. They're alright. I took a year off after . . ."

"I know," Lisa interrupted.

I appreciated her deference. It was a sore subject with me. My first year of school had been marred by a momentary lapse of judgment, followed by a leave of absence. Due to extenuating circumstances I had been allowed to return the following fall with a clean slate and an empty record folder.

"Well, anyway, my grades are probably good enough to be competitive, but there's always the matter of my board scores and the suitability of my CV. I need to shore it up with some research. This project should help."

The rest of the trip consisted of Lisa talking about her desire to leave the drudgery of the third year behind and get into the electives she had selected for her senior year. Her interest, not surprisingly, was obstetrics and gynecology.

I dropped her off at her apartment building, which was diametrically opposite mine in the same complex. She thanked me for the ride and then disappeared around the corner, her long brown hair bouncing in a gentle breeze. One part of me wished that I had been more bold and asked about the status of her engagement. Another reminded me that I was the ultimate dweeb, with limited social skills and even less judgment as to when to leave a subject alone. Still, it would have been nice to have found out what where she stood availability wise.

After microwaving a frozen dinner and wolfing it down, I took the shuttle bus back to the medical center. By now I was familiar enough with the staff to walk through the dermatology clinic doors without checking in with the receptionist. Julie was seated at her desk with the customary stacks of patient charts surrounding her. She smiled when I knocked on her partially open door.

"Come in," she invited. "Have a seat. All ready to get to the first patients of the day?"

I sat down in a wooden chair opposite her desk.

"You bet," I said enthusiastically. I hoped she couldn't tell I had ulterior motives for my participation in the study.

"Dr. Jennings was by earlier," she said. "He seemed to be impressed with your work."

It was music to my ears.

"Well, good," I stammered. "It's nice to know that I haven't been screwing things up too badly."

"On the contrary. We're ahead of schedule thanks in large part to your efforts. That's something of a minor miracle for a drug study of this caliber."

Out of the corner of my eye I saw someone filling the doorway to Julie's office.

"Are we ready to go?" Galen Hart asked. He sounded restless, suggesting he had better things to do.

Julie's smile faded. "Dr. Hart," she said flatly. "I had forgotten you would be here this afternoon."

<u>Sort of like being reminded you're about to get a root canal, isn't it?</u> I thought.

"Yeah. Jennings and Franklin wanted me here to teach the med student how things are supposed to work."

"I think you'll find Dr. Douglas sufficiently up to speed. Maybe he'll even show you a thing or two."

Hart chuckled sarcastically. "Sure he will." Turning to me he said, "How's it going Jeremy?"

"Justin," I corrected him.

"We aren't going to be here later than 4:30 are we?" he asked Julie.

"Well, that depends on how many patients show up and how quickly we get through the paperwork."

"I have an appointment at 5:00 so if we're running behind I'll let Wonderboy here finish things up."

"The first patient is in room 7 so why don't we get down to business?" Julie said.

The three of us walked down the hall to the examination room. Hart knocked on the door before entering. I stayed at the back and out of the way straining to hear since apparently I would be flying solo sooner than I had planned.

"Are you Alicia Prentiss?" Hart asked.

A woman looking to be in her mid 40's was seated on the end of the examination table. She had been thumbing through a well worn a copy of *Vogue* but set it behind her after we entered the room.

"That's correct," she responded.

"I'm Dr. Hart and this is Julie our nurse coordinator for the study." The resident's tone was professorial, obviously intended to convey to the patient that he was in charge of things. "Have you read through all the material we sent you?"

The woman didn't answer. Instead, she looked past Hart at me.

"This is Dr. Douglas," Julie interjected. "He's working on the study with us as well. He'll probably be the one you see at some of your future visits."

Ms. Prentiss smiled at me and nodded. Her face bore an expression more of sympathy at my position in the pecking order than friendliness. Still, as a medical student I was readily accepting of any kindness directed my way.

"Yes," she answered. "I put the disclosure form and release on the table."

"Great," Hart said. "Did you get a chance to look over the video the company sent you?"

"I did."

"Do you have any questions about what the weekly procedures will entail?"

"Let me see if I have this straight. I take two of the patches, peel off the backing and put one on each side of my forehead just above my eyebrows at bedtime. In the morning, I remove them, wash my face and apply a layer of the sunscreen you're going to give me. Is that correct?"

"That's all there is to it," Julie said. "We will also give you a daily diary for you to jot down any side effects or other symptoms you notice. Anything, and I mean *anything* that occurs out of the ordinary whether you think it's important or not, we want you to write it down in the diary. We will be reviewing it with representatives from Omega and we'll decide after the study is finished if whatever you experienced had anything to do with the medication."

"Fair enough," Prentiss said.

"In the packet with your patches is a card with our phone numbers on it. You can reach us 24-7 if you have any questions or problems."

"Okay."

The rest of the visit consisted of completing paperwork and giving Prentiss the box containing her materials. Arrangements had been made with the University's medical media department to photograph each participant using a special camera. The patients were to contort their faces into three different expressions with shots done at a variety of angles. These photographs would later be evaluated by independent observers looking for a statistically different outcome between patients receiving the active drug or placebo.

"Did you get all of that?" Hart asked me after Mrs. Prentiss had left.

"It seems pretty straightforward," I answered.

"I would hope so. The company designed the study so that even a chimp could do it."

I hadn't heard that one before. The wit just never ended.

"He'll do just fine, Dr. Hart," Julie chimed in. "Why don't you go see the next patient."

Hart ignored her for the moment but eventually put his Blackberry away and ambled down the hall.

The remainder of the afternoon consisted of 4 more patients with 4 more visits not remarkably different from that of Mrs. Prentiss's. The three women and one man were affable enough and seemed excited at the prospect of receiving some cutting edge cosmetic procedure without anesthetic and scalpels. The fact that it was free no doubt contributed to their enthusiasm. By the time all the paperwork was completed it was close to 5:30. Hart, of course, was long gone. He reminded us no less than three additional times of his need to vacate the premises for his "appointment" which likely was a tee time or a reservation for a squash court. When all was squared away, I told Julie goodnight, walked to the bus stop and went home.

MacGregor had been on the phone all morning procuring laboratory supplies. Most of the calls had been successful. He'd been assured of a stock of prime *Clostridium botulinum* organisms from a laboratory in Stockholm. A potential choke point involved the constituents for the patch diffusion matrix. Without an appropriate chemical gradient, a measured delivery of the toxin into the skin was impossible. Scientists at Omega's home offices had tested and developed a complex system using cow serum, microsphere gel technology and vector pH buffers. Its production was straightforward, providing all the components were in place. Bovine, or cow serum had been gradually becoming a scarce commodity. Most industrial houses were strapped for raw materials and backorders were the norm. It was a problem Mac-Gregor could not have foreseen. By mid morning he was frustrated and more than a little nervous. The higher ups in Omega had faxed him a proposed production schedule. Normally, it would have provided for more than enough time to complete the work. However, an insufficiently stocked laboratory would make progress nearly impossible.

In the late afternoon, a research collaborator who owed him a favor supplied him with the name of a vice president in a biotechnology firm. After filling out the appropriate paperwork and faxing it to the company he received an email finalizing the transaction and a promise that the serum would be at his doorstep no later than noon the next day.

Getting the laboratory up and functional had been amazingly trouble-free. MacGregor had spent the better part of a week demonstrating how he wanted things done. His new employees had proven to be capable learners, typically acquiring a given skill the first time. All the materials and machines had arrived on time and in good condition. Within a week the first culture media had been produced. It registered a 98th percentile purity index, well beyond what MacGregor had hoped for or what would be required for FDA approval.

On Friday of their second full week of production, Mac-Gregor received an email from Gary Page. Page wanted an update on the status of the plant and asked MacGregor to place an overseas call whenever convenient, meaning today. After closing out his server, the Scotsman picked up the phone and punched in the numbers. Getting to Page required three transfers and nearly ten minutes on hold. The man was definitely well insulated.

"So how are things in the Old Country?" Page said cheerily.

He must be having a good day, MacGregor surmised.

"Quite well. And yourself?"

"Splendid. Lots of sunshine and in the middle 70's," Page replied. "What can you tell me about the toxin production?"

"Well, sir, we've just completed some of our initial testing. The stocks of organisms have been excellent leading to good growth in our larger media containers. On Monday we should have the spectrophotometer figures on the final purity of the product. However, our preliminary results show readings in the high 90's."

"Wonderful," Page exclaimed. "If that data pans out when do you think you'll be able to ship us the finished product?"

MacGregor thought for a moment. "I would think within 10 days or so."

"Fabulous. As you know we have sufficient quantities for the first round of patch production but that's not going to last very long. Our stocks will be exhausted within a month, so at that point we'll be completely dependent upon you and your laboratory for continued supply."

"Yes sir, I understand. I don't foresee any problems. All of my vendors are aware of our requirements and have promised no interruption in the flow of substrate materials."

"Very well then," Page said. "I'll let you get back to work. I'll alert the folks producing the patches to expect your initial shipment within two weeks."

Patrick Murphy stood by the gate to his stock pens, a slow drizzle falling from the overcast skies. He had taken the morning off to meet a buyer for his cattle. After kissing his wife and sons goodbye for the day he distributed the last of the feed to his animals. Obtaining more would be problematic leaving him with little wiggle room in negotiating the price of his heard.

After a few minutes of waiting, Malcolm Craig, the local livestock wholesaler, appeared driving the same Ford pickup he'd owned for the past 16 years. Despite his trappings of modesty everyone knew he made considerable money with his operation. He had a virtual stranglehold on the local market. Families raising cattle in the area were typically small, independent operations without the means for transporting their cattle elsewhere for a more favorable price. They usually had to accept whatever Craig was willing to give them for their livestock.

"'Morning Malcom," Murphy said as the man stepped from his vehicle.

"Rotten weather, today, isn't it?" Craig responded.

"Indeed."

Murphy's mood was subdued. He had talked over his plans the previous evening with his wife. She had been understanding but reticent about the matter, unable to fully support an idea she lacked confidence in.

"So what have you got for me today?" Craig asked, his yellow and misshapen teeth visible through a thievish smile.

"Just what we spoke about on the phone. We have 18 head we need to sell."

"Let's see what we have here, shall we?" Craig said as he opened the gate to the pen.

Gathered around a circular metal feeding rack were the animals in question. They stood silently in the foggy morning air, their coats gradually becoming soaked from the rain. Some turned to look as the men approached them but most simply continued chewing on the remaining meal nuggets.

Craig spent a few moments inspecting the small herd, but it was all a performance. The man had already decided what he would pay for the lot. It would be well below their market value. The wholesaler had Murphy at a disadvantage and knew it.

"Well, I can give you 85 pence per kilo for them," he finally said.

Murphy's mouth dropped open in shock. Even his worst case scenario didn't involve a figure that low.

"What?" he exclaimed. "That's only two-thirds of the going market price!"

Craig shrugged his shoulders as he reached into his coat pocket for his cigarettes.

"Cattle futures are down, m'boy."

"I talked with Gerold Garvey last week and he told me you were offering 105 per kilo."

Craig fumbled with his lighter as he struggled to get his smoke lit.

"That was last week. Most of the farmers around here are selling off their livestock in large numbers if not cashing out altogether. That drives the prices down. And it's not just in this area. It's happening throughout the country. It's a buyer's market and I can't get the same prices at slaughterhouses now I could even three days ago." Craig exhaled blue cigarette smoke upward into the air. "I'm afraid it's a matter of take it or leave it. I've got three other stops to make today with families who are going to be getting the same speech. They'll likely find the prices even lower than what I'm quoting you. My advice would be to lock in now."

Patrick Murphy surveyed the herd in front of him with pangs of melancholy and frustration. He had no great affection for the beasts but in selling the animals he would be closing a chapter in the farm's history extending back to the times of his grandfather and perhaps before. He had used the cows to teach his sons about responsibility and discipline as his father had taught him. He could impart the same lessons with other mediums but not as well. The care and tending of livestock was a unique learning experience.

"I'll take it," Murphy said quietly without looking away from the cattle. "Lock us in."

Evan Leitch was in a foul mood. Drinking, usually able to sooth some of his rancor, tonight only seemed to make things worse. Sitting alone in his favorite watering hole waiting for his companions to arrive wasn't helping matters.

Leitch worked in an animal food manufacturing plant. With his tenure of 15 years, he had sufficient seniority to warrant assignment to the day shift. However, over that 15 years his drinking problem had steadily worsened and he had begun showing up for work drunk. The first few infractions had been overlooked but they had become more frequent. He'd been warned by the plant's management to get his act together. Eventually, his union bosses told him the same thing. The final straw had come 3 weeks earlier. After arriving for his shift with bloodshot eyes and slurred speech, he'd been taken aside by the company night manager and his union shop steward and informed that he was being put on the graveyard shift. One more mistake and he'd be out of a job. He'd taken the news poorly.

Never one to assign blame to himself, Leitch began to search for ways to even the score. One day his eye caught a newspaper article regarding an animal rights group upset over the treatment of sheep and cattle at slaughtering houses. At the local library he accessed their web page and made contact. Within a few days they reached out. Several telephone conversations ensued confirming for the activists they had more than a willing accomplice in their pursuits. Tonight's meeting was designed to set things in motion.

When he heard the tavern door open, Leitch looked up from his whiskey spotting two young men who definitely didn't belong there. No question these were the fellows he'd been talking with. Leitch slid off his barstool and wobbled towards them.

"This way," he said motioning with his arm.

The three men made their way to the back of the room settling into a booth which reeked of cigarette smoke and beer.

Leitch set his drink on the table and stared at the two men in front of him. Neither could be older than 30. Both sported scraggly beards and woolen caps emblazoned with the logos of well known English soccer clubs.

"You'd be Trevor and Dermot, I take it?"

"Something like that," Trevor replied. "Our names aren't really important. We understand you're employed at a local animal food plant, is that correct."

"It is," Leitch said, draining the last of the whiskey from his glass.

Dermot raised three fingers towards the bartender signaling a request for drinks at the table.

"Is it fair to say you're willing to help us impress on your employers the errors of their ways?"

"Something like that."

"It's our understanding that of late you haven't gotten on well with either your union or the plant management."

Leitch squinted his eyes. "How do you know about all that?"

"We do our homework. We're young but we're not stupid. How far are you willing to go in your quest to 'get even' as it were?" Dermot asked.

"Well, I ain't killing nobody if that's what you're asking."

"That's not the sort of statement our organization makes. It tends to complicate matters. We believe bollixing up the corporate bottom line gets our point across better."

The waitress arrived with three glasses of whiskey, setting them down in front of the men and removing Leitch's empty.

"Well, I don't understand much of what you're talking about but they demoted the wrong man and one way or the other, they're going to pay."

Trevor and Dermot smiled at each other. Another useful idiot had come to the party.

"Give us an idea of what your work entails and how the plant is structured."

Leitch gave them a thumbnail sketch in a rambling 5 minute speech. By the time he was done, his glass was again empty.

"So you have access to most if not all of the machinery directly involved in the manufacturing of these products. Is that correct?"

"Yep."

"Excellent. How difficult would it be for you to pour a thermos full of liquid into one of the large mixing machines? Obviously, without being seen."

"No problem at all. What's in the thermos?"

"I don't think you need concern yourself with that. I can assure it's nothing of potential harm to you. Would you be willing to undertake such a mission?"

"What's this going to do to their business?"

"In a word, devastate it. I doubt it will force them to close but it will take millions of pounds to correct and months to do so. In the meantime, according to your union contract, you'll be furloughed at full pay until the plant re-opens."

Leitch looked over at the bar. A rugby match was on the flat screen television above it. After thinking for a moment, a slight smile spread across his face.

"When, boys?" he said.

"Sometime next week, a green thermos will be placed during the night on the front stoop of your home. Simply take it to work with you, pour the contents into the largest mixing machine available and return the thermos to your front stoop. It will be picked up the next evening. Couldn't be simpler."

Five days later, Leitch returned to his home as dawn was breaking. There on the cement stoop sat a medium size green thermos. The next evening, he deposited the liquid it contained into the number 4 mixing machine just after midnight. Trevor and Dermot had been correct. It had been simple.

Three days later, Leitch failed to show up for work. Given his penchant for hard drinking, the conventional wisdom was that he had simply gone on a bender and fallen into a river somewhere. Absent a wife and children, the local authorities wasted little time and few resources trying to locate him. Within a week, the case was officially listed as "pending".

The group of animal rights activists waited patiently to view the fruits of their labors. None, however, had any idea its effects would be as far reaching as they were.

By the second week of the study things had settled into a stable routine. I would show up at the clinics a little before 1 o'clock, go over the patient list for the day with Julie and then review the accumulated laboratory data. According to the protocol, each patient was required to undergo a series of psychological tests to ensure no undiagnosed mental illness existed which might skew the results and standard blood work evaluating the function of their kidneys, liver and bone marrow. So far everything looked good with no significant abnormalities. Dr. Hart's signature was required on the forms but my job was to pre-screen everything.

Beginning at 2 o'clock the patients would arrive in 20 minute intervals. Initially, there was some down time but eventually all the slots were filled and we became quite busy. Ordinarily, a study such as this would have 2 or more days per week without patient visits. This protected time would be dedicated to tying up loose ends and other endeavors. However, Jennings and Franklin were anxious to proceed at full speed with this project. Omega Pharmaceuticals was slated to disperse their payments to the University incrementally with the first installment to be released after half the enrolled patients began their visits.

Since neither the patients nor the investigators knew which subject was receiving the active ingredient and which were receiving a placebo, it was difficult to tell if the medication was working. However, some of the patients definitely began to show diminished numbers of wrinkles on their foreheads, a fact which thrilled Jennifer Maddux who stayed in touch with us almost daily via email. Julie had sent her a note announcing the positive effects. Maddux wrote back within hours, bubbling at the news. Most of the other sites lagged behind us and ours were among the first preliminary results she had received. The big boys at Omega Pharmaceuticals were pleased as well, she wrote.

I was under whelmed. So the drug got rid of a few wrinkles? Big deal. It's not like we were finding a cure for cancer. Still, I realized that while this might be of some tangible benefit to someone, somewhere, I was happy things were proceeding smoothly and, hopefully, glowing reports were being relayed to the brass about my role in the study. I did, after all, have ulterior motives for my participation.

One night, after returning home, I was at my desk studying for the mid rotation test in psychiatry when my doorbell rang. It was Lisa, an unexpected and appreciated reason to interrupt my scrutinizing of another dry textbook.

"What's up," I said after I opened the door.

"Do you have a minute?" she asked.

Lisa was wearing a T-shirt and running shorts. Sweat had beaded on her forehead which she was wiping away with a towel.

"Sure," I responded. "Been jogging?"

"Yeah. I try to get in a few miles each day when I can. As you know, it's not easy these days," she said with a smile.

"I used to run," I said, trying to sound like physical fitness was an integral part of my lifestyle. The truth was, I hadn't exercised to any significant degree since my freshman year in college. I had thought it would be a good way to meet girls but when that didn't pan out, I dropped it like a bad habit.

"Can I come in?" Lisa asked with an air of feigned exasperation.

I realized we had been holding our conversation in the doorway of my apartment.

"Oh, yeah. Absolutely," I said opening the door for her and backing away. I scanned the contents of the apartment. My relief at having gotten the kitchen cleaned up was quickly deflated at the sight of my *Calvin and Hobbs* boxer shorts draped over the cable box atop my television. There was no way to covertly retrieve them so I could only hope she would fail to notice.

"Nice shorts," she said pointing to the boxers. Her face was flush with a smile. Mine was bright red.

"Wasn't really expecting company," I parried. "It's the price you pay for not calling first."

Lisa chuckled. "Fair enough. You shouldn't be expected to be both a medical student and keep an immaculate apartment." My guest sat down on the couch, flipped off her running shoes and began massaging her feet.

"Want something to drink?" I asked. "Coke? Beer? Hemlock?"

Oh, yeah. I was pretty smooth.

"Ah, no thanks," she responded. "I wanted to talk with you about dermatology."

I procured a bottled water from the refrigerator. I had read somewhere that women admire men who cultivate nutrition and good health. The last thing I wanted her to know was that

I went through 3 cans of Copenhagen a week and my diet consisted largely of fried food.

"Shoot," I said as I slid into an overstuffed lounge chair in a man-of-the-world sort of fashion.

"How hard is it to get into?"

Her inquiry took me by surprise.

"Pretty nasty," I replied. "Radiology and ophthalmology used to be hot residencies. Actually, more competitive than dermatology. But with the Medicare cutbacks in reimbursement the average income for specialists in those fields has stagnated. Consequently, the competition for dermatology training positions has gone off the charts. Some institutions don't even consider applicants not in the top 5% of their class. People are failing the match 2 and 3 times before getting in. Publication oriented research is all but required. In short, it's completely out of control."

As my outline regarding the lay of the land had proceeded Lisa had stopped massaging her feet. When I finished, she was methodically biting her lower lip.

"Wow," she said. "I had no idea it was that bad."

"It's awful," I said as I sipped my water. "Look what I'm doing to boost my competitiveness. Investing my time in some anti-wrinkle study. It's not like I'm going to derive any life-altering experiences and insights."

Lisa sat up on the couch. "Well, I need to get into it."

"And that means what exactly?"

"I need to get a residency position."

"Here?" I asked.

"Anywhere. I'm not particular."

While part of me warmed to the notion of Lisa and I having a common interest, another part of me, the petty and selfish aspect, didn't want any more competition in the field than already existed. Lisa was very well thought of and a member of Alpha Omega Alpha, the medical school honor society. Although she might find herself playing catch-up competing for a residency, she was more than capable and could sprint past me in a second. Besides, her father was in academic medicine. Granted, it was in Nebraska but it was still academic medicine and who knew how far his reach extended.

"I thought you were looking at pediatrics or obstetrics?"

"I was. Things change." Lisa said flatly. "So what are the steps for getting into a derm residency?"

I set my bottle of water on the coffee table between us. "The first order of business is meeting with the chairman of the department and making your wishes known. Jennings will give you the usual song and dance about the difficulty of getting a position and how there were giants in his day. Your job is to maintain eye contact, nod appropriately and try not to yawn. When he's done with the fluff he'll probably ask about any research interests you have. This is where you tell him you are interested in almost everything. He'll suggest you talk with one of the faculty members with some ongoing project requiring copious grunt work. You'll meet with them, find out what they want you to do and you're on your way."

"That's about what I figured," Lisa said. "Not too much different than pediatrics or OB-GYN. Well, except for the increased competition I suppose."

"Yeah, that can be a problem," I said with a soft chuckle. "You do realize you are getting a late start in the game, don't you?"

"Sure," she responded. "But like I said, things change."

Clayton Murphy was the younger son of Patrick Murphy. At 9 years old, he was a budding soccer star, at least in his own imagination. Adorning the walls of the room he shared with his older brother, Michael, were posters of English and Irish football idols. The only thing occupying his mind more was the cattle his father raised. One in particular, a calf, had captured his fancy. He had been present for its birth and promptly named it Peter in honor of Peter Tench, the goalie on the Irish national team. He visited the calf daily, usually more than once. Peter became fond of the young boy, knowing his arrival meant a vitamin cookie would be in his pocket.

After Patrick Murphy had procrastinated as long as possible, he informed Clayton that when the stockyard truck arrived, Peter would be accompanying his brethren to the slaughterhouse. Clanton threw a fit. Following a protracted discussion with tears and foot stomping Patrick gave in, allowing the single cow to remain on the farm. In truth, it comforted him knowing he had not entirely divested the family enterprise of something which had been such an important part of their livelihood. Perhaps in time he might use Peter to begin rebuilding the herd.

When the large tractor trailer arrived at the Murphy property, only Patrick was present to witness their departure. The whole of the family had been distressed with the turn of events and it had been all that Patrick could do to convince them of its necessity. It would be better, he told himself, if no one were to see what took place.

The driver of the truck also served as its loader. Not much for conversation, he quickly maneuvered the beasts up the walkway and into the waiting trailer.

"I guess that should about do it," the man said as he swung the large metal doors into place and locked them. He retrieved a clipboard from the truck's cab before providing a Murphy a receipt.

"Sure you don't want me to take the calf?" he asked.

Murphy glanced towards the holding pen at the small animal taking advantage of his now unobstructed access to the feed trough.

"No," he said shaking his head. "That one's sort of a family pet. My son would have a meltdown if I got rid of him."

"Uh-huh," the man grunted as he climbed behind the wheel. "Mr. Craig will have you a check first part of next week, after the animals have been sent to the slaughterhouse."

"Okay," Murphy said despondently.

When the truck had rumbled out of sight Murphy walked into the pen and began stroking the calf's neck and shoulders.

"Sorry about the way things turned out, fella" he said softly. "Seems I say that a lot these days."

Before clinic the next day, I was picking up my mail at the medical school when I spied Lisa in the hallway. She had changed clothes since our morning duties at St. Joes and appeared dressed for some sort of interview.

"Hey stranger," I said as I approached her near the stairwell. "Don't you look nice."

"Thank you," she replied, her cheeks blushing a bit. "I'm glad I ran into you. I'm on my way to a meeting with Dr. Jennings."

"So, are you going to make a run at dermatology?"

"I think so. I'm sorry for having been so vague the other night. I'll fill you in when we have a bit more time."

I was touched she was willing to confide in me.

"I should be finished about 5 or so. You can call the apartment tonight if you like. I should be home studying for the psych exams."

"Thanks," she said as she turned to go. "Wish me luck."

"Will do," I responded.

The time in clinic went by quickly enough. Julie was complementary of my efforts which made me feel good. Galen Hart remained at the periphery of the process, making frequent calls on his cell phone to consult with the decorator working on his condominium and whoever else needed checking up on. He was becoming less interested in the project and had to be goaded by Julie into seeing patients and signing off on their laboratory data. I kept my nose to the grindstone and my profile low.

When clinic was finished I was sitting at a table in the break room completing the last of my notes when Julie stuck her head in the door.

"Dr. Franklin's on the line. Says she wants to speak with you."

My blood pressure instantly rose about 20 points. Dr. Franklin had never called me in the past. I didn't know if this was going to be good news or bad.

"Trouble?" I asked.

Julie smiled. "I doubt it. Dr. Franklin doesn't usually deliver bad news on the phone. She does it face to face."

<u>Lovely</u>, I thought. Well, there was nothing to do but grab the bull by the horns. I picked up the receiver from a phone on the wall and pressed the hold button.

"This is Justin Douglas," I said, trying to sound confident.

"Justin. Dr. Franklin here. I just got an email from Dr. Jennings about the Omega study. He wants to add another student onto the project. Lisa Penning. You know her?"

"Yes ma'am," I responded. "She's in my med school class."

"I'm aware of that," Franklin said sharply. "What I need to know is if she's a good student. Hard worker. Reliable. That sort of thing."

"Oh, quite. She's one of the best in our class. Very bright. Makes good grades. Gets along well with everyone. I can't speak to her previous involvement in any research efforts . . ."

"That's all I needed to know," she interrupted. "Sometimes the old man sends me a medical student or resident he's trying to unload so he doesn't have to deal with them. I gave Lisa a copy of the protocol and told her to contact you. I assume you can get her up to speed?"

It was less of a question than a command but I was in no position to pick and choose my assignments. If the dragon lady wanted something taken care of, I would have to comply.

"I can do that," I answered.

"Good. She should be calling you today or tomorrow."

Turning past a set of large iron gates at the front of the property, two limousines wound towards a 5 story stucco building near the back of the facility. On the neatly manicured lawn outside was a polished platinum sign bearing the logo of Omega Pharmaceuticals.

The limousines slowed to a stop in front of the building's portico. A doorman quickly appeared and opened the vehicles' doors. One by one, the passengers exited making their way towards the building's lobby. Each was either the chairman of a dermatology department or the second in command at one. Ten people in all, they represented some of the top medical schools in the country. They had been invited and flown first class to Omega's headquarters in Florida. Each would receive an honorarium of $5000, paid in cash before returning home. None had disclosed the reasons for the meeting to anyone beforehand. While not strictly off the books, it was definitely well below the radar and for good reason. This sort of blatant fraternization with pharmaceutical companies was, if not outright forbidden, certainly taken a dim view of. Some of the attendees had even expressed opinions in the professional and lay press railing against such relationships but none of the others would hold that against them. They were simply doing what they needed to get ahead. All were now at the feeding trough and there would be enough slop for each to eat their fill.

Although the Omega property wasn't expansive, it was unquestionably state of the art. Encompassing just over 8 acres, the campus was rimmed by 40 foot palm trees with posted warnings that the grounds were patrolled by security officers and protected with infrared detection devices. Each building was new, or nearly so, and immaculate. The windows were polished to a bright sheen as was the copper and zinc flashing around the rooftops. At any one time there were no less than 4 groundskeepers maintaining the lush St. Augustine grass and flowering foliage.

The morning air had become sticky with the rising temperatures making the air conditioned building a welcome respite. Gary Page was not in the office having taken the company plane on an early flight to Birmingham for a meeting. Omega's official hostess for their stay, Kelli Patton, had assured them he would be back by lunchtime for their seminar. In the interim, they would be shown around the facilities by Bob Harrington, one of the senior vice presidents.

The infrastructure was spectacular. Everything was state of the art, from supply intake to the assembly rooms to the tracking system for monitoring product dispersement. The computer systems were first rate, equipped with the latest software to ensure an efficient and safe workplace. Harrington explained in some detail the painstaking efforts made by Omega's human resources division to supply the company with well-trained, highly educated and motivated personnel. It seemed to have paid off. According to their host, the workforce ranked in the top 15% nationally in comparable wages and benefits. *US News and World Report* had given them high marks as an employer. As a result, they had little trouble assembling a qualified labor pool. There was a company cafeteria, subsidized daycare, exercise facilities and a profit sharing plan. Everyone the men met seemed pleased to be part of the company.

Lunch was being served in the boardroom when Gary Page arrived. He made the rounds with each of his guests greeting them by name. Page had been given an extensive dossier on the group's background which he had committed to memory during the morning flights. He knew enough about the men's spouses and children to ask how their son or daughter was doing at college or if their wife had made partner in her accounting firm. It was a trick he had learned from his original business partner, Jerry Fields, and had engendered considerable good will over the years. "People love to talk about themselves", he had said. "And they love to talk to a receptive audience even more."

After 20 minutes of schmoozing, Page walked to the small lectern at the head of the table. His guests dutifully turned to look at their host who gently held up his hand requesting a subsidence in their conversations.

"Thanks for coming," Page began. "I hope you are enjoying the accommodations. Please feel free to stay as long as you like. Omega writes off the costs of your rooms . . ."

The men chuckled and looked at each other.

". . . so it's not like we're out any real money," he said smiling. "When we finish here, I'll be glad to entertain any questions you have on anything related to Omega or the project. If you've heard enough and wish to relax, the resort has a top flight golf course and tennis courts if you are so inclined. They also have a really crackerjack masseuse on staff which I can recommend personally."

Having concluded his opening remarks, Page turned to the matters at hand.

"I realize you are all busy men so I'll get down to business. Each of you has been asked to attend this meeting for two reasons. First, you are in leadership positions in dermatology departments with influence in your specialty. Second, your departments have either off-site clinics or you have a relationship with clinicians in private practice. These are the venues for testing we wish to concentrate on. We found out long ago the red tape associated with performing drug studies within medical institutions was, shall we say, tedious. It is simply too difficult to get anything done what with the minions of administrators obstructing progress at every turn. To be sure, the testing of our drug delivery device will be done through such institutions in the time honored fashion, however, the patient numbers will be small and the amount of invested resources will be restricted as much as possible."

"Private practices are another story. Unfettered by an association with large medical centers, they are capable of a much more time and revenue efficient means of evaluation. It's in these practices we wish to test our patches. What we need from you is access to them."

"Why not simply contact them yourselves?" the man from the University of Pennsylvania asked.

"Time," Page responded. "The number of drug detail personnel vying for access to a practicing dermatologist's attention has doubled in the past 4 years. As you know, your specialty is almost exclusively office based. Seeing as many patients per day as feasible generates the maximum revenues. Pharmaceutical reps barely have enough face to face time with the docs to pitch their newest cream or pill, much less speak to them effectively about becoming involved in our study."

The head of the dermatology section at Stanford spoke next.

"What about a dinner and presentation at a nice restaurant?"

Page smiled and nodded his head. He'd been anticipating the question.

"We've considered that as well. Unfortunately, some medical societies and institutions frown upon such events. Besides, our research has shown most practitioners at the end of the day wish to leave the office and go home. Attendance at such dinners is at best stagnant and at worst, diminishing."

"Gentlemen, we are on a tenuous time table. We want to have this patch on the market within a year. That means we need to have the research done, collated and submitted to the FDA no later than 8 months from today."

The audience members looked at each other with raised eyebrows. The Food and Drug Administration was notoriously slow to approve new drugs and medical devices. Omega's schedule, if accomplished, would be nothing short of a miracle.

"Isn't that a bit unrealistic?" one guest asked. "I mean, even phase III studies usually take twice that much time, if not more and that's if everything goes well."

"Without disclosing my hand, I have it on good authority we may expect an expedited review of the data such that we will be on schedule."

Everyone in the audience caught Page's meaning. He had someone on the inside to push the project through.

"What we need is access. Access to private practices unfettered with institutional red tape. It is my belief you gentlemen can accomplish that."

"Why the rush?" asked a balding man at the far end of the table. "So the patch comes to market in 18 months, or even 24? Is waiting a year longer really that big a deal?"

"Competition. Two weeks ago I learned that a group in Canada is experimenting with the same delivery device. We have some idea how far along they are but not the complete picture. As you may or may not know, the testing oversight for such products under Canadian law is much less stringent. It's conceivable they might have a botulinum patch ready for market in 18 months or less. If so, while the physicians on this side of the border will not have direct access to their product, it will be available indirectly. More importantly, consumers with means will simply travel to Canada and purchase it there or on line. We need to beat them to the punch."

"This is all quite cutting edge" another of the guests said, "but you're asking us to trade on our good will with the private practitioners in our communities. Some may be interested but the time frame is going to be a big problem. It will require a significant refiguring of their practice's way of doing business. It could be a tough sell."

"That's true," Page acknowledged. "This proposal is an aggressive one and not for every practice. The participating physicians will be well compensated with a sizeable amount of cash up front. This should help soothe any negative impact on the conduct of their practices. However, there is an additional incentive for those willing to sign on. Exclusivity."

Page paused for a moment to take a sip of water.

"Until now, Omega's product line has largely involved chemotherapeutic agents and antibiotics. Most patients receiving our drugs either didn't know what they were getting or were too sick to care. They were relying on the judgment of their physicians to do the right thing by them. Consequently, our emphasis was on convincing the docs to prescribe our drugs. That's going to change 180 degrees. When these patches are approved, Omega Pharmaceuticals will embark on a massive media blitz. We'll be advertising in all the major media, particularly print. *Elle, Glamor, Cosmo,* you name it. There will be a 2-4 page advertisement in each issue. Additionally, infomercials, the Home Shopping Network, direct mailing and billboards will be employed. You name it, we'll be there."

"And where will we direct the public for the purchase of this product? Why to the clinicians who did the testing on it, of course. We will not be making these patches available to anyone with an 'MD' after their name. There has to be some sort of discretion. Imagine the foot traffic in Dr. Smith's office when the public learns not only that he or she did some of the original studies on the product but the only place to obtain the patches in the greater Dallas or Portland area is their office alone. The return will be substantial, to say the least."

The men in the room looked at each other with wry smiles and arched eyebrows. Substantial would be an understatement. Coercing the private practitioners in their communities would be considerably easier with that sort of incentive. They liked what they had heard but the best was yet to come.

Page looked around the room with satisfaction. He had gotten his audience's attention. It was time to go in for the kill.

"Before anyone asks the obvious question, I'll answer it for you. Five hundred thousand dollars. That is what each of you will receive in the event you are able to provide Omega with an appropriate forum for our testing. It will be deposited anywhere you wish and no one the wiser, including ex-wives."

The audience chuckled.

"I'm certainly no lawyer," the department head at Yale said, "but isn't this illegal?"

"Not at all," Page responded. "My attorneys tell me there are no limitations on what pharmaceutical companies may pay for 'consulting'. Informing your parent institutions about that income is another subject. I assume they wouldn't be pleased to learn of the financial transactions but then again, if the money is wired to say, an off-shore bank, the matter need never come to light. I'll be completely candid, Omega has never before operated in this manner. However, we've never had a product such as this."

The audience stared at Page and each other in disbelief. This sort of payday was something they could have only dreamed about.

"Obviously, no arm twisting will be involved. Everything discussed here will stay here. I'll trust you to your own discretion. If you don't wish to be involved that's up to you. There are a few things that will be required of you such as the number of patients needing to be enrolled and your personal assurance their testing will be completed on time. However, I think you'll find them to be minimal and Omega has a well-trained support staff in place to help move things along."

Page could see his announcement had captured his audience's imagination. He had known all along what would catch their attention - money. While professing to be in their field for the science and teaching, those rarely translated into mortgage and child support payments. He would allow them the remainder of the day to mull the matter over but he knew most if not all would eagerly proceed forward. It had been a successful meeting.

CHAPTER 7

Patrick Murphy's cattle were held in their pens overnight. The next morning they were herded, along with their brethren from surrounding farms to the floors of the slaughterhouse. The adults were quickly whisked away for immediate processing. A different fate, however, awaited the calves.

Several men physically separated the younger animals, moving them down a long corridor to a large, well-lit room. They were strapped to the sides of thick steel pipes firmly cemented into the floor. With the animals secured, a technician inserted a large bore needle into the jugular vein in their necks. The calves' blood was siphoned into large sterile vacuum bottles. As the crimson liquid rapidly filled the containers, new ones were cycled in. The blood loss caused the animals to become stuporous, eventually losing consciousness and slumping in their restraints. The blood letting now complete, the calves were hoisted onto the bed of a mechanized cart. When full, it would be driven to the slaughterhouse floor where the calves would be processed along with the older animals.

Each bottle was appropriately labeled, dated and a tracking number written with indelible ink on its side. The technicians placed the containers into a temporary mobile cold storage unit. Later it would be transported to the loading dock where a refrigerated truck would pick it up and carry the materials to the waterfront for the trip east across the Irish Sea to a biochemical supply company. Testing and sterilization of the blood required several days. Different components were extracted during separation, all in the confines of a painstakingly sterile "clean room". Within a week the company would begin shipping these components, primarily the serum, to different laboratories around the world.

***

After clinic was finished I went to the grocery store to pick up some essentials, in this case the typical frozen dinners, canned fruit, breakfast cereal and chewing tobacco. I had just arrived back at my apartment and was in the process of stowing my purchases when there was a knock at the door. I looked through the peephole. It was Lisa.

"Come in. Come in," I said, opening the door.

"Is this a bad time?" Lisa asked. She was again in her running attire wiping the sweat off her arms with a towel.

"No. Not at all. I was just doing the domestic thing."

"I can come back later if that's more convenient."

"No time like the present," I said with a smile. Unaccustomed to having attractive women in my apartment I'd have to be bleeding from an aneurysm to refuse such an offer.

"Have a seat," I said as I motioned to one of my two recliners. I had found them at a garage sale the first weekend after my arrival in Houston. What they lacked in taste they more than made up for in deterioration. To their credit, they were excellent for napping. I had come to like them so much I had given them names. Bob and Larry. Lisa was sitting in Larry, my personal favorite.

My guest adjusted the seat before folding her towel and placing it in her lap. "I guess you heard I'm going to be involved in the Omega study," she began. "I hope that I'm not stepping on any toes."

I could see in Lisa's eyes her concerns were genuine.

"Not at all," I said waving my hand in the air. "The more the merrier."

The truth was, I did have some hesitations. I liked Lisa a great deal, but my competitive nature was a difficult beast to tame. Obviously, she was interested in pursuing dermatology. Why else would she be getting herself involved in this project? Lisa was a top flight student. She had been elected to Alpha Omega Alpha as a third year medical student, a distinction afforded only 2 or 3 of the best students annually. My grades, although good, were not nearly as stellar. If it came down to a choice between myself and Lisa for a residency position I couldn't imagine a scenario where I would win out.

"Well, I did have some reservations, Justin. My decision to seek a dermatology residency has come at a late date. Certainly at least compared to yours."

"Better late than never."

Lisa chuckled lightly and looked at the floor. Something was troubling her and it was more than just concern over our sharing any kudos emanating from the research project.

"You probably were under the impression I had an interest in obstetrics," she began. "That was the case. I always admired what my father did for a living. His tales of difficult deliveries were fascinating to me. He was a hero, at least in my eyes, for having gotten the women he attended to through a harrowing time. Not to mention what he did for their babies."

She paused for a moment to refold the towel in her lap. Speaking to me seemed difficult for her, as if she was about to unload some sort of bombshell. I didn't have to wait long to discover what it was.

"I talked with my father a few days ago. He was diagnosed with Parkinson's disease last month." Tears began welling in her eyes and shortly dripping down her cheeks and off her nose.

"I'm sorry," I said softly. "Obviously, I didn't know that."

Lisa emitted a short laugh as she used her towel to dry her face.

"Thank you. Dad told me he'd been having symptoms for a while and suspected Parkinson's might be responsible. He wanted to be certain of the diagnosis before he spoke with me. He's very much the stoic type. Doesn't talk a lot about his feelings or problems. Apparently, he's in the early stages of the disease. He's taking medication for it but he had to inform the department chairman of his condition, so for the foreseeable future his duties on the obstetrics floor have been suspended. He'll mostly be working in the clinic. I guess his call duties will be less but knowing him, he'll feel like he's letting the department down not being able to shoulder a full load. The man has worked all his life. It's what he does."

"I know the type," I responded.

Lisa continued wiping the tears from her face. She sat up in the chair, set her shoulders back and tried to regain her composure. After taking a deep breath, she continued.

"Anyway, his phone call changed a few things. I obviously don't know what the future holds. How slowly or quickly his disease will progress, what effect his medications will have, if he'll get involved in some type of treatment or surgery protocol. It's still pretty early on. But it has caused me to re-evaluate my choices for future medical practice. The time investment for obstetrics and gynecology residency isn't much different than other disciplines. But, as you know, the work schedule after finishing is. I'm going to need a practice where I can be available to help look after my father. I'm not going to turn over his care to some nursing service. I want to be available for whatever he needs and spend what time with him as I'm blessed with."

The further talk of her father had once again filled her eyes with tears. Her nose was running so I rose from my chair, tracked down a tissue and handed it to her.

"Thank you," she replied before blowing her nose. "You can see why I'm interested in dermatology. I confess to not having a burning passion for the field. I simply don't know much about it other than the hours are good and that's my overriding concern at this point."

Her plight touched my heart. She was genuinely frightened and hurting.

"I have to be honest, Lisa. Getting involved in a drug study like the one with Omega is a good way to get a suitable letter of recommendation but it's not going to give you much of a feel for the profession. What goes on in our clinics is a far cry from the day to day practice of dermatology."

"Oh, I realize that," Lisa said dabbing her eyes. "I've spoken with the Dean about getting my fourth year electives changed to dermatology. That shouldn't be a problem. But I needed to start somewhere and I know research is all but required to be competitive for a residency spot. My father plays golf with the vice-chairman of the dermatology program at Nebraska. I'm hopeful that connection will get me an interview and a leg up on a position but without a better foundation I don't stand a chance there or anywhere else for that matter."

"Point well taken," I responded. "Like I said, the more the merrier. What do you want to know about the study?"

Sean McMillan was checking the serial numbers on a load of nutritional supplements when the buzzer from the front door sounded. Placing his clipboard on some nearby sacks of feed he walked back inside the store. His visitor was a man he'd never seen before, wearing a three piece suit and carrying a briefcase. Rarely was anyone in his store dressed in anything other than jeans or coveralls.

"Are you Sean McMillan?" the man asked.

His accent was British. McMillan considered answering negatively if for no other reason than his inherent distrust of people not from the area.

"Who's asking?" he said suspiciously.

"My name is James Leister. I'm an attorney representing a group of agri-businesses in Kent, England."

"Uh-huh," McMillan replied.

"I apologize for interrupting you in your work but I was wondering if we could chat a bit."

"What about?"

"Well, it's really rather a long story. Could I buy you lunch at the pub down the street?"

McMillan's abhorrence of lawyers stemmed from his particularly nasty divorce 5 years previous. He'd managed to keep his store but little else, including much visitation time with his daughter. The mere fact that one had traveled such a distance to talk with him, however, was intriguing.

"Alright," he replied after looking at his watch. "I suppose it's a bit early but I can close up for a while."

After hanging a "CLOSED" sign on the front door, McMillan and Leister walked to the Red Dog Pub, a favorite local watering hole with better than average fare. When they were seated with a pint of Guinness in front of them, Leister retrieved a photocopied invoice from his briefcase.

"Do you recognize this by any chance?" he asked.

McMillan studied it for a moment before answering. "It's an invoice."

"Do you recognize the company listed on the third line?"

McMillan replaced his reading glasses and again looked at the paper.

"It's a commercial livestock feed manufacturer," he said. "If I'm not mistaken their headquarters is in Wales."

"Cardiff, to be exact. Hamilton Manufacturing has been there for some time. Is it safe to assume you've purchased their products in the past?"

"I guess so. Some of their line is pricey. Not much call for it around here. I can't remember buying any recently."

"Have you ever purchased Surrey brand livestock feeds?"

"Yeah. They're cheaper." McMillan waved his hand in the air. "Look, I'm a man of limited patience. What is this all about?"

"Quite right. You've been more than considerate, Mr. Mc-Millan," Leister said with a smile. "As I'm sure you know, mad cow disease is quite a problem in the EU, particularly England. Some of the cattle growers and other agri-businesses have been hard hit by the disease. Many proprietors have declared bankruptcy or closed down altogether. About a year ago some of these entrepreneurs contacted my firm regarding a lawsuit against the feed manufacturers. It was their contention the materials supplied to them had been substandard, causing a loss of their livelihood."

Leister paused for a second to take a sip of his beer.

"This is quite good," he remarked. "Brewery around these parts?"

"Down the road 6 kilometers," McMillan responded impatiently. "You drove past it on your way into town."

"Anyway, our firm agreed to consider the lawsuit but frankly, after discussing it in a partners meeting, it generated very little enthusiasm. In the first place, these plaintiffs had previously been rejected by 6 different legal firms. If they weren't willing to undertake the project, given their extensive resources, it didn't make much sense for us to do so either. To buy a bit of time, we gave the project to two Cambridge students who were interning with us. We assumed it might be good practice for them and when they turned up little or nothing, we could at least tell the clients we had tried. As it turns out, we underestimated these students. One of them discovered a little known change in the manufacturing process of livestock feed implemented in the early 1970's. This new technique allowed for greater recovery of proteins from the flesh and internal organs of rendered animals. With these proteins came an increased number of viral particles responsible for mad cow disease which were incorporated into the agricultural products of Europe and elsewhere. It is the opinion of our firm these companies are legally liable for this error and we are preparing to bring suit against them."

McMillan sat listening carefully, intermittently taking a drag off a cigarette he'd lit.

"You done now?" he asked

"I think that about sums it up, yes."

"Is there something in this that deals with me?"

"Our quest is a simple one. Tracking feed shipment lots and their ultimate dispensation."

McMillan emitted a short, sarcastic chortle. "I'm the only retailer for livestock feed in this area. As a consequence, I move a lot of materials. I don't track what goes through the warehouse. The products I purchase are done through a wholesaler. It costs me more but I get to choose which product lines I want to bring in. Since the prices fluctuate, I usually just pick the cheapest ones."

"But surely you have some means of tracking what you purchased and who you sold it to?"

"Well, yes. But that would take a bit of digging."

"Do you have it on a computer somewhere?"

McMillan sighed as he crushed out his smoke. "This isn't a particularly high tech area of the world, Mr. Leister. I have a computer but so far as what comes in and where it goes, I never had much reason to keep count. The only way to obtain that information would be to look over the old invoices and match the product to the customer."

"What would it take for you to undertake such a project?" Leister said with a smile.

I explained as much of the study to Lisa as I could. She already had a large 3 ring binder of documents spelling out all the gory details of the research but seemed to appreciate my taking the time to go over the day to day aspects of the project. When I was finished she thanked me profusely before leaving.

The next day we met again in the clinic. She seemed nervous. Julie did her best to put Lisa's mind at ease, outlining the protocol and what would be expected of her. Actually, having another person available to help with the mounting paperwork proved quite helpful. Dr. Hart had become progressively more useless, showing up late for clinic and often leaving early citing some pressing need to attend a "meeting". My hope was that Julie was relaying his lackadaisical attitude to Drs. Franklin and Jennings. Not that they would be able to do much about it. Dismissing a resident for poor performance was all but impossible and in Hart's case, even less likely given the relationship between the chair of the department and his father.

We were well into the clinic when Hart blessed us with his presence. Julie was clearly irritated with his tardiness.

"Clinic started 40 minutes ago, Dr. Hart," she said testily.

"I had a meeting that ran late," he replied as he took off his sunglasses. "Sue me."

Lisa was exiting an exam room having finished her evaluation of the afternoon's second patient when she caught Hart's eye. His eyebrows arched upwards.

"Who's the babe?" he asked.

I stepped between the resident and Lisa with my temper rising. While we had no official relationship, I took issue with him speaking of her in that manner. Lisa was an attractive young woman and I was protective enough to feel compelled to defend her honor and dignity.

"'Babe' was the name of a movie," I said, staring him straight in the eye. "Perhaps you've seen it." I had raised my voice and Julie quickly moved closer to us presumably in the event we began throwing haymakers at one another.

My remarks surprised Hart. He wasn't accustomed to be addressed like this by a subordinate. His shock quickly gave way to anger.

"Watch your mouth, boy," he said through clenched teeth. "Or I'll have you pulled from this study so fast you'll wonder if you were ever in it."

I was about to say something I would regret when Julie interceded. She placed a patient chart between us and gently nudged me away from Hart.

"Mrs. Fields is in room 4, Justin. She's here for her third visit. Since we're running a bit behind," she said looking back at Hart who seemed to take little notice. "Would you see her so she can get on with her day?"

I took the chart without looking at her, my gaze remaining fixed on the resident in front of me. He, likewise, continued to stare at me. Turning to walk down the hall I passed Lisa who had a puzzled expression on her face.

I don't remember much of my visit with Mrs. Fields. I was so angry I could have spit nails or 'passed 'em sideways' as my uncle was fond of saying. When I emerged from the room Hart was gone or at least out of eyesight. I considered asking Julie where he was but thought better of it.

My temper had been a thorn in my side for as long as I could remember. When I was in kindergarten one of my classmates taunted me while we were at recess. After the bell had rung heralding our return to the classroom, I rushed inside and hid behind the door. When the boy appeared, I grabbed his arm, swung him around the room and let him fly. To this day, I don't know what I had hoped to accomplish by my actions. Unaccustomed as I was to being picked on, my outburst was a misguided attempt to lessen the anxiety of the situation. However, I certainly didn't consider the possibility he would launch headfirst into a desk opening a 2 inch gash above his left eyebrow.

I don't recall whether he bled very much. He should have considering the location of his wound. Nor do I have any recollection of what happened after his screams of pain brought the teacher running in from the hall. What I do remember is the reaction from everyone around me, except perhaps my father. That I had started down the road to a life of crime and incarceration appeared to be a foregone conclusion. Only the faintest chance for redemption existed. Of course, he never bullied me again. Or anyone else for that matter. In the ensuing years I nurtured bitter feelings about the entire incident but it did teach me an important lesson. I had a problem with my temper. Discovering this at a young age was overall to my benefit. I managed to subdue my flash points, keeping my anger in check largely with sheer discipline. Only rarely did it elude my grasp anymore.

Julie could see I was fuming and wisely decided to let me gather my thoughts.

"Dr. Hart had to leave," she said calmly. "Well, actually, I asked him to take the rest of the afternoon off."

I considered making a caustic remark but decided against it.

"I see," was all I said.

Lisa was sitting across from me at the table finishing her note on the patient she had just interviewed. She looked up from her writing, put her pen down and placed her hand atop mine. I was surprised at the calming effect it had on me. In truth, I was embarrassed by my anger and worried she would view me as some sort of hot head gone off the deep end over a perceived insult of a relationship which didn't exist. When I looked up she was staring at me.

"Julie told me what you said," she remarked softly.

I wasn't prepared for what she said next.

"Thank you. That was a kind thing you did."

Dr. Martin Goldstein sat in the office of a young woman who had several years earlier been one of his residents. Karen Mahoney was now out on her own and, from the look of things, was doing quite well. Mahoney had been an MD/PhD candidate from Stanford when she applied to the dermatology residency in Dallas. Her research had involved the immune system and its role in the skin of persons who suddenly began losing its pigment vitiligo. As Goldstein had some interest in the subject, he had insisted she be invited for an interview after review-ing her application. Her grades were acceptable as were her let-ters of recommendation and during her interview she professed an undying interest in pursuing further research in her chosen field. As with most such candidates, that interest died abruptly upon entering the residency. Goldstein had taken it with a grain of salt. He had seen it before and would surely see it again. The siren song of big bucks and private practice had captured her. If abandoning her roots in the laboratory ever bothered her, it didn't show.

After graduating from the program, she joined another der-matologist in a well-heeled section of town and never looked back. Eighteen months later she severed ties with her partner and began her own practice. Armed with every imaginable la-ser available and a newly opened spa, she had become success-ful. Quite successful as it turned out. Unlike most women in the field, she worked full time. She had to. Between a million dol-lar new home and round the clock domestic help she had con-structed a fortress-like golden prison. Her practice now owned her.

"To what do I owe the pleasure?" Mahoney asked as she strode into the room. Dressed in freshly starched lab coat and every hair in place, Goldstein had to admit to himself, private practice seemed to agree with her.

Rising to his feet, he shook her hand.

"Thanks for seeing me, Karen. I realize you're busy."

Mahoney sat behind her desk. It was immaculate as well. No piles of paper or stacks of unread medical journals for her.

"Not too bad," she responded smiling. "Mostly HMO and PPO patients this morning. They can wait. Besides, that's why God gave us nurse practitioners."

Goldstein shifted in his seat. "I assume you got my email?"

"I did. I'm not sure we have much room here for another drug study. We already have three in progress with two more scheduled to begin in the next several months."

"You might want to put as much as possible of that on hold after you hear what I have to say."

Goldstein laid out the nuts and bolts of the patch study. When he came to the part about the exclusive license to prescribe the product, Mahoney's eyes widened.

"Are they serious?" she asked.

"Oh, I can assure you, they're quite serious. Omega envisions this as a large part of their corporate future. I can't say for certain if they are putting all of their eggs in a single basket but it would appear so."

Mahoney stared out the window for a brief moment. Goldstein could see the wheels turning in her mind, mentally calculating how much money it would infuse into her already lucrative practice.

"As you know, we dispense botulinum injections here. It's quite profitable but obviously something not involving needles would be a giant leap forward. I can't envision a scenario where patients wouldn't be lined up around the block to get a patch instead of a shot."

"Indeed," Goldstein said with a grin.

"I have to admit, I haven't heard anything about this product. Before I would agree to become involved, I'll need to see some of the data."

Goldstein opened his briefcase, removed a thin manila folder and handed it to this host. Mahoney glanced through it briefly before closing it and placing it on her desk.

"I'll go over it more in depth later," she said as she stood.

Goldstein rose as well, recognizing the meeting had come to an end.

"One other thing," he said as he picked up his briefcase. "This will be an exclusive contract."

"Meaning what?"

"Omega wants to have their patches dispensed by a single practitioner. You would be the only one in the Metroplex with the rights to sell this product. Obviously, if you don't want to become involved, that's up to you. But I need an answer in the next 48 hours so I can pitch it to someone else if you decline."

Mahoney nodded her head. "Thank you for coming to me with this first. I'll let you know tomorrow what my decision is."

Goldstein smiled. She was in.

Sean McMillan arrived at his shop the next morning at 6:45 A.M., the same time as always. James Leister was sitting in his rented automobile across the street drinking coffee with an associate. When they spied the proprietor unlocking the front doors, they exited their vehicle and walked hurriedly toward him. He had just gotten his key in the lock when Leister called out to him.

"Mr. McMillan!"

Sean turned to see the barrister and a woman he'd never met before quickly closing the distance between them. He mustered a half hearted wave in their direction.

"Mornin'," he said, his cigarette bobbing up and down in lips as he spoke.

The trio walked into the store and McMillan switched on the overhead lights.

"This is Helen Jamison," Leister said. "She's an associate of mine here to work on the project we discussed yesterday."

McMillan was terminally "old school" and generally inclined to interact with the fairer sex as infrequently as possible. When Leister had said he would have someone going over the invoices he had naturally assumed it would be a man. This surprise wasn't a welcome one.

"What's she doing here?" McMillan said gruffly.

If Jamison was offended by the remark, she didn't show it.

"I'll be evaluating your purchase orders and sales receipts," she said cheerily. "It's a pleasure to meet you." She thrust forward her hand.

McMillan reluctantly shook it noting that she had a firm grip, at least for a woman.

"As I promised," Leister began, "we'll try to stay out of your way. Is there somewhere we could set up our computers?"

"Yeah, there's a small office in the back near the loading dock. You can camp there for the time being."

"Is there a door to this office?" Leister inquired.

McMillan looked at his guest quizzically.

"There is. Why?"

"We thought you'd be more comfortable if as few people knew about our presence as possible," Jamison said.

McMillan thought for a moment. "I suppose that makes the most sense. How long you two plan on being here?"

"That would depend," Leister responded. "If we can find out what we need to know, perhaps only a day. On the other hand, if your records require a more thorough evaluation, a bit longer."

"Well, as I told you yesterday, this isn't a high tech operation. I rarely have much need to recheck invoices so I don't have them organized."

"Oh, we understand," Jamison said. "Would you like me to make some coffee?"

Now McMillan was completely confused. From what he had read, women in today's workplace, at least those in the big cities, were loath to stoop to such pedestrian pursuits as procuring coffee. Perhaps he'd come to enjoy having her around the shop after all.

"Yeah. I could use some. There's a coffee pot in the office."

Jamison and his protégé walked into the back of the business which consisted of an expansive concrete floored room and a single truck bay with a retractable metal door. Stacks of feeds and animal supplements lay atop wooden pallets on the floor. Birds could be heard fluttering in the building's rafters. Several had built nests within the steel girders. The chirping of their progeny echoed around the room.

Jamison had been in enough of these warehouses over the past year to watch where she stepped. It wasn't a fear of tripping that provoked her vigilance. It was a terror of rodents. Once while inventorying a business in Brighton a mouse had run across her foot sending her into a full fledged panic. Since then she had taken to wearing closed toed boots at the job site and carefully searching for telltale evidence of mouse infestation – small tears in feed sacks near the bottom of the stack, well placed rodent traps, droppings and, most important of all, a cat. Larger operations no longer used them, but the smaller and mid sized businesses did. Jamison was walking deliberately across the concrete floor when she saw a flash of dark whisk along the edge of a bag of horse food. Looking upward she discovered it belonged to solid black cat with white on its nose, front paws and the tips of its ears. The animal was lying still atop a mountain of 75 pound sacks looking regal and bored with the goings on around him.

Jamison, like many women, had a soft spot for cats and the site of one in the workplace was all the more appealing. She moved quickly towards the animal.

"Kitty," she said playfully.

"Good grief," Leister mumbled under his breath.

"Is this your cat?" Jamison asked McMillan.

"Guess so," he replied. "I keep feeding him and he keeps hanging around."

"How friendly is he?"

McMillan shrugged his shoulders. "Friendly enough, I suppose. Unless you're a mouse. He's never bitten me or anything. Course, I don't sit around and pet him either."

Jamison was leaning over the animal, scratching it under the chin. The cat, in return, responded with a loud purring sound, rubbing its head over the woman's hand and wrist. It was clearly enjoying the attention.

"What's his name?" Jamison asked.

"Stan," McMillan answered.

Jamison stopped petting the cat and looked back at McMillan. "What kind of a name is Stan?"

"In this case, his kind," McMillan responded with a note of irritation in his voice. "My daughter was here one day when the useless fleabag wandered up and she named him. I wanted her to take him home but her mother nixed the idea. He's been pretty good company. Keeps the vermin population down and doesn't talk much. I can't complain."

Jamison hadn't heard the last half of what her host had said, so intent was she on stroking Stan and rubbing his face. The animal was more than happy to let the woman do so, occasionally looking over at McMillan as if to say 'see, this is how one properly treats a cat.' When she had finished Jamison followed Leister and McMillan into a small office adjacent to the bay door.

McMillan switched on the overhead light. Inside the room was a desk cluttered with pieces of paper, empty soft drink cans and junk mail. Boxes crammed with sheets of pink invoices rested on the floor. In the corner sat a file cabinet corroding around the edges. Atop it was a coffee maker with the remnants of its previous brewing still in the pot.

"There's a can of coffee in the top cabinet," McMillan said gesturing towards the appliance. Jamison opened the file cabinet and peered inside.

"Where are the filters?" she asked as she rummaged through the open drawer.

"Aren't any," McMillan answered. "Just use paper towels. There's some in the bathroom around the corner."

Jamison glanced at Leister who shrugged his shoulders. <u>Well, I did offer</u> she said to herself. Backing out of the office she walked to the restroom and pulled the chain attached to an overhead light socket. To her pleasant surprise it wasn't as ill kept as she had anticipated. Jamison rinsed the liquid thoroughly from the pot before refilling it with clean water and grabbing a single paper towel from a stack atop the toilet. When she returned to the office Leister and McMillan were loading boxes onto the crowded desktop.

"Thanks," McMillan said as the coffee maker spun up and began spewing hot water into the plastic housing. The smell of the freshly brewed liquid began filling the room. It took the two men only a few more minutes to organize the boxes. When they were done, McMillan backed out of the cramped space into the warehouse.

"Well, there you have it," he said. "I'm going back to the front. Some of my customers are early risers. You two have fun."

Jamison and Leister looked at each other and then back at the boxes full to overflowing with invoices. They had their work cut out for them.

By the end of clinic I had calmed down, aided in no small part by Lisa's compassionate words. Hart had not returned to the premises but I hadn't expected him to. I suspected he had long since forgotten about our encounter. Or at least I hoped he had. As the clinic wore on I increasingly worried that word of the momentary flare of my temper might get back to Drs. Franklin and/or Jennings. I suspected neither liked Dr. Hart much more than I did but he was after all, a resident in their program and their loyalties would undoubtedly lie with him. Snagging a position in a dermatology program was difficult enough without hamstringing myself by getting a reputation as a hothead.

When clinic was finished Julie asked Lisa and I if we wanted to see some of the before and after patient photographs. Omega Pharmaceuticals wanted the progress of the study's participants charted visually, presumably for use in publishing the results as well as hastening its FDA approval.

We sat down at the table before a large screen computer terminal while Julie loaded a CD. After a click or two the photographs began to appear side by side. The results were impressive. The "before" photographs showed enrollees, largely women, with various lines and furrows on their foreheads. Some were more apparent than others but the photographic equipment clearly was adept at uncovering many more than were visible to the naked eye. Even more telling was the effect of the patches despite the short time of their use. Many, if not all of the lines had been reduced or eliminated. The decrease in the perceived age of the participants was stark. Most looked at least 3-5 years younger and in a few cases, more so. We had appreciated some changes but nothing as conspicuous as those depicted on the computer screen. Equally obvious were those patients we believed were receiving the placebo. Their photographs were virtually unchanged.

At the conclusion of the study a second computer software package would statistically analyze the effectiveness of the toxin but it was clear a change had taken place. The absence of any untoward side effects and normal blood evaluations would make it all but impossible for the FDA to stall its approval. Omega Pharmaceuticals had a winner on its hands.

CHAPTER 8

Jamison and Leister worked the rest of the morning collating the invoices in McMillan's office. By noon they had segregated the paperwork chronologically and were ready to begin critically evaluating its contents. Their semi-covert efforts mandated a degree of secretiveness requiring lunch be ordered out. They were kind enough to procure something for their host who closed the shop for the dinner hour and joined them in the back. All three sat in the warehouse, McMillan perched on top of a palate of horse feed and Leister sitting in a rickety wooden chair. Jamison sat on the floor eating her salad and petting Stan the cat who, once again, basked in the attention. Every few minutes she would reach into her Styrofoam container and select a small fragment of chicken which she fed to her new friend.

After a brief discussion of things political, all three returned to their tasks at hand; McMillan manning the front counter of the shop and Leister and Jamison sorting through the piles of paper. Just before 6:00 P.M. McMillan returned to the back office, knocking softly on the glass prior to turning the doorknob.

"Closing up," he announced.

Jamison opened the door. "You're preparing to leave?" she asked.

"Yeah. It's 6:00 o'clock."

"We were wondering," Leister asked. "If we might talk with you a moment before you headed home."

"I guess so." McMillan's voice had a hint of irritation to it. He'd been a congenial host but entertaining visitors for the entire day had been wearing. He was accustomed to having the place to himself and was anxious for a return to business as usual.

Leister rose from his chair, stretched his back and picked up a sheaf of papers sitting in front of him. "May we go to your counter up front?" he inquired. "I'd like to spread these pages out and we don't have the room for it here."

"Fine," McMillan grumbled.

The proprietor and his guests walked through the door separating the warehouse from the store. The daylight outside had all but disappeared, leaving the room bathed in the sickly glow of its fluorescent lighting. On the long countertop adjacent to the back wall Stan sat grooming himself. He glanced up when his bathing was interrupted and immediately launched into an audible purr when he spied Jamison. McMillan nudged him off onto the floor. The cat landed on all fours, rewarding his owner with a disdainful look before slowly ambling off.

Leister carefully placed five different stacks of papers in neat piles on the countertop.

"Here's what we've been working on for the past few hours," he began. "As you can see, over the past year you've purchased different lots of animal feed from quite a number of suppliers. By our calculations, and this is just a preliminary evaluation, I want to make that clear . . ."

McMillan shook his head slightly. <u>Always the bloody disclaimer</u>, he thought to himself.

". . . it appears you've received around 40% of your merchandise from Surrey Manufacturing in Cardiff and another 25% from Manchester AgriFeeds. The remainder come from a variety of other providers. Most of this has been for cattle, pigs and horses. Surrey and AgriFeeds are the ones we're most interested in. According to the information they provided us and your invoices, none of the lots match up. Apparently, you were never sold any products known to be potentially contaminated. I'm sorry."

"You're sorry?" McMillan asked. "For what?"

"Well, that you won't be able to be a party in the ensuing lawsuit, of course."

"I'll live."

Leister raised his eyebrows in surprise. "You're certainly taking this much better than some. I dreaded giving you the news. Others in your position have viewed this as a winning lottery ticket. When they discover they won't be in the running, they've become quite irritated."

"I've got enough money as is. Besides, it would just mean another encounter with the ex in court and I've been around lawyers enough. No thanks."

Leister picked up the sheafs of paper and began straightening them. "I must confess, I find your attitude not only refreshing, but altogether quite rare. However, we do feel compelled to reimburse you for the time and trouble we've put you through."

"Fine," McMillan said. "Send me a check or something."

Jennifer Maddux sat at her desk in the Omega office complex composing a memo for her boss, Gary Page. In the weeks following his meeting with the dermatology department gurus, the confirmations had steadily flowed in. All but one had found someone in their community willing to undertake the testing protocol. Maddux had been busy flying from one locale to the next speaking with the clinicians who had signed on the dotted line. Most were cordial and eager to get started.

Maddux kept her remarks to a single page of paper. There wasn't really much to tell anyway. She listed the names of the practitioners, their location and affiliated institution. There were 9 in all, more than enough to generate the numbers needed to get the data past the FDA. Maddux had been working late each evening making certain the supplies were sent to the right places and the accompanying paperwork would be filled out correctly. In addition, she had arranged for an on-site photographer to be present each day to take pictures of the study patients and log their digital images into the computer. It had to be costing Omega a fortune to set all this up but she had been assured by the corporation's bean counters the funds were available and to spend whatever necessary to get the job done. Besides, that part of the company wasn't her concern. She had enough on her plate.

After typing the last of the memo, she proof read her composition, printed a copy and gave it to her secretary to forward to Page. He would be pleased.

"I'm Dr. Ewan Calcote," the man said. "I believe Mr. Walsh is expecting me."

The security guard on duty eyed the 30-something man with suspicion. In the first place, he was unaccustomed to having many visitors at the south end of the Fairlyn Meats processing plant. Most of the traffic consisted of incoming live cattle and the departure of dead ones. In addition, he had been upbraided a few years previous after some animal rights activists had shown up and he had been slow in closing the sliding, 12 foot steel gate. A few of the protesters had made it onto the grounds. After launching into their well rehearsed discourse, they realized the protective shield of police officers were on the other side of the fence leaving them alone with plant workers who took a dim view of those advocating their unemployment. Things had gotten messy with several of the activists receiving cuts and bruises. Since then, anyone the guard didn't know or didn't possess the appropriate paperwork was scrutinized. Besides, the visitor was driving a Ford Escort and had government weasel written all over him.

"I'll have to call the office," the man responded. He returned to the concrete guardhouse, making sure the steel gate was closed and locked. The phone call to the main office, a small two-story affair dwarfed by the large slaughterhouse adjacent to it, took less than 60 seconds. Mr. Walsh's secretary informed the guard her boss was indeed expecting the man, and since he was a government official who could make trouble for the company, he was to be treated more than respectfully. The guard mumbled under his breath as he hung up the phone and pushed a button on the wall opening the gate.

"Right," the guard said, with a strained smile on his face. "They're expecting you at the office. That's the smaller building on the left about 200 meters down the drive. Should be some parking in front."

"Thanks so much," the visitor responded as he rolled up his window. He put the car's transmission in gear, roared down the road and into the parking lot. Five minutes later he was sitting in Jeffrey Walsh's office having tea served to him by his host's secretary.

After a brief amount of small talk, Walsh decided to break the ice.

"So, you're here to begin the sampling, correct?"

Calcote sipped again at his tea. "That's right. I assume you received the memo from the Minister of Agriculture?"

"I did," Walsh responded.

"Well, it's pretty much all there in chalk and cheese. Our offices will be sending out inspectors to every meat processing and packing plant in the country for the next 6 months. The visits will be unannounced, no more often than twice monthly and for a total of 10 visits. Each inspector will procure samples to be processed at the home offices. Nothing has changed since the minister released the memo."

"Well, I suppose it's a sign of the times," Walsh said as he rubbed his neck. "I assume we'll be given a copy of your findings."

"Certainly."

"And a final report, when you've compiled it?"

"Absolutely."

"Very well then," Walsh said rising from his chair. "Let's get you on with your job so I can return to mine."

Walsh walked from behind his large wooden desk beckoning Calcote to follow as he opened the door to his office. The two men strode down a single flight of stairs and out a service door to a small parking area behind the building. Adjacent to a large dumpster were three well traveled golf carts which the office staff used when their duties required them to visit the processing plant. Calcote couldn't help but notice that the carts were immaculately maintained. If animal matter was ever splattered on the vehicle's exterior, it had been efficiently removed.

Walsh climbed into the driver's seat, Calcote dutifully seating himself beside his host. The morning was chilly and as the two rounded the corner of the office building, a blast of cold air hit the men causing them to instinctively secure the top of their overcoats. It took less than a minute to arrive at a large loading dock with an ascending concrete ramp. Forty yards away were the holding pens for the cattle. Most were milling around with a vacuous look in their eyes, oblivious to what was about to befall them.

Walsh maneuvered the golf cart up the ramp before parking at the far end. Both men exited the vehicle, walked into the building and down a long hallway. After their arrival at the phlebotomy room, Walsh held the door for his guest who walked inside, a large industrial-looking briefcase in his hand. The place was empty, something Calcote found surprising.

"Why aren't there any workers here?" he asked.

"We thought you might like to have the place to yourself. Fewer distractions," Walsh responded.

Along the near wall was a long bank of mobile metal shelves. One-gallon clear plastic buckets with adherent masking tape strips rested on the metal rods. Each contained pink, wax-like calf brains bathed in an amber liquid. The tape strips bore the date of the animal's death and a series of numbers corresponding to the lot from which it had been taken.

"I think you'll find everything here self-explanatory," Walsh said. "When you're done, I can provide you with a printout of the tracking numbers you'll need."

Calcote nodded his head. The surroundings were similar to those in other plants although he had to admit, not having any company would make for a less hectic work environment.

"How long do you think this will take?" Walsh asked.

Calcote looked at the long array of shelves. "About an hour should do it."

Walsh glanced at his watch.

"Fine. I'll send someone back around with the golf cart in an hour then. Enjoy."

Calcote placed his briefcase on a nearby table, rolled in the combination and pulled open the flaps. He removed a small box containing 25 glass tubes each containing a small amount of fluid and a red rubber stopper. After donning a pair of latex gloves, Calcote rummaged through his briefcase until he located the sterilized packet of surgical instruments his assistant had given him the day before. Finally, he placed a small clipboard on the tabletop before turning his attention to the specimens themselves.

There was no set protocol for selecting which of the calf brains he would sample other than to make the choices randomly. A minimum of 48 hours in formaldehyde was required for suitable fixation. Firmer brain tissue made for more easily evaluated specimens.

Calcote approached the first rack of buckets. The dates here were recent, some having been placed there only the day before. He began moving down the row searching for older specimens. He removed a single container, checked the date and held it up to the light. The tissues appeared to be in good condition so he carried it back to the table, removed the lid and peered inside. Satisfied that the brain was up to standard, he picked up a large pair of tweezers and a disposable scalpel. After removing a pencil eraser sized fragment of tissue, he dropped it into the first glass tube, resealed the stopper and transcribed the information from the masking tape to a paper sticker before affixing it firmly to the glass tube. He repeated this process until 25 specimens had been procured. Calcote was repacking the materials into his briefcase when Walsh's secretary knocked on the closed door.

"Come in," Calcote said loudly.

The middle age woman stuck her head timidly past the metal doorframe. "Have you finished or do you require more time?"

Calcote chuckled to himself. "No," he said. "I'm just wrapping things up."

When the refrigerated transports containing the calf serum arrived at Balwynn Biomedical Supplies they were unloaded from the trucks, the men and women on the docks quickly moving the materials to the freight elevators and up to the 2nd floor for processing. The individual canisters were catalogued with bar code stickers corresponding to their site of origin along with the date of their procurement and arrival.

Once inside a sterile laboratory, the thick liquid was removed from it's near zero frozen confines and decanted into large glass tubes for sterilization, a process requiring most of the day. The first step was to allow the fluid to assume room temperature. This promoted adherence of the clotting proteins to one another, initially into microscopic aggregates and eventually into larger, visible ones. Upon completion, the tubes were centrifuged in a large metal structure the size of a washing machine. After spinning for 15 minutes at several thousand rpms the containers were removed and the clots extracted manually. What remained was serum, a compilation of water, proteins and various trace elements including calcium, potassium and sodium. While not the end product of the process, this liquid comprised the starting material of the bulk of Balwynn's product line.

A small amount of heparin was added to the serum preventing residual clotting proteins from clogging the machinery. The faintly pink liquid was then sterilized using radiation from a high intensity light source. After cooling, it was decanted into sterile plastic bottles for storage and shipment.

***

"Just some headaches," the woman said.

"Just some headaches?" I asked.

"Yeah, that's pretty much it."

The study was in its ninth week and with the patient enrollment complete, our clinics had become full. Part of my job was to interview the participants and ask them a series of questions provided by Omega. It was a laundry list of side effects, some of which made sense to me since the patients were being treated with a neurotoxin but most seemed baseless. I assumed the queries were more for the FDA oversight committee than for any real interest in how the drug might be adversely affecting the test subjects.

Seated in front of me was Helen Rubin, a middle aged woman who had been one of the study's first enrollees. She had done well to date. No problems with the patches and a visibly marked reduction in the wrinkling on her forehead and temples. I had seen her during her previous visits but she seemed different this time. Here eyes were lifeless and her affect blunted. Something was troubling her.

"Have you had problems with headaches in the past?" I inquired.

"Not really. I get an occasional one when I'm stressed out but it usually responds to aspirin or ibuprofen."

"Do these?"

"Sort of. I mean, they eventually go away but not like they have in the past."

"Is the pain in the same place as your other headaches?"

Mrs. Rubin shook her head. "No. In the past the pain was usually near the back of my head. You know, like with tension. These seem to be on the top of my head."

I decided to focus on the neurologic symptoms addressed on the checklist.

"Any visual problems? Difficulty focusing? Blind spots? That sort of thing?"

"Not that I've noticed. It could be all work related. I'm in the middle of a project that has kept me strung out the past 3 weeks."

I glanced back down at my clipboard. "Weakness anywhere?"

Mrs. Rubin furrowed her brow. "You mean like with walking or something?"

"Well, certainly that, but also in any of your muscles. Difficulty standing up. Problems with swallowing. Earlier onset of fatigue while fixing your hair. That sort of thing."

Mrs. Rubin thought for a moment. "Well, now that you mention it, I have noticed that my arms are more tired in the morning after blow drying my hair. I just attributed it to getting older."

Her brief laugh was a poor attempt at dismissing the subject. I could tell I'd hit pay dirt.

"Any changes in your medication?" I asked.

"Yes," she answered. "My internist put me on Zoloft this week."

"Zoloft," I said as I jotted down the name of the anti-depressant. "You've been having some problems with depression?"

She rolled her eyes and glanced out the window at some pigeons preening on the windowsill.

"I guess so. Dr. Henry thought it might help with some of my symptoms."

"What kind of symptoms?"

"From what Dr. Henry said, they're pretty classic for depression. I had been getting easily irritated. Not sleeping well. Sort of sitting around in a funk when I wasn't at work. Problems with concentration. That sort of thing."

"These would be new experiences for you?"

"Oh, yes," she said with a pained smile. "I'm typically a real go-getter. Nothing much gets me down but in the past month things changed."

"Like what?"

"Well, the first thing I noticed was while driving. Someone would cut me off and I'd fly into a rage."

I could relate. Not only did the volume of traffic in the Bayou City boggle the imagination, the drivers' aggressiveness was legendary.

"Well, the traffic around here can be trying," I responded sympathetically.

"True. But it's not like me to launch into a cursing spree or shoot someone the bird." Her eyes bore an expression of bewilderment.

"Has the Zoloft helped?"

"Not that I can tell," Mrs. Rubin said shaking her head. "At least not yet but then I've only been on the medication since last Friday. Dr. Henry told me it would take a few weeks to kick in."

"That's true. This problem didn't begin overnight and it won't be solved overnight either."

I consulted my clipboard again, ready to resume my checklist of signs and symptoms. When I looked up, Mrs. Rubin was in tears, her head in her hands. Emotional outbursts from women was something I had little experience with. My mother and sister were pretty stoic, in fact all the women I knew growing up were that way. My father called it the "Little House on the Prairie" syndrome. Crying was something I had seen only at funerals and occasionally at weddings.

"Are you okay?" I asked hesitantly. I didn't know whether to pat her on the shoulder or sit quietly while she got it out of her system.

"No," she answered after blowing her nose. "I'm not. My husband keeps telling me I'm forgetting things."

"Forgetting things?"

"Like where my car keys are. What time church starts. Whether I fed the dogs or not. Stuff I've been doing without any problems for the last 20 years."

"Well, that could be an element of the depression," I said, hoping my words would be of some reassurance.

"I realize that. But this came on over a period of 3 weeks. That's pretty fast, don't you think? And what if it doesn't resolve? I'm afraid I'm losing my mind."

She again put her head in her hands and wept openly. I felt completely powerless to help the woman so I did the least intrusive thing I could think of. I let her cry. When she was done I offered her a tissue. It was then I noticed her palms. Standing up, I took her right hand and ran my fingers along the surface of palm. The skin was red and peeling.

"What's the story with your skin here?" I asked.

Mrs. Rubin sniffled as she used her free hand to wipe her nose and blot her eyes.

"I don't know," she said dejectedly. "They've been like that for the past month. Just gradually getting worse."

"Any symptoms?"

"Some burning and tingling, I suppose."

"No itching?

"Not really."

"Have you been putting anything on them? Lotion or something?"

"Yeah. I got this stuff from the drugstore that's supposed to be good for dry skin but it hasn't helped much." Mrs. Rubin sniffled some more and blew her nose. "Do you think this could be due to the patches?"

I shook my head. "I suppose so, but I doubt it. I'm not aware of the botulinum toxin causing these sorts of effects. Let me do this. I want to get someone else to look over what you've told me. I'll be back directly."

Mrs. Rubin nodded her head and continued to dab at her eyes with the tissue.

I opened the door and stepped out in the hall. Julie was at the nurses' station. Upon seeing me she arched one of her eyebrows.

"You were in there a while," she said.

"I think we may have a problem," I answered.

Dr. Calcote stopped by the offices before leaving. True to his word, Walsh had provided a sequential list of the brain specimens with his secretary. Calcote sat in a small lobby with the clipboard resting on his knees reading the material he'd been given. It took him only a short while to jot down the necessary information in the appropriate spaces. When he was done, he returned the clipboard to the secretary who barely looked at him. She had been in the middle of some transcription and apparently didn't care much for being disturbed.

Calcote walked down the hall adjacent to her desk and stuck his head in the doorway of Mr. Walsh's office.

"I'm all finished," Calcote announced.

"No problems, I assume?" Walsh asked as he removed his glasses.

"None whatsoever. I appreciate your hospitality. Having the room to myself was definitely conducive to completing the task."

"And you have all the numbers you require?"

"Yes, sir. I'll be leaving now. I don't know what the time frame will be for the sample analysis but it shouldn't be more than a few weeks. I have your fax number so I'll ask the laboratory chaps to shoot you a copy straight away after they're finished."

"Splendid. Have a safe trip."

"Will do," Calcote said buttoning his overcoat.

<u>Good riddance</u>, Walsh thought.

Clayton Murphy sprinted between the barn and his family's home, jumping on the porch and letting the screen door bang loudly behind him.

"Dad," he said, out of breath. "Something's wrong with Peter."

Patrick was sitting at the kitchen table working on the family's budget for the month. The cash infusion from selling the livestock had been less than he'd hoped for but enough to cover the costs of putting in the new crop of potatoes with a small amount remaining to pay off some of his bill at McMillan's feed store. If the harvest to come didn't pan out, however, he had no idea what he would do to keep things afloat. Another potential problem from his young son wasn't welcome news.

"What do you mean 'something's wrong'?" Patrick said.

"He won't get up," Clanton answered.

Patrick looked up from his spread sheets and removed his glasses. "He won't get up?"

"No. He just lays there in his pen. I tried giving him a cookie but he didn't want it."

Patrick could tell his son was worried. Clayton was a typical 8 year old boy. Headstrong and fearless on the soccer field, he possessed a soft spot for his calf. The animal had remained a part of the family almost exclusively at his insistence. Clayton's concern touched his father. The paperwork would still be there when he returned.

"Let's go take a look," Patrick said softly.

The two Murphy men walked briskly to the barn, a ramshackle affair built entirely of wood by his father and grandfather. Some of the neighbors had larger steel buildings but Patrick had always loved the look and feel of timber. Over the years he had put in more hours than he could remember replacing the side boards, patching the roof and shoring up the frame. His wife often remarked her husband felt more at home in the barn than in the house.

When Patrick peered into the animal's stall he realized his son had reason to worry. Peter was laying motionless on a bed of fresh hay, his eyes glazed and his breathing labored. The animal's lips were swollen, the surrounding hay damp from the steady oozing of saliva.

"Let's see what we've got," Patrick said, trying to sound upbeat. He stroked the animal's head gently but Peter barely responded to his touch. Normally a spirited animal, it was unlike him to be so lethargic. Something was definitely wrong.

"Maybe he's got a twisted gut," Clayton said hopefully.

"Could be."

Patrick placed his arms around the calf and lifted him to his feet. For a moment, it seemed like getting him upright and active might help. The calf took several wobbly steps before slumping into the wall and sliding back down onto the ground. He could barely hold his head up.

"Did you try getting him some water?" Patrick asked.

"Yes. But he didn't want any."

"And he was okay last night?"

"He seemed sort of tired," Clayton answered. "He didn't want to chase me around the pen like he normally does."

Patrick glanced at the feedbox hanging on the adjacent wall. It was still full from the previous evening.

"He doesn't seem to be very hungry either," Patrick noted.

"What's wrong with him, Dad?" Clayton asked. His eyes were brimming with tears.

Patrick placed his hand on the boy's shoulder.

"I'm not sure. Let's call the vet and see what he has to say."

I told Julie about my encounter with Mrs. Rubin. She listened attentively before asking any questions. To my satisfaction, her queries all regarded subjects I had covered with the patient. When our conversation was done she turned to Dr. Hart who was fixated on a brokerage website.

"Did you hear what Dr. Douglas was telling me?" she asked.

"Not really," he answered. "Did Dorothy screw up again?"

Hart's comment didn't rile me. Well, not much, anyway. He was always good for a few caustic remarks per clinic. Most of them at my expense and, to his credit, some occasionally witty.

"Get over here!" Julie said, raising her voice. Apparently, she'd had enough of the resident's lagging interest in the study. Hart was surprised by her tone. He jerked his head away from the screen and swiveled around in his chair.

"Okay!" he said, raising his hands. "Cool your jets. I'm here. What's the problem?"

I gave the resident a brief synopsis of my encounter with Mrs. Rubin who did his best to look bored at my recitation.

"That's it?" he asked.

"Well, don't you think that's significant?" Julie asked, incredulously.

"She's probably just going through the change."

"Going through the change?" I asked.

"Yeah, nimrod. You know. Menopause. They do still cover that in medical school, don't they?"

Julie stood staring at Hart, her mouth agape, too stunned to say anything.

"Did you ask her about night sweats? Hot flashes? Her menstrual periods? That sort of thing?"

"She had a hysterectomy 9 years ago," I retorted.

My knowledge of Mrs. Rubin's medical history took Hart by surprise.

"Oh," he said, with an air of embarrassment. "I didn't know that."

"Well, there's a shocker," Julie said.

"I can't be expected to keep up with every meaningless detail on each patient in this study, you know!" Hart said defiantly. "Give me the chart. I'll get to the bottom of this."

Hart ripped the folder from my hand as he set off down the hall at a brisk pace. Five minutes later, he emerged from the examination room.

"Well?" Julie asked.

"She's nuts," Hart announced.

"Is that a medical opinion or just one of yours?" Julie inquired.

Hart ignored her.

"Who's the psych resident on consults?"

"Why?" I asked.

"Well, I'm making this chocolate soufflé for my significant other and I need some tips on how to keep it from falling."

If Hart's gaze had been a laser it would have bored a 6 inch hole through my brain.

"Because I want to get a consultation on this woman, that's why."

"Wait a minute," Julie interjected. "Before we do that we need to get approval from Omega. We're authorized to do routine lab work but not psychiatric evaluations."

"Swell," Hart said. "You do that. But in the meantime, I'm calling the psych resident."

Dr. Ian Kellor stared at the calf lying on the ground. Peter's condition had changed little since Patrick had contacted the veterinarian. He continued to drool copious amounts of saliva, breathe laboriously and for the most part, lay motionless. Patrick hadn't tried to lift him again, instead preferring to let him rest as much as possible. The calf's appearance was pathetic.

Kellor examined the animal's eyes, tongue and mouth as best he could. When finished, he removed his stethoscope from his bag and listened to Peter's heart and lungs. With Patrick's assistance he pulled the calf to its feet. Peter took three steps before collapsing again in a heap, this time emitting a small, pitiful groan. At his father's insistence, Clayton had remained at the house, peering out the window at the barn.

"Ever seen anything like this before, doc?" Patrick asked.

"Not very often," the veterinarian said shaking his head. "I don't think it's any sort of infection, at least not one of the more common ones. He doesn't have a temperature or any open wounds. His bowel sounds are appropriate so there's no reason to suspect an impaction or malrotation. You said he'd been fine until last evening?"

"That's what Clayton told me. He visits the calf at least twice every day."

"The best guess I can make is that it's some sort of encephalopathy," Kellor said.

"What's that?"

"His brain function is being abnormally affected by the buildup of a toxic substance within his body."

"Like what?"

Kellor shook his head. "Could be any number of things. If he's in kidney or liver failure that could do it. But the timing isn't consistent with a metabolic encephalopathy. Normally the onset of those conditions is more protracted. Weeks, even months. A virus could be responsible but there's typically other signs of infection."

The veterinarian paused for a moment.

"What have you been feeding him?"

Patrick looked away.

"Is there something I should know about?"

"I needed some feed to tide me over a few days so I got some from McMillan."

Patrick was silent again, tracing circles in the ground with the toe of his boot.

"And . . . ?"

"And the stuff I bought was off the books."

"What does that mean, exactly?"

"McMillan did me a favor and let me have some sacks that were out of date. I got them for cost."

"Were they on the embargoed list?"

"The embargoed list?"

"Yeah, you know. The inspector general's list of all the companies producing feed suspected of causing mad cow disease."

Murphy was confused. "I . . . I don't know. I don't think so. I assume McMillan wouldn't do something like that. I thought you were concerned that some of the feed might have been spoiled or something. Do you think this could be mad cow disease?"

Kellor stared at the animal. "It's a consideration. Again, the onset of this calf's condition has been a bit quicker than that of bovine encephalopathy, but I can't rule it out. Fortunately, there haven't been any confirmed reports of that condition in this area."

The veterinarian stood up, brushing the dirt and hay from his trousers. "Well, whatever the cause, I don't think this calf is going to live. Once these animals develop an encephalopathy, the odds of survival are slim."

Patrick stared at Peter. The calf's breathing was noticeably more strident than earlier in the day. Dr. Kellor's last remark hadn't surprised him. He'd been around farm animals long enough to know when one was going to die.

"Want me to put him down for you?" Kellor asked.

Patrick shook his head. "No. I'll take care of it after I talk with Clayton. Never an easy thing."

Murphy walked with the veterinarian back to the man's pickup. He placed his satchel into the passenger seat and fished his keys from his coat pocket.

"Patrick, I'm going to have to do some testing on the calf." Kellor raised his hand as if to deflect any protest. "But don't worry. It's going to be on the government tab. Anytime I come across a farm animal with an encephalopathy the law requires I try to find out what caused it. I'll just need some tissue samples to send to their lab. I can drop back by later and get them if that's okay with you?"

"That'll be fine. Thanks for coming out so quickly, doc," Patrick said before Kellor closed the door.

Murphy had taken only a few steps towards the house when Kellor called out to him.

"One more thing, Patrick," Kellor said over a partially rolled down window. "Was the calf the only animal to eat any of that feed?" he asked.

CHAPTER 9

had to hand it to Hart. He had managed to obtain a psychiatry evaluation in record time. The hospital consulting service was notoriously slow. I assumed obtaining a similar patient evaluation in an outpatient setting would be all but impossible. However, within 30 minutes the chief resident was in our clinic examining Mrs. Rubin. Julie, Hart, Lisa and I were standing in the nurses' station awaiting Dr. Kovach's proclamation when he emerged from the examination room and walked towards us.

"Strange," he said as he put her chart down on the countertop.

"Meaning what?" Hart asked him.

"Well, it's difficult to get an accurate grasp on what's going on with her but she appears to be experiencing a fragmented break with rational thought."

"A psychosis?" I asked.

"In a sense, yes," Kovach said, raising his eyebrows. "I performed an abbreviated Mass U index assessment for depression which was positive. She has limited awareness of her surroundings, impaired short term memory and I never could get her more than 65% aligned on orientation. In summary, she's got a real problem. Your medical student is correct, Galen. She definitely has an element of psychosis."

"So what do we do now?" Hart asked.

"I think she needs to be admitted to the hospital," he answered. "This appears to be the first time she's had this sort of problem meaning she needs a complete workup. Thyroid evaluation, toxicology screen, CT scans looking for a mass lesion. The whole shooting match."

Kovach looked at the four of us, presumably for some indication of our willingness to undertake such a process.

"What did you find out from Omega?" Hart asked Julie.

"Nothing," she responded. "I left a message on Ms. Maddux's voice mail but she hasn't returned my call. Frankly, this is new territory for me."

"Does she have health insurance?" Kovach inquired.

"Yes, through her husband's employer" Lisa said. The four of us looked at her. "At least that's what her chart says."

"Well, that's good enough for me," Kovach remarked. "I spoke with her briefly about hospitalization and she's amenable to it. All I need from you folks is the go ahead."

Kovach scanned our faces searching for some affirmative response.

"Put her in," Hart responded after a moment.

The brisk winds prevalent in the earlier part of the morning had subsided only to be replaced by the slow and steady falling of snowflakes. The temperatures in the previous few days had been well above freezing causing the ground to absorb the small particles of frozen moisture. Nothing was sticking at the present but, of course, that was subject to change if the snow showers continued and the thermometer readings dropped.

Patrick Murphy barely noticed the weather as he drove into town. He was distracted, replaying his conversation with the veterinarian over in his mind. When Dr. Kellor had asked him about the feed, Murphy admitted he had given it to the other animals. If it was indeed contaminated, he was in a world of hurt. Not only would he suffer the embarrassment of having to admit his mistake to the people he'd sold them to, he'd surely have to return the money and assume some degree of liability for the outcome.

When he entered McMillan's feed store he was relieved to find the place empty aside from its proprietor.

"What's the weather like out there, Pat?" McMillan asked, looking up from his computer. His business had slowed as it always did at this time of year.

"Rotten," Murphy replied as he stamped his feet on a large woolen mat just inside the front door. "Got a minute?"

McMillan didn't like the tone of the question. Between the visit he'd received from the attorneys and the thought of having nearly dispensed a contaminated product, it had been a trying few days. He'd intended to call Murphy about the matter but had been procrastinating.

"Sure," he replied. He shut the top to his lapbook. "Want some coffee?"

"No, thanks."

Murphy walked towards the counter where McMillan was putting a second helping of sugar in his cup and agitating it with a plastic stirrer.

"What's up," he asked as he brought the steaming liquid to his lips.

"I've got sick calf on my hands, Sean. I had Dr. Kellor out this morning to take a look at him and he thinks he's got some sort of brain problem."

"Brain problem?"

"I can't recall exactly what words he used, but he thinks his brain is sick. He won't walk or move much. Just lays there drooling with dead eyes. I'm going to put him down later today. After that, the doc wants to do some testing on his brain."

"I see."

"I told him I'd bought some feed from you that was off the books."

McMillan stared at his coffee while deciding what to do next. "I was afraid of this," he said after a few moments.

"Afraid of what, exactly?"

"That you'd be back in my store with this sort of tale. I got a visit the other day from some lawyers from England. Said they were investigating a few businesses there turning out suspect livestock feed. Mad cow disease and all. They were going to file a lawsuit against them on behalf of a few agri-businesses that had taken a hit from the bad product."

"What did you tell them?"

"Not a lot. It was the first I'd heard on the subject. They looked over some of my invoices to see if I'd done business with the manufacturers in question."

"Did you mention my name?"

"No. They never asked."

Murphy stuck his hands hard into his pant's pockets.

"Look, Sean, I'm sorry about this. I was the one asking for the feed and bought it knowing full well it was off the books.

I only wanted to give you a heads up. I'm going to have to tell Craig."

McMillan snorted a sarcastic laugh. "Yeah, he'll be thrilled. Probably launch into a full fledged fit. Then promptly burn any paperwork associated with the transaction. Worthless git."

"How did you leave it with the lawyers?"

"They said they would call me if they needed anything else but I don't expect to hear from them. They got what they came for and left just as fast. You know how they are. Besides, none of the lots matched."

"What?"

"Apparently, the stuff I bought wasn't contaminated with mad cow disease."

"Well, that's a relief, I suppose," Murphy said, breathing easier. "But it still doesn't shed any light on what's wrong with my calf."

Within an hour Dr. Kovach had Mrs. Rubin out of the clinic and into the hospital. He notified her husband which had to have been an unpleasant task. She was slated for a slew of tests later in the day. The last I saw of the woman she was shuffling down the hallway behind Dr. Kovach, her head down, intermittently blowing her nose. The rest of us returned to our duties while Julie busied herself in paperwork. I had just returned to the nurses' station when her cell phone rang. It was Maddux.

"Julie. Sorry I didn't phone earlier. I'm in Atlanta meeting with some of the folks from Emory. What's up?"

"We have a problem with one of the patients in the study."

"What kind of problem?"

"Well, it's difficult to say. Helen Rubin is her name. She's been in the study for over a month and has done well until now. When Dr. Douglas was speaking with her this morning she became tearful and related a story of some significant depression. Dr. Hart met with her for a few moments and arranged for a psychiatric consultation. The chief resident came . . ."

"A psychiatry consult?" Maddux interrupted.

"Yes, a psychiatry consult. The resident who evaluated her was concerned about her mental status and suggested she be hospitalized. Mrs. Rubin left about a half hour ago for admission. Obviously, I thought this was something that should be brought to your attention. I need to know how you want this situation handled."

"Well, for starters, she's out of the study."

"I realize that," Julie said. The woman's short sightedness had begun to wear on her. "Have there been any reports of similar occurrences at other testing sites?"

"Not that I'm aware of," Jennifer said. "How wacko was this woman?"

"According to Dr. Kovach, the resident who evaluated her, she's disoriented with some short term memory impairment. At this point, we don't know what's going on with her. Let me have you speak with Dr. Hart."

Julie glanced towards the computer to find Hart again online checking the stock ticker. "Do you suppose you could tear yourself away from your investments long enough to talk with Jennifer Maddux?" she asked.

Hart looked up from the screen disgustedly. "It's called day trading."

"I stand corrected," Julie said as she pushed the phone in Hart's direction. He took it reluctantly, continuing to stare at the constantly changing numbers in front of him.

"This is Dr. Hart."

"What's going on with this Rubin patient?"

"Who knows? It looks like she's had some sort of psychotic break. There wasn't anything in her past medical history to suggest something like this but then I suppose you never know."

"So you looked over her medical chart?"

"Well, not exactly," Hart said sheepishly. "The clinic has been pretty full this morning."

<u>What a piece of work</u>, I thought. The guy did less work around the place than anyone but he was first in line to make it sound like he'd been slaving away.

"I pulled a few strings and got her seen by the resident on the psychiatry consultation service, no easy task in an outpatient setting, I might add. He wasn't clear on why she went over the edge but suggested she be admitted for a full workup."

"Which includes what?"

"More in-depth evaluation of her cognitive deficits. Blood work looking for endocrine abnormalities. MRI scans. Toxicology screens. That sort of thing. She'll be on the psych floor."

"Any reason to think this was due to the patches?"

"No. I'm going to do a search of the medical literature on line later today and see if I can turn up anything. My guess is it'll be a dry run."

"You haven't done that already?"

"Not yet. As I said, we've been swamped around here."

"Right. You mentioned that."

The phone line was silent for a moment.

"Well," Jennifer continued, "I'll have to take this to Omega and fill them in. I'm going to need a daily update on Mrs. Rubin's condition as well as what her workup is showing."

"The medical student will make sure you get . . ."

"No. Not the medical student. You."

"Me?"

"In case it hadn't occurred to you yet, this is a substantial bump in the road. Omega wants this product on the market in the next 6 months. We've gotten fast track approval from the FDA which comes with an obligation to submit weekly reports on the project. Incidental associated side effects like a rash or a headache they might ignore. However, since we're dealing with a neurotoxin, some sort of psychiatric meltdown is going to engender a lot of scrutiny. Frankly, we don't need that. There's going to be a big paper trail on this one and it will require lots of signatures on it with the initials 'MD' after them."

"Do you have any idea how much time that's going to take?"

"Not really and to be honest, I don't much care. Your university is being compensated handsomely for this project."

"Well, I'm not!" Hart said defiantly.

"Then ask for a raise," Maddux snapped. "One of the risks of performing drug studies is that when an unexpected side effect occurs it gets dealt with according to our rules. All this was spelled out in the prospectus you signed along with the other members of the department."

"This is ridiculous."

"So noted. I'll speak with Dr. Franklin after we hang up but you'll need to fill her in on the details. By the end of the day, I'll email you a web address where you can begin submitting your daily patient updates. There are spaces to fill in all relevant information as well as a narrative of the patient's progress and condition. You'll need to forward a copy to Dr. Franklin."

"Including Saturdays and Sundays?"

"Right. The last time I checked, 'daily' encompassed all seven days of the week."

By this point Hart was seething. Although I could only hear his half of the conversation, I could tell it wasn't making him happy. His face was red and the veins in his neck were bulging. He had stopped looking at the computer screen and was pacing back and forth in front of the desk. When the conversation was completed he angrily snapped the phone cover closed and thrust it back to Julie.

Julie allowed him a moment to calm down. When she deemed enough time had lapsed she asked Hart about the plans for Mrs. Rubin.

"Mrs. Rubin," Hart said through clenched teeth, "Will remain on the psychiatry service for the foreseeable future. I will be providing Jennifer Maddux, Dr. Franklin and Omega Pharmaceuticals with daily updates as to her condition. When her health permits, she will be discharged and we will follow her as an outpatient."

Although the memo hadn't generated much excitement when Ewan Calcote had signed off on it, it was quite a relief to Jeffrey Walsh. The message, in the form of an email, had emanated from the laboratories of the Agriculture Ministry for Northern Ireland and pertained to the samples of bovine brain tissue sampled at Fairlyn Meats 4 weeks earlier. All were free of any known proteins associated with bovine spongiform encephalopathy or mad cow disease. Although Walsh had expected a clean bill of health, he was relived to put the experience behind him. Almost no mad cow disease had been reported in Northern Ireland and the few rare cases had been in the southern counties near the border. He gave the document to his secretary to file. Within a few days he would forget about the matter entirely.

Julie's email and Dr. Hart's phone conversation ignited a firestorm of activity. The last thing the suits at Omega Pharmaceuticals wanted was to have it leak out that one of the patients in their clinical trials had experienced some sort of psychiatric hiccup. The correlation between the woman's participation in the drug study and her mental illness was tenuous at best but Omega was circling the wagons. Within an hour Dr. Jennings called informing us there would be a meeting of all involved parties that evening in the department library. Jennifer Maddux was flying in on Omega's private jet and would be in attendance. Jennings told everyone to prepare to stay well into the evening. Even Frau Franklin herself stopped by the clinic in the late afternoon, presumably preferring to hear about the patient encounter first hand. Julie's description of the events didn't elicit much of a reaction from her. I got the impression she considered this much ado about nothing - that Jennifer Maddux and the rest of Omega people were overreacting. Frankly, I concurred, but kept my opinion to myself. No one cared what I thought.

There was so much commotion around the clinic that Hart couldn't launch into one of his tantrums. He continued to mumble under his breath and spit out the occasional disparaging remark. Lisa and I gave him a wide berth. When Dr. Jennings announced that our evening had just been co-opted, Hart was mad enough to eat dirt.

Julie told us we could leave around 5:30 to get something to eat so long as we were present in the department library no later than 6:30. Since we had no idea how long the evening's festivities would last, we took advantage of the opportunity.

Lisa and I walked into the department library just before 6:30. Jennifer Maddux, Dr. Jennings and Dr. Franklin were already present. We sat at the back of the room in chairs against the large built in bookshelves, well under the radar. We may have been mere medical students, but we weren't stupid.

At the front of the room, Maddux paced back and forth. She carried a cell phone which was hooked to a listening piece in her ear. I hadn't been around the woman enough to know her well, but I suspected she was upset. She was also visibly worn. Despite her camouflage attempts with makeup, the circles beneath her eyes were unmistakable. With the responsibility for overseeing 15 test sites she'd been forced to burn the candle not just at both ends but in the middle as well. This sort of "crisis" was the last thing she needed. The one saving grace was that it had taken place in the city where she resided. At least she could sleep in her own bed.

When 6:30 rolled around, Jennifer removed her earpiece and placed the phone back in her briefcase. She checked her watch before scouring the room. Hart was missing in action.

It wasn't like him to be late for such a sit down. Clinic, yes. Grand Rounds, definitely. But not this kind of meeting. Failure to show would be viewed dimly. He was pushing the envelope.

At 6:37, Hart made his appearance. It was memorable. At least to me it was. Back in Rotan, I had a couple of friends who made extra money performing as rodeo clowns. It wasn't very glamorous work. They weren't even particularly good at it. But they could whoop and holler with the best of them. At least enough to distract the bulls from the riders who seconds before had been holding on for dear life and now lay in various states of disarray in the dirt.

Jimmy Stargill, a fixture on the rodeo circuit in the small towns of north central Texas, invariably performed his duties as a rodeo clown three sheets to the wind. He wasn't falling down drunk and he always managed to maintain enough professionalism to continue to get work. When the rodeo would begin he was usually in pretty good shape. As the barrel racing began winding down, he would disappear to his trailer ostensibly to begin applying his makeup and donning his costume. By the time the bareback and bull riding commenced, he was thoroughly lit. So much so that he earned the nickname "Ginny" Stargill. With his eyes vaguely glazed, a flush to his face and a much more colorful vernacular in place, he would take to the arena to begin plying his trade. We all learned to recognize when the man was hammered.

"He's drunk," I whispered to Lisa.

"How can you tell?"

"Trust me."

"Nice of you to join us," Dr. Franklin said as Hart made his way past her.

Hart didn't reply. If the others in the room noticed his condition, they didn't mention it.

Jennifer Maddux, seeing that everyone who needed to be there was present, began.

"Thank you all for coming. I realize that this is on short notice and I'll try not to keep you longer than necessary."

She leafed through some papers on a small lectern in front of her.

"As you know, one of the subjects in our study, Helen Rubin, has been hospitalized with an acute onset of psychiatric problems. I took the liberty of breaking the code to assure myself she had been receiving the patches containing active drug and indeed she has. I also contacted some of the other sites in the study asking if they had any patients with similar symptoms. They have not. While I think this is almost certainly an isolated case I wanted to go over her symptoms, get an update on her condition and discuss where we go from here. Dr. Kovach what can you tell us about Mrs. Rubin?"

Kovach rose from his seat and cleared his throat. "She seems to be somewhat of a mystery, at least to us. We did a magnetic resonance scan of her head which revealed normal findings. Her spinal tap was equally unremarkable and so far, aside from some mild anemia, her blood work has been normal. She had an electroencephalogram performed this morning. I spoke with the interpreting neurologist although the final report won't be available until tomorrow. Apart from some mild slowing of the brain waves there was nothing specific about her examination. A toxicology screen of her blood and urine were also negative aside from the medications she said she'd been taking."

"So there's nothing really to report?" Jennings asked.

"Well, I didn't say that. We sent some of her serum off to a reference laboratory looking for botulinum toxin. That report won't be back until the end of the week, at the earliest. We also performed a battery of tests designed to better define her depression. The changes are compatible with those of an organic etiology."

"Meaning what?" Franklin inquired.

"The list of etiologies associated with an organic based psychotic depression is extensive. Some are endogenous such as depleted thyroid reserves or abnormal adrenal activity. Since those are the most likely source of the problem, we're investigating them. However, chemical contaminants are also capable of inducing this type of depression."

"Such as?" someone asked.

"Well, heavy metals for one thing. Admittedly, it's a rare occurrence but something definitely worth evaluating. Again, we've sent off some of her serum and a 24-hour urine collection to a reference lab."

"I think her husband works for an industrial tool and dye company, doesn't he?" Julie said.

"In fact, he does," Kovach responded with a smile. "But he's an executive with the company and the patient isn't sure if he has any contact with the production facilities. I have a call into his office and hope to speak with him later this evening."

Jennings appeared visibly relieved. "So this could be due to nothing more than some type of exposure she had at home?"

"That's a possibility," Kovach said. "Another is she was deliberately poisoned but obviously, that's all speculative. Before we proceed further we need to get her labs back. However, I have a question for the dermatology brain trust here. Are her cutaneous findings consistent with that from heavy metal exposure?"

"I didn't know she had any skin findings," Jennings said. "What about it, Dr. Hart?"

To my surprise, Hart had yet to utter a peep. When I first saw him entering the room I would have bet real money that the liquor would have loosened his tongue and transformed him into a virtual fountain of useless information.

"No," was his succinct reply.

Julie was thumbing through Mrs. Rubin's chart when she came across the page she was searching for. "I think Dr. Douglas noted some changes on her palms," she said.

"Well, what about it?" Jennings barked.

"Her palms were red and peeling," I began. "I asked if it had been going on for very long and she said they had been chapped like that for the last two weeks. No symptoms or anything. She'd been applying some lotion to them but it hadn't helped much."

"Did you concur, Dr. Hart?" Franklin asked.

Hart sat up straighter in his chair. "She had some faint redness and scaling on her palms. I thought it was a bit of hand dermatitis. Nothing out of the ordinary."

Neither Dr. Franklin nor Jennings appeared much taken with Hart's observations. Apparently, it showed since he continued.

"I believe her skin changes and many of her other symptoms could be due to menopausal conditions."

To my surprise he then offered additional thoughts.

"I seriously doubt we're looking at some sort of heavy metal toxicity here."

For a first year resident to put forth such a statement, given their limited experience in the field of dermatology, was a demonstration of considerable arrogance. It was an unspoken rule that when discussing more esoteric skin conditions, residents, particularly those in the beginning stages of their training, were to keep quiet and listen.

"Oh, and why not?" Franklin inquired sarcastically.

Hart had been called on to defend his position, something he was ill equipped to do in his condition.

"Statistics. The condition is simply too rare."

It was a poor defense and everyone in the room, with the possible exception of Hart, knew it. They turned their heads back toward the front of the room which Hart interpreted as a dismissive gesture. That, combined with his impaired capacity for rational thought was like applying a lit match to spilled gasoline. Hart leapt to his feet and began speaking loudly.

"So you're just going to take this medical student's word for it?"

The initial reaction around the room was one of shock. It was unusual, even in the most tense of discussions, for someone in an academic medical department to raise their voice. Moreover, it was an unspoken rule that only the brass were afforded that luxury. A junior professor might be permitted if the stakes were high enough but never a resident. Jennings' head rocked back slightly in surprise. Franklin's mouth was open, a look of stunned disbelief on her face. Seemingly the only person in the room unconcerned by the outburst was Jennifer Maddux. Standing in front of the marker board she merely folded her arms and looked over the top of her reading glasses.

"Here we go," I whispered to Lisa.

Although Jenning's first reaction had been one of shock, it was quickly replaced with anger.

"Lower your voice, Galen!" he yelled. "I don't know what your problem is . . ."

"I know what his problem is," I said under my breath.

". . . but get a grip boy! No one here is taking anyone's word over anyone else's. We're just trying to find . . ."

"I evaluated the patient <u>thoroughly</u>," Hart interrupted, jabbing his finger in the air. "Just like I do all the subjects in this pretentious little drug study. That the oversight faculty is implying I neglected my duties is more than a little insulting considering the baggage I've been saddled with!"

To this point, Hart had kept his condition hidden. Apparently, no one in the room, besides me, could tell he was hammered. After his tirade commenced, however, it became obvious to everyone present, he wasn't all there.

"And I wanted it noted for the record," Hart continued. "That I was the first person to consider she might be experiencing some sort of toxic episode."

"Must be contagious," I muttered. Apparently, I didn't mutter it softly enough.

"Lillian, is this resident on some type of medication I don't know about?" Jennings inquired of Dr. Franklin.

I only heard part of Jenning's question and none of Franklin's response as I had other matters vying for my attention.

Hart, using his hand to steady himself on the table, turned around and faced me. His eyes were watering, his face was flushed and he bore the unmistakable look of someone, as the old timers back home used to say, "with blood in his eye." As luck would have it, I was seated directly behind him.

I've always thought I could read people reasonably well. I'm not clairvoyant or anything like that, but I can usually tell when someone is going to do or say something substantive. Like the time I was trash talking to the left tackle for the Decatur Bulldogs about his lazy eye. Although it wasn't one of my finer moments, I was able to predict when he was going to come out of his three point stance and try to choke me. It allowed me to protect myself and feign innocence while he was ejected from the game and our team enjoyed a 15 yard penalty. Unfortunately, my skills had apparently diminished with age.

Hart picked up a large plastic notebook and swung it level with my head. With the short distance between us I had no time to react. The edge of the binder struck me above my left eye opening a two inch gash over my eyebrow. The bleeding started almost immediately which coincided with my fit of rage. Leaving the wound to do what it would, I leapt from my chair and buried my shoulder in Hart's chest, knocking him off his feet and onto the table. Papers and notebooks flew everywhere. As Lisa would tell me later, it resembled an ice hockey fight. I tried to get an arm free to smack Hart in the face but the blood obscured my view. I don't think I ever got a clean shot in but then I didn't have much of a chance. Before I knew it Jennings had grabbed my shoulders while Dr. Kovach and Julie began pulling on various aspects of Hart's anatomy. Mostly, I think they were trying to get the resident safely away from me before I killed him which, given my frame of mind, was my intent. When they had sufficiently separated us and I had begun to cool down I glanced at the table and my opponent both of which were smeared with blood, all of it belonging to me.

"What on earth is wrong with you, Galen!!" Jennings was shouting. "Get him out of here!"

Julie and Dr. Kovach hustled Hart out into the hall. He half stumbled and half lurched his way through the door. The resident, realizing he had bitten off more than he could chew, seemed grateful for the distance between us.

"I want that punk fired!" Hart screamed in the hall.

"Go home, Galen," Kovach said.

"He had no right to embarrass me like that!"

"Get out of here, now!" Julie interjected. "Or we'll let Justin have another go at you."

Apparently, a spark of lucidity made its way through Hart's clouded mindset long enough for him to realize the wisdom of the women's suggestion. Mumbling to himself, he staggered down the hall and out of sight.

"Are you alright?" Jennings asked.

My sense of pride dictated I downplay the significance of my wound but as I stood there panting and dabbing at my hemorrhaging forehead I became aware of how much it hurt.

"I'm okay," I said.

"I think you're going to need stitches to close that, son. Why don't you head down to the ER and see if they can't sew you up."

"Sorry about messing up the meeting," I said apologetically.

"Well, it certainly was one of the more memorable ones," Jennings responded, a faint smile on his face. "Lisa, can you make sure Dr. Douglas has this attended to?"

"Yes, sir," she responded.

It was then I noticed that she had taken my arm. Whether it was an attempt to steady a bloodied combatant or to comfort me wasn't clear. All I knew was that it felt pretty good.

As we made our way down the hall Lisa asked, "Did you know he was going to do that?"

"You mean Hart?"

"Yeah."

I considered lying to her and lauding my prognostic skills regarding human behavior but thought better of it. Besides, she'd see right through me. I was, after all, a terrible liar.

"No," I responded. "I didn't."

"Well, it was considerate of you to push me out of the way."

I stopped walking and looked at her. "What?"

"When you stood up to barrel into Dr. Hart you used your arm to nudge me back."

Her recollection of the events was news to me. I had no memory of doing anything of the sort.

"I don't remember doing that, but it seems like the least I could do given that I had probably egged him on with my comments."

"I suppose so," Lisa responded. "Still, it was nice to feel protected."

CHAPTER 10

Malcolm Craig wasn't pleased to hear from Patrick Murphy, but then he wasn't pleased about most things. To the farmer's surprise, Craig volunteered that the situation wasn't altogether unique. It had happened before and would in all likelihood happen again.

"Well, it's not something we publicize much, but having a cow with an encephalopathy isn't all that unusual," Craig growled.

"Aren't you concerned this is mad cow disease?" Murphy asked.

"Not really. You probably didn't know it, but the Agricultural Ministry has been randomly sampling cow brains at meat packing plants for the past 18 months. I have a source on the inside who supplies me with the results for this district as well as the whole of the UK. We've not had much problem with mad cow disease to this point. The Brits, now that's another story," he said with a brief laugh. "It's actually much more common for cattle to have a herpes infection in their brains. We run across that two or three times a year. I'd have to look, but so far as I know, the lot containing your animals went to the slaughterhouse over 2 weeks ago. They have already been evaluated and so far I've heard nothing."

"What a relief," Murphy said. "I was certain this would become some sort of major incident."

"Did the vet come and pick up the animal?" Craig asked.

"Yes. Earlier this week. He said he hasn't heard from the pathology lab but that he'll contact me as soon as he does."

"Well, I'll wait to hear from you then. Call me when you know something," Craig said before hanging up.

After Lisa and I left the dermatology offices we walked to the ER. I was anxious about the impending encounter. The hospital emergency room was notorious for long waits particularly if you weren't dying. Although I was still bleeding, it wasn't serious enough to put me at the head of the line. I feared having to wait as Lisa, being the considerate person she was, would choose to sit with me, further occupying time she might prefer to expend on more enjoyable pursuits, such as laundry. The last thing I wanted to be was a burden to her.

We walked into the back of the ER looking for the head nurse. I had expected some 260 lb battle axe to pointedly tell us to get into the waiting room, check in and wait like the rest of the unwashed masses. To my surprise, we encountered a soft spoken, pleasant woman who genuinely seemed concerned with my wound.

"Why don't you come with me," she said and began walking down the hall. I assumed we were headed to the receptionist to check in but instead she lead us to a suture room, opened the door and told us that one of the residents would be with us momentarily. "I'll see if I can't locate an ice pack somewhere."

"She was nice," Lisa said.

"She's a body snatcher," I responded.

"Oh, she is not," Lisa said laughing. "Not everyone is dark, psychiatrically challenged and out to get you."

"I never said *everyone* was out to get me. Just *most* everyone."

"I stand corrected."

Lisa opened a small cabinet, removed a washcloth and soaked it with water before wringing it out. "Here," she said handing it to me. "You might want a fresh one of these."

"Right," I said as I took it from her. She had a big smile across her face. I couldn't tell what she was thinking but then my head was killing me. The initial rush of adrenaline which had helped to blunt the pain had long since subsided leaving me with a pounding headache.

I used the damp washcloth to dab at my forehead. Fortunately, most of the bleeding had stopped but I could feel the edges of the defect. Manipulating it wasn't painful but it did make me slightly sick at my stomach. I decided to leave it alone since all I could do was make myself more nauseated and get the thing infected.

I was about to lie down when the exam room door opened. To my relief, the resident in the ER that evening was one I had worked with during my surgery rotation. Better yet, he was someone I liked and admired.

"Douglas!" the resident exclaimed. "Long time, no see."

Jason Robbins' 6'5" frame easily filled the door. A former baseball player from Auburn University, he had managed to maintain most of his physique from his playing days. Possessed of a mid 90's fastball and nasty change-up he was a potential first round draft pick when he developed a partial tear in his rotator cuff. Surgical repair should have been routine but there had been complications. He developed a wound infection which damaged some of the nerves in his shoulder. Within the span of a week his baseball career was over. Though remaining on scholarship, he never played again. The turn of events required a re-assessment of his long term plans, ultimately propelling him towards sports medicine in general and orthopedic surgery in particular.

Unlike many of his colleagues in surgery he was what we in Rotan termed, a "good guy." He treated medical students with respect and collegiality, something rare among the house staff in his chosen profession. Robbins and I had always gotten along well. I was relieved to see he had been assigned to sew me up.

"Bar fight?" he asked.

"Worse. Dermatology departmental meeting."

"I've heard those things can get pretty nasty. What with all the controversy about topical steroids and such."

I realized Lisa hadn't said anything since his arrival so when he glanced her way I took the opportunity to introduce her.

"Lisa, this is Jason Robbins. He's one of the orthopedic surgery residents and all around decent guy."

"It's nice to meet you," Lisa responded as she shook his hand.

"Likewise. You need to do a serious re-evaluation of the people you hang around."

"So I've heard."

Robbins turned his attention to the clipboard he carried.

"Says here you were struck with a notebook?"

"Something like that," I answered. "Could have been a gardening tool."

"It was a three ring binder," Lisa added.

"Who hit you?" Robbins asked as he pulled on some examination gloves.

"One of the dermatology residents."

"A dermatology resident? Boy, you are a rowdy bunch. I'm not sure I'd let that get out. Which resident?"

"Galen Hart."

"Galen Hart? Captain Happy Pants?"

"Captain Happy Pants?" I asked, a grin spreading across my face. "I've never heard him called that before."

"That's the pet name we have for him in the ER. He's been down here a few times doing consults. One afternoon he arrived wearing a double breasted sports coat and striped pants. A nurse gave him the nickname and it stuck. Not a real people person."

"Not as such."

Robbins took the washcloth from my hand, set it on the examination table and began inspecting the wound. "What did you do to set him off?"

"Well, he was loaded and didn't appreciate my . . ."

Robbins stepped back and looked me in the eyes. "He was drunk?"

"Yeah. It's a long story but the short version is he showed up for the meeting hammered."

"I have to change residencies," the resident said as he returned to poking around on my forehead. "Sounds like you guys are having too much fun."

"Anyway, the conversation was about a patient in one of our drug studies who developed some psychiatric problems and when it turned out I knew more about her condition than he did, he snapped."

"Did our boy here lose consciousness?" Robbins asked Lisa.

Lisa laughed out loud. "Not hardly. He threw his shoulder into Dr. Hart and they went flying up on the conference table."

"Why Dr. Douglas, I think it's fair to say my opinion of you has increased substantially. Does the good Dr. Hart have any wounds as well?"

"I doubt it. I never got a shot in. The grownups broke things up pretty fast. They sent him home so I can't say for certain. Maybe his head hit the table or something."

"Well," Robbins said removing his gloves, "Your laceration appears pretty textbook. Should take about 8 stitches or so to close it. You want me to do it or should I call the plastics fellow?"

"You do it. I just want to get out of here. My head hurts."

"Yeah, I should think so."

Lisa's pager went off and after looking at the number she said, "It's Dr. Franklin. She probably wants an update on your condition. If it's alright, Justin, I'm going to step out and return the page."

"Fine with me. Give her my best but you're going to miss watching me experience excruciating pain when he numbs up the wound.

"I think I'll pass," Lisa said as she left the room.

"Nice looking girl," Robbins said after the door had closed. "You two a couple?"

"Not yet," I said watching him fill a syringe with lidocaine.

"Well, it's good to have a dream."

Ian Kellor's pickup pulled in front of the Murphy home and rolled to a stop. Patrick was pulling on his jacket as he sprinted down the front steps. The weather continued to be foul with thick gray clouds intermittently spitting rain or freezing drizzle.

"Thought I'd find you here," Kellor said. It was just past 6:30 in the morning, a time when only farmers and apparently veterinarians were awake and about their duties.

The men shook hands and Murphy continued buttoning his coat before pulling the collar up close to his neck.

"I assume you're here about the calf. I hope this doesn't mean bad news."

Kellor chuckled. "I suppose it depends on how you look at it. The lab got back to me yesterday just before I closed up. To make a long story short, they didn't find anything definitive."

"What do you mean 'definitive?'"

"Well, I had suspected the cause of the calf's problem was some kind of viral infection in his brain. Herpes or something along those lines. Turns out it wasn't anything of the sort."

"So what was it then?"

Kellor shrugged his shoulders. "Who knows? The lab wasn't able to pin it down any more than to say that it was an encephalopathy, an inflammation of the brain and spinal cord."

"That doesn't do us much good, does it?" Murphy asked.

"Not really. As you might suspect, the Agriculture Ministry doesn't have an unlimited budget. Their overriding concern is detecting animals with mad cow disease. Beyond that they typically don't look much further aside from evaluating for infectious causes. The chap I spoke with on the phone suggested we consider either chemical imbalances or some type of poisoning."

"What?"

Kellor leaned against the hood of his truck. "An animal with a metabolic problem sufficient to cause this degree of encephalopathy would have been either pretty sick for a while or visibly abnormal from birth. Obviously, neither was the case with your calf so I think we can rule that out. Poisoning is another matter."

"I can assure you the calf was not poisoned," Murphy said definitively.

"Oh, I understand that. I know your son took excellent care of him. Is it possible he got into something toxic? Vermin bait or insecticide? Something along those lines?"

Murphy thought for a moment before answering. "I suppose anything's possible but it's pretty unlikely. I keep all the chemicals in a separate shed. We have a cat who keeps the mouse population to a minimum so there would have been no reason for any vermin bait in the barn. The calf was born in an adjacent pen and to my knowledge, was never anywhere else in his life."

"I thought that might be the case. Which brings me to my next question. What about the feed you gave him?"

The police and paramedics were quick to arrive at the Texaco Mini-Mart. In a small town such as Port St. Joe there typically wasn't a lot happening at this time of year with the tourist season several weeks in the future. Paul Nobles knew the police officers on duty that day. He had gone to high school with Jimmy Lyon's younger brother, David and Larry Bowen had umpired some of his little league games.

"Seen her around here?" Bowen asked. He was standing in the bright sunlight wearing wrap around mirrored sunglasses and doing his best impression of a big city cop. Fifteen years earlier he had been just another officer in a Podunk Florida town scratching out a living in obscurity. But that was two marriages and 50 pounds ago. Now he was a senior member of the police force and while he was never going to pass the lieutenant's examination, he possessed enough tenure to restrict himself to the day shift.

"No," Nobles replied. The events of the morning had shaken him and he had begun chain smoking cigarettes.

"So she just mentioned the lights and water?" Lyons asked without looking up from his clipboard. As the junior member of the dynamic duo it was his job to handle the paperwork and driving.

"Yeah, that's about it. Wasn't making much sense. I tried to talk with her but that went nowhere."

The paramedics were quick and efficient. The woman had regained consciousness by the time they arrived but was no more lucid. One of the young men had inserted an intravenous line and taken her blood pressure while the other prepared to load her into the vehicle for the short trip to the hospital in nearby Apalachicola when Bowen walked up.

"How's she doing?" he asked. In truth, the policeman could have cared less but being a closet voyeur, he was curious.

"Okay, I guess," one of the men said. "She's not making much sense but some of these homeless people are pretty out of it anyway."

"Any idea what caused her to pass out?"

"Not really. We'll let the docs at the hospital sort that out. We just scoop 'em and run."

"Fair enough. I'll call the ER later today and see if there's more information for my paperwork."

"Sounds good."

The ambulance driver closed the door and made his way to the cab. Bowen waddled back towards Nobles and his partner who was busy scribbling.

"What did the bus boys have to say?" Lyon asked.

"They didn't know much. I told them I'd call this afternoon to see what's up."

Bowen turned to Nobles who was using the lit end of his cigarette to fire up another one. "You said she wasn't carrying a purse or a bag or anything, right?"

Nobles shook his head. "Not that I saw. She had a small fanny pack around her waist. I didn't go through it."

Bowen laughed. "Good decision. Who knows what you'd have found in there."

When Lyon was finished writing, the policemen bid Nobles' goodbye and returned to their squad car. To them, the case was just a vagrant who'd had too much to drink or done too many drugs. Nothing out of the ordinary.

"Another day in paradise," Bowen said as the officers drove off the parking lot.

After Jason Robbins finished sewing up my head, 13 stitches in all, Lisa and I left the emergency room to return home. Robbins had suggested I get a cat scan of my head but I declined. I'd had enough for one day and besides, getting hit in the noggin wasn't anything new to me. I'd had worse on the football field.

Lisa saw me to my apartment and into Larry the recliner. Before leaving she made me promise to call her in the night if I needed anything. Using as much macho bluster as I could summon, I told her that wouldn't be necessary although in truth, I appreciated her concern.

The next morning I awoke with a terrific headache making me reconsider the wisdom of not getting a cat scan. After drinking some coffee and taking a couple of ibuprofen the pain subsided enough for me to function, albeit in slow motion manner. Lisa had kindly agreed to call the psychiatry service and tell them I wouldn't be in that day. We both assumed it would take the better part of the morning for me to get my bearings. I had hoped she would come by the apartment and check on me but either she did and I didn't hear her knock or she had decided to let me sleep.

I tried to plow through some of the required reading for my psychiatry rotation. A test was scheduled on the diagnosis and treatment of depression the next week. My attention to the assigned material had suffered as more and more of my energies were devoted to the drug study. At 10:00 A.M. the phone rang. I was hoping it would be Lisa. It wasn't.

"Have you checked on Mrs. Rubin yet?"

In my befuddled state it took me a moment to recognize the voice on the other end of the line. Jennifer Maddux.

"I'm fine, thanks. The headache is gradually getting better and the doc says I can get the stitches out sometime next week."

It was comforting to know my brain hadn't been rattled so badly as to completely erode my capacity for sarcasm.

"Oh, right," Maddux replied. If she felt a tinge of remorse, it wasn't evident in her voice. "How are you feeling?"

"Above ground."

I considered giving her a brief synopsis of what had transpired in the ER but decided to let it drop. Maddux clearly wasn't interested in matters not concerning her, least of all the trials and tribulations of a medical student.

"In answer to your question, no. I haven't seen Mrs. Rubin today. I was planning on visiting her before clinic began this afternoon."

"After you left last night, we decided you would be the best person to ride herd on her condition. Obviously, Dr. Hart won't be in a position to oversee her progress, at least not anytime in the near future."

I had wondered what punishment awaited Captain Happy Pants or if that was even discussed after my departure. I assumed I'd learn everything in due time. It wasn't much comfort to be told I'd been given extra work because the person who assaulted me could no longer perform his duties. I thought about asking Maddux exactly what was expected of me, but prolonging our conversation held little appeal.

"Well, I should be up on the psych floor between noon and 1:00. I'll get back to you after I've seen her."

"Thanks. Make it in email form and forward a copy to Drs. Franklin and Jennings."

Our chat now completed, I attempted to return to my reading but the thought of all the work waiting for me at the hospital prompted me to shower and begin my trek to the hospital. As the water began to heat up I glanced at myself for the first time in the mirror. It wasn't pretty. Although most of the swelling had subsided, I had a huge bruise on my cheek and forehead. Not since I went a few rounds with Tommy Thurman in 6th grade had I looked this bad.

After showering and applying a bandage to my forehead I took the shuttle bus from the apartment complex into the Medical Center. Getting onto the locked psych ward wasn't difficult. I'd been there before and most of the nurses knew me. The news of the previous evening's events was apparently the topic of the day. Those familiar with Dr. Hart were quite interested to hear from the horse's mouth if I had managed to land a complementary blow. I found myself almost apologetically acknowledging that I had not, in fact, punched him out.

In the middle of the hall was a work station with a few tall chairs, a flat countertop and two computer terminals. It was there I found Dr. Kovach writing in a patient's chart. He looked up as I approached.

"Ouch," he said as his eyes widened.

"It looks much worse than it is," I responded.

"I should hope so because it looks terrible."

"Thanks. I had to cancel my modeling photo shoot obviously."

Kovach chuckled and smiled. "Heard from Dr. Hart yet?"

"He sent flowers and nice card. Very caring fellow. Shallow, but caring."

I decided to change the subject to matters at hand. "What's the story on Mrs. Rubin?" I asked.

"None of her pending lab work is back. I don't really expect it for another day or so. She's resting comfortably. I spoke with her husband after the meeting. Considering last night's discussion and his possible involvement with her condition, it seemed warranted."

"And?"

"And not much. I'm certainly not an expert in forensic psychiatry but from what I can determine, the man didn't have anything to do with her current situation. I assume an investigation will take place if we suspect she was exposed to some systemic toxin but I don't think he's involved. Of course, that's just my opinion."

"How's her mental status?"

"Don't know. She wasn't in her room when I went to check on her. We loaded her with an intravenous dose of haloperidol last night and according to the nurse's notes, she calmed down quite a bit. We've also started her on oral lithium. I think she should be stable enough in the next few days to go home. That's assuming the rest of her workup is negative."

"But what's the long term game plan if you don't find any underlying reason for her break?"

"Management."

"That's it?" I asked incredulously.

Kovach smiled at me as leaned back in his chair, resting his face on his open palm.

"This may come as a surprise to you, but patients experiencing an acute psychiatric disease, even to the point of a psychotic break but without a defining reason is common. Statistics show that an 'idiopathic' cause in these cases approaches a third of the affected populace. Somewhere in the recesses of their brains things begin to short circuit, the neurochemical transmitters start firing abnormally and the next thing you know, they're ranting and raving like a lunatic. In those situations, it's our job to make sure they don't have a tumor in their head or an overactive thyroid gland and get them started on medication to address the problem both in the short and long term."

"So what you're saying is you may never know what caused this problem?"

"That's exactly what I'm saying. Like you've been told since the first day of medical school, the practice of medicine is often more art than science."

Kovach closed Mrs. Rubin's chart before handing it to me. "Enjoy," he said as he walked down the hall.

I pulled up one of the stools at the charting station and began rummaging through the paperwork in the patient's file. There were a few routine laboratory tests pending which I checked on in the computer. None were helpful. The nurse's notes were comforting, suggesting a gradual normalization of her mental outlook. After fifteen minutes of reading I walked to her door, knocked on it and slowly swung it open.

The first thing I noticed was that the bed was both unmade and empty, something not out of the ordinary. Hospital patients are often not in bed or in their rooms for that matter. They walk the halls for a bit of exercise as well as travel outside for some fresh air or to smoke. The most common reason for a patient to be AWOL is a trip to another part of the hospital for testing. Except, in those instances, the patient's chart always accompanies them. No exceptions. My having her chart precluded her being in radiology or anywhere else.

"Mrs. Rubin?" I asked as I pushed the door open wider.

There was no answer. Her television was on, flashing colored light on the ceiling and walls. I walked further into the room as I continued to call her name. The next most logical place for her to be was the bathroom. I didn't want to disturb her but it was nearly 1:30 P.M. meaning I had to be in clinic soon. I took another step towards the bathroom door.

"Mrs. Rubin? It's Justin Douglas from the dermatology clinic."

I waited a few seconds to see if she would respond.

"Are you in there, Mrs. Rubin?"

The lack of audible movement within the room concerned me. The door was slightly ajar. I knocked on it but received no response. As a last resort, I pushed the door open as I called out her name one final time. It was a relief to find she wasn't there. I was about to turn and leave when I noticed a drop of red fluid on the tile adjacent to the shower. The curtain was pulled shut. As much as I didn't want to, I felt compelled to check behind it.

I wasn't prepared for what I saw. Lying on the floor in what had previously been a white bathrobe was Mrs. Rubin, dead. Blood was everywhere. Folded in her hand was a razor blade still covered with the slowly congealing crimson liquid. She had gouged open the large vessels in her neck, including the carotid artery and had bled out in a matter of minutes. The woman was ghostly pale, her eyes still open but without any signs of life. I stumbled out of the room running for the nurses' station. A code would be called but there would be little point. Helen Rubin was gone.

Questioning his son about the death of his pet calf was something Patrick Murphy could have done without. The boy was still upset about the animal's demise. Murphy had wisely put the calf down when Clayton was at school but telling him about his decision had been difficult. The boy cried uncontrollably for several minutes. In the ensuing days he had kept mostly to himself, not wanting to do much around the house and certainly having no interest in the barn. Murphy comforted him as best he could but realized he would have to work it out for himself. The birth of livestock on a farm was a wonderful learning opportunity for children but the animals' deaths were a part of the same experience. Reliving the matter was certain to be painful for the little boy.

Murphy walked from the kitchen into the den where Clayton was sitting on the floor watching cartoons. It was late in the afternoon meaning his chores were supposed to be done but Murphy and his wife had given him some leeway in recent days considering what he'd been through.

"Clayton," his father said clearing his throat. "I need to talk with you for a minute."

The boy said nothing, his gaze fixed on the television in front of him. Murphy picked up the remote and turned it off. Clayton looked up at his father.

"How are you doing?"

"Alright, I guess. Why can't I watch my program?"

"Because I need to ask you a few questions. Some things about Peter. Can you talk about him with me?"

"Yeah."

Murphy was struck by how small his son appeared. Despite his prowess on the soccer fields he often had to remind himself that Clayton was, after all, only 8 years old and still a child.

"I talked with Dr. Kellor about Peter," Murphy began. "He said he had been pretty sick for a while."

"What made him sick?" Clayton asked.

Murphy was encouraged his son was conversing with him. He'd been so quiet the past week he had worried this might turn out to be a one sided affair.

"He wasn't quite sure. He thought he might have had some kind of infection."

"Like a cold?"

"Something like a cold. He also thought Peter might have gotten into some poison."

Clayton's eyes grew wide as saucers.

"Poison?"

"No, no," Murphy said rubbing his son's shoulder. "Dr. Kellor just thought he might have eaten something he wasn't supposed to. You didn't let him out of the pen or the barn, did you?"

Clayton shook his head. "No, sir. You told me not to."

Murphy smiled. The one thing he could always count on with his youngest was his truthfulness. He knew time would change that and he would begin experimenting with shading matters in his favor. Most boys eventually did. For now, however, he could take his son at his word.

"Well, there's also the food that we were giving him. I know we don't have any more of it left, but . . ."

"I still have some," Clayton announced.

The declaration surprised Murphy. "You do?"

"Yes, sir."

"Where?"

Clayton rose from the floor and scurried to his room. A minute later he rounded the corner carrying the metal trough that had previously been in Peter's stall. Within it were a half dozen brown lumps of cattle feed.

"You were keeping his bowl?"

"Yes, sir. I didn't want to lose it. It reminds me of Peter."

Murphy scratched his head. "Well, that makes sense. You didn't eat any of it did you?"

Clayton scrunched up his nose and smiled. "No. Why would I do that?"

"Just wondering. If it's alright with you, I'd like to have a few of these nuggets to give to Dr. Kellor. I think he might be able to test them and perhaps tell us if this is what made Peter sick."

Clanton thought for a moment. "Okay. But I still get to keep the trough, don't I?"

Murphy tousled the hair on his son's head. "I wouldn't have it any other way."

Larry Bowen and Jimmy Lyon had finished their shift and were sitting at their desks completing the requisite paperwork. The highlight of the day had been the crazy woman at the Texaco Mini-Mart and Bowen had taken an interest in her disposition. He picked up the phone, placing a call to the emergency department at the hospital in Apalachicola. He was eventually connected to Adam Price, one of the ER docs on duty. The two had conversed before.

"So what's the story on the lady we sent you this morning?" Bowen asked.

"She's nuts," was the terse reply.

"Really? I hadn't noticed."

"I'll bet. We haven't been able to find out much. Some of her lab work has come back but we're still waiting for a bunch of other stuff. Her liver enzymes are off the chart and she's dehydrated and anemic but that probably doesn't account for her mental status changes. She won't or can't tell us much. We gave her some thorazine about an hour ago so she's less agitated."

"Did you do a toxicology screen?"

"Yeah. Nothing remarkable. No cocaine, marijuana or amphetamines. I suppose there's always the possibility she ingested some designer drug but she doesn't fit the profile. We did find a doctor's card in her belongings. Some fellow at the University of Florida. Other than that, we don't know squat."

"Are you going to keep her?"

"For the time being. One of the internists has agreed to take over her care. New doc looking to build his practice. I imagine after he finds out she's genuinely crazy he'll ship her to Tallahassee. She should be here for a few days though. Anything else?"

"Not really. Just looking to round out my shift report. Well, that and sort of curious too."

"Uh-huh," Price said.

"Actually, I keep a running tab on what's wrong with the nut jobs we find here. Sort of like a hobby."

"You don't get out much, do you?"

"Not as much as I'd like," Bowen said with a chuckle.

After I made it to the nurse's station the charge nurse called a code. Several of the orderlies moved her body to the bed and began chest compressions while they waited for the code team to arrive. When they did, their efforts were half hearted. Mrs. Rubin was gone. Wide open intravenous lines and electrical shockings of her heart weren't going to bring her back. With the code well under way, Dr. Kovach and his attending physician showed up. They knew better than to get involved in the resuscitation efforts. They waited with me in the nurse's station for the inevitable pronouncement of their patient's demise. When it came, Kovach looked at the floor and shook his head. We stood around in silence for a few moments before the attending began making some final notations in Mrs. Rubin's chart.

After watching the orderlies transport Helen Rubin's remains to the morgue, I left the floor and made my way to the dermatology clinics. I was nearing the main lobby when my pager went off. It was the dermatology offices. Rather than walk across the street before returning the call I turned around, climbed back up 2 flights of stairs and headed towards the main office. In the hall I was greeted by Drs. Jennings and Franklin. Both had somber looks on their faces.

"We heard about Mrs. Rubin," Franklin began. "What on earth happened up there?"

I took a deep breath before relating what I had seen and done. Jennings stood stoically in the middle of the hall, fiddling with the change in his pocket like he always did when he was nervous or bored. When I had finished, they asked me a few questions which I answered as best I could. There was still a lot of information regarding Mrs. Rubin's condition which had yet to be learned. Most notably, the toxin screens on her blood.

"Have you contacted Jennifer Maddux about this?" Jennings asked flatly.

"No, sir," I responded.

"Well, don't. I'll call her. Maybe I can sweet talk her into keeping the study open. We haven't received the initial installment of our reimbursement and if we get shut down now, we may never get paid."

The man's concern at the financial fallout of Mrs. Rubin's death was appalling. I didn't know if her participation in the study had played a role in her death but to openly ponder the downside to the department was beyond crass. I was learning more about the inner workings of a medical school department than I had bargained for.

"You didn't mention her involvement in the drug trial, did you?" Franklin asked.

I shook my head. "No ma'am."

"What about notations in her chart?"

"No. I assumed everyone involved in her care knew about it already so I didn't think it was relevant. It was mentioned in her original history and physical by the psychiatry resident, though."

Jennings pursed his lips and looked away. "Well, we could have surmised as much. My only hope is that in the event of a lawsuit, Omega takes as much of the heat as we will."

"Oh, I would think so," Franklin added. "They have the deep pockets. Besides, our legal department signed off on the consent forms. We should be okay." I couldn't tell by the tone of her voice if she was trying to reassure Dr. Jennings or herself. In either event, it didn't involve me and I was anxious to get away from them and on with my day.

I couldn't help but notice that neither had inquired about my experience in the emergency room the night before or the large bandage covering my forehead. I concluded my assault by one of their residents was simply another problem requiring their attention and more of an annoyance than anything else.

"Why don't you go ahead and get to clinic," Jennings said. "Dr. Franklin and myself will oversee the fallout from this mess. For now, just keep your head down, work with Julie on the remaining aspects of the study and refer any questions about Mrs. Rubin to either of us. I'm sure there's going to be some unwanted press in the coming days. You are to plead ignorance on all counts. Got it?"

"Yes sir," I said before turning to walk over to the clinic.

The weather outside was beautiful. It was one of those rare springtime days in Houston where the temperature was in the low 70's and the humidity had yet to climb to its torturous summertime levels. As I walked from one building to the next it occurred to me that I used to be outdoors quite a lot on days such as this. Growing up in a small town, most if not all our extra-curricular activities involved being outside. On occasion, when the weather was particularly nice, our teachers would hold class under the spreading branches of a nearby oak or elm tree. If the winter had been overly harsh the school principal could occasionally be persuaded to dismiss school early, usually when spring plowing on his farm required his attention. This type of weather occasionally sparked regret on my decision to pursue an indoor profession. My angst wasn't relieved by having to return to the dermatology clinic and face everyone there. I was certain the questions would be fast and furious and, frankly, I didn't feel like getting in to it. The one bright spot was that Lisa would be there and I'd get to see her.

Upon entering the clinic's back hallway the first person I saw was Julie. She gave me a warm smile and then, surprisingly, wrapped her arms around my shoulders and gave me a warm, lingering embrace. It was a pleasant surprise. I had never been one much on physical contact. My family wasn't the touchy feely sort although to hear my father tell it, we were practically Oprah clones compared to his parents. I could count on one hand the number of times my father had hugged me, the last one being the day I loaded my pickup for the trip to Houston.

"You okay?" she asked staring me square in the eyes. Behind her Lisa looked my direction and gave me a wink.

I nodded my head. "I'm alright. Had better days but had worse ones as well."

"Ready to get to work?" Lisa asked. "Might be the best thing for you."

"I couldn't agree more," I answered. I removed my lab coat to hang it on a hook when the door behind me opened. It was such a common occurrence I scarcely noticed it any longer.

Since it was the only private entrance to the clinic, nurses, medical students and residents were constantly coming and going. As I slipped on one of the light blue lab coats given to us by Omega Pharmaceuticals I happened to glance over at Lisa whose expression had changed in the past 30 seconds. In place of what had been a warm and inviting smile was a tight lipped look of concern. Before I turned to see who had entered the clinic I already had my suspicions.

"Evenin'" came Hart's greeting.

Julie was quick to intercede. "I don't think you're supposed to be here, Dr. Hart."

"I wasn't aware that you thought at all, Julie," Hart replied. "Wouldn't that interfere with your duties in the clinic?"

The resident continued walking deliberately down the hall towards the resident's room.

"Do I need to call security?" Julie asked.

"Oh, I shouldn't think so," Hart answered without turning around. When he got to the end of the hall, he turned to face the three of us. "I'm simply here to pick up my Palmpilot. No need to have a cow, ladies."

"What's the story, Lisa?" I asked quietly.

"Maybe you need to talk to Julie," she answered.

I turned to Julie. "What's up?"

Julie shook her head as if to say, 'not now.' In a few moments, Hart emerged from the resident's room his backpack swung over his shoulder and a smarmy smile pasted across his face. If he felt any remorse over the events of the previous evening, he was managing to keep it under wraps.

"Well, I suppose you should get it straight from the horse's mouth," he said, looking at Julie. "But I'll tell you instead. Due to my irresponsible and inappropriate behavior last evening I've been suspended from the study and, instead, assigned to cover the clinics at the VA."

Hart's declaration infuriated me. I had stitches in my head and a possible concussion and all he received for his assault was a slap on the wrist.

"That's it?" I asked incredulously.

The resident laughed. "Marsha, Marsha, Marsha," he said derisively. "When are you ever going to learn? Money talks. Might want to jot that one down for future reference. Have fun with the patch people."

Hart turned to leave the clinic but after taking a few steps he stopped. "Oh, by the way. You might want to watch your back, Dougie."

"Meaning what?" I asked.

"Just some friendly advice," Hart said with a smile.

Although my mind was swimming and my head was throbbing I felt Lisa instinctively put her hand on my chest as if to hold me back from going after Hart. It felt nice. At least something did.

CHAPTER 11

Startled by the ringing of the phone, the secretary hurried back to her desk and lifted the receiver from its cradle. It had been a hectic morning and the last thing she needed was another call to deal with.

"Dr. Haverson's office."

"Good morning," the man's voice said. "This is Adam Price. I'm one of the emergency room physicians in Apalachicola. I was wondering if I could speak with Dr. Haverson?"

"May I ask what this call is regarding?"

"Well, we have a woman in the hospital here with Dr. Haverson's card in her possession. We don't know her name but I was wondering if he might be able to shed some light on the matter."

"I see," the secretary said. "Let me see if he's available."

After putting Price on hold, she walked around the corner, stuck her head into the open door of an office and addressed the man sitting behind his desk.

"Dr. Haverson?" she asked.

The man looked up from his work with a scowl on his face. Apparently his day hadn't been progressing any better.

"Yes?" he said tersely.

"There's a Dr. Price on the phone from Apalachicola. He says they have a patient in the hospital that had your card with her and he wants to ask you a few questions."

Haverson sighed and shook his head. Just what he needed this morning. Something else to deal with.

"Fine."

"He's on line 3."

Haverson picked up the phone and punched the blinking red button.

"This is Gerold Haverson," he said.

"Dr. Haverson, my name's Adam Price. I'm one of the ER docs here in Apalachicola. I'm sorry to bother you, but our hospital admitted a woman yesterday I wanted to discuss with you."

"Sure. What's her name?"

"Well, that's part of the problem. We don't know. She was transported here from Port St. Joe yesterday after she passed out at a convenience store. She didn't have any identification but she did have your card in her possession."

By now, Dr. Price had Haverson's complete attention.

"Was the card white with black lettering?"

"Yes, sir. It was."

"No mention on it of any academic appointment or affiliation?"

"Correct."

"And on the back are a few dates with times listed next to them."

Price turned the card over, examining its other side. "Yes, sir. I assume all this means something to you?"

Haverson closed his eyes before rubbing them with his free hand. His day, already well on its way to being a trying one, had just taken a turn for the worse. "She's a study patient," he said finally.

"What does that mean?" Price asked.

"Our department has a number of ongoing drug studies," Haverson explained. "When patients are enrolled and assigned an appointment time, we give them one of the cards like you have in your possession. It helps distinguish them from the general clinic population. What was the last date and time recorded on the back?"

Price turned the card over and glanced down the row of numbers. "April 19, 2:00 P.M."

Haverson jotted the information down on a scratch pad. Turning to his computer screen he punched in a few numbers before selecting the correct document.

"According to my spreadsheet, that date and time belonged to Emma Truett. Caucasian female, fifty four years of age, 5 foot 3, 105 pounds, brown curly hair and hazel eyes. How are we doing?"

"Sounds about right. I'm guessing you know her?"

"I've met her but most of the face to face time in the study is done by the nurse coordinator and the research fellows. Can you send me her photograph in an email?"

"Sure, why not?" Price said. "I'll try to shoot it over to you early in the afternoon. By the way, what was the nature of the research she was involved with?"

"She was in our botulinum toxin patch study."

Ian Kellor was wrapping up his day. It had been a long one. Accustomed to working mostly with large animals on surrounding farms his clinic had been congested with dogs and cats. He had no aversion to such creatures but their owners were another matter. People could become so attached to their pets that having a rational conversation about them was occasionally difficult. When one of the animals needed to be put down, the owner often balked. This typically led to continued suffering for all parties and more strident demands from its master to "do something." Farmers were usually more reasonable. When the animal needed to be destroyed, it was.

He was at the door ready to lock up when his telephone rang. Normally, he would have let the machine take a message but he had been waiting for laboratory work on a large steed owned by one of his regular clients so he decided to pick up.

"This is Dr. Kellor," he said.

"Dr. Kellor. My name is Barbara Gates. I'm with the Agriculture Ministry. Do you have a moment?"

Intrigued, Kellor placed his briefcase on the counter and plopped down in the receptionist's chair.

"Certainly."

"My call concerns the cattle feed you sent to our office for analysis. I apologize for having taken so long to contact you but our laboratory performed its testing twice to be certain of the results. Before I get into the findings, may I ask where you obtained the sample?"

"Patrick Murphy, one of my clients. He had a calf that died recently with some sort of encephalopathy. At first I suspected it might be herpetic in nature but an analysis of brain tissue from your laboratory ruled out that diagnosis. His son had a few of the foodstuffs remaining so I mailed them to you."

"Well, that would make sense, I suppose. We did a molecular examination of the material to determine if there were any elements which might be responsible. In short, we found significant amounts of mercury."

"Mercury?"

"Ethyl mercury, to be exact. It's not widely available anymore for obvious reasons. In fact, aside from some research chemistry laboratories it hasn't been in use for the better part of two decades. Clearly, it had no business being in the cattle feed nor the processing plant."

"How contaminated was the material?"

"Quite. The readings were off the chart. We've had similar cases where toxic amounts of heavy metals, usually lead or arsenic, were detected in animal foodstuffs but nothing like this. There's no possibility this could have been an accident. It was clearly tampering."

The woman's words stunned the veterinarian. He had wondered if the animal had been accidentally poisoned but never imagined mercury would be responsible. He was mulling over how he would break the news to Patrick Murphy and his son when Gates began speaking again.

"I'm assuming this is a new experience for you?" she asked.

"Absolutely. I've seen animals poisoned from herbicides and pesticides but not with mercury."

"Obviously, we will need to speak with the family who owned the animal and contact the manufacturer of the feed. I don't suppose you would know where the foodstuffs originated?"

"I don't but Mr. Murphy likely has a record of it. If he doesn't, surely the vendor will."

"Again, I apologize for calling after hours but I thought you would want to know. What our office needs now is for you to contact Mr. Murphy, tell him someone from our office will be there tomorrow afternoon to speak with him."

"Certainly," Kellor replied. "I'll stop by on my way home and tell him the news. Mercury, huh? What a pity."

"Are you kidding me?" Jennifer Maddux asked incredulously. On the other end of the phone was Leon Spangler, one of the vice presidents at Omega Pharmaceuticals. Mrs. Rubin's suicide had been bad enough but now there was news of another ill patient.

"I wish I were. I just got off the phone with Gerold Haverson in Gainesville. He's about to have a stroke."

"Did he say what happened?" Maddux was leaning back on the headrest of her seat. She had cracked the windows of her BMW to allow the breeze from what had turned out to be a beautiful spring day pass over her face and neck. If she was going to receive bad news at least she could be comfortable doing so.

"He's still not certain. All he knows for now is his patient is hospitalized in a tiny town in the Florida panhandle with some sort of psychiatric meltdown. He hopes to learn more soon but you know how these things work."

"But this one's still alive, correct?"

"For the moment," Spangler answered. "Of course the day is young."

"Terrific," Maddux muttered under her breath. "I suppose Page knows."

"Not yet. I thought I'd give you the heads up before I told him."

"He'll be thrilled."

"Delighted. What do you think he'll do?"

Spangler's voice belied more concern than curiosity. He'd been with Omega for 10 years and knew where the company skeletons had been interred. Most were relatively inconsequential - a matter of lost paperwork or reconfigured data, which in the end made little or no difference to the well being of any patient, current or future. But there were a handful of others as well. Screw-ups for which the company could have, and in some instances, should have received an FDA investigation. Omega's brass had become skilled at concealing such matters. What most worried Spangler was the recent number of well publicized legal cases involving upper management in health care related industries found guilty of federal transgressions and sent to prison.

"I suppose it depends on how bad it is. There are still some loose ends to be tied up on the suicide patient here but if there's any association with the patches, it's going to be a problem. Any idea when we'll know more about the woman in Florida?"

"Nope. But I'll keep you in the loop."

"Thanks," Maddux replied before hanging up.

"This is just what I need," she mumbled as she turned the key in the ignition.

When the afternoon clinic was finished, I grabbed my back pack and headed for the elevators. Julie had assigned me a lighter load, perhaps out of sympathy for my wounds or the lousy way my day had begun. Either way, it had been an act of mercy I appreciated. I was dogmeat tired. Between the pain from the head wound and the stress Helen Rubin's suicide, I felt as if every bit of my body's energy had been siphoned off.

After gathering my mail, an assorted collection of supermarket flyers and advertisements for cellular phone service, I walked to my apartment and threw my things on the couch. Collapsing into Larry, my favorite recliner, I picked up the television remote and began scanning the tube. Nothing much was on, or at least nothing worth watching. I considered reading some of the course material for my psych rotation but passed, deciding instead to check out ESPN's Sports Central. The NHL Stanley Cup playoffs were beginning and I wanted to catch up on who was doing what. I'd been watching for less than ten minutes when there was a knock at my door. I hoped it might be Lisa but when I glanced through the curtains I saw it was Mark Kovach, the psychiatry resident. *This is odd*, I thought.

"Got a minute?" Kovach asked after I opened the door.

"Sure. Come in."

"I received some information regarding Helen Rubin and thought you might be interested."

"I am."

"I got tired of waiting for her blood work results, so I called the reference lab myself and spoke with the clinical pathologist on duty. It seems Mrs. Rubin's blood contained over 7 times the normal amount of mercury."

While I had wondered about an association between Helen Rubin's demise and some sort of toxic exposure, the agent responsible shocked me.

"Wow."

"Yeah. That would explain most if not all of her symptoms."

"I guess so. Pretty bizarre."

"Indeed. Of course the 64 million dollar question is how she was contaminated."

"Her husband?"

"That seems to be the direction the police are taking. They interviewed me this morning but I didn't have much to tell them. I think Mr. Rubin is in for much of the same."

"Do you think he did it?" I asked.

Kovach shrugged his shoulders. "Who knows? From my interactions with him I'd say no. He didn't really seem the type but then what do I know about criminal investigations? Another reason I dropped by was to give you a heads up."

"Me?"

"Yeah. The detectives said they would be interviewing everyone associated with her recent medical care so I'm assuming you're on that list."

"I don't know what I can tell them about other than her time in the study."

"Well, that begs another question. Is it possible she was exposed to mercury from the patches she was using?"

Kovach's question surprised me. When she became ill, I wondered if it was an abnormal reaction to the botulinum toxin. That possibility had been exhaustively explored, however and since her symptoms didn't fit with its known side effects, it had been all but ruled out. The presence of other contaminants had never occurred to me.

"I don't see how," I answered. "The ingredients in the transdermal matrix contain almost no inorganic materials and certainly no heavy metals. If there were mercury in the patches it would have been an adulterant."

"That's what I figured. I suppose the autopsy should tell us more when it's completed."

"She's going to get an autopsy?"

"Oh yeah," Kovach said, arching his eyebrows. "Big time. The police have labeled her death as a poisoning meaning by law, an autopsy is mandatory. I've been in touch with the pathology department about it. They're supposedly going to do some special studies of her organs to determine the extent of mercury contamination, including the skin of her face and forehead."

"Good grief," I said softly.

Patrick Murphy's response to Dr. Kellor's news was initially shock followed by fear. His thoughts were for his family. If the cattle feed he'd been using was contaminated, wouldn't the human beings living around it be at risk as well? When he voiced his concerns, Kellor quickly put him at ease. Yes, there could potentially be increased amounts of mercury in their blood but it would be unlikely and even if there were, it could be evaluated and treated. The family would require some blood tests but that would probably be the extent of it. The next matter involved the cattle sold to Fairlyn Meats. Kellor offered to accompany his friend to visit Jeffrey Walsh when he broke the news but Murphy declined, something which didn't surprise the veterinarian. Murphy was an independent sort and accustomed to solving his problems on his own.

As it turned out, the weather had prevented Walsh from his usual Thursday afternoon golf game. An avid duffer, he was unfortunate enough to live in an area of the world with limited climatic support for the sport. During the colder months he pined to be on the course making the onset of better weather something which greatly lifted his spirits. He had been scouring the Internet weather sites daily for good news. At the beginning of the week, the outlook was promising. The forecast called for mostly sunny skies with cooler temperatures and little wind. As luck would have it, the predictions had been mistaken. Wednesday afternoon saw the entry of a cold front with spitting rain and low clouds. It had been enough to send the businessman into a blue funk, something not lost on his secretary who knew when to stay out of his way.

Murphy arrived at the plant's office unannounced and without an appointment.

"It would have helped for you to call ahead," Walsh's secretary said bluntly.

"The situation only presented itself in the past 24 hours," Murphy responded.

The woman rose from her chair, walked down the hall and stuck her head into Walsh's open door.

"There's a Mr. Patrick Murphy here to see you," she announced.

"Who?" Walsh replied. It was becoming clear, his day wasn't going to improve.

"Patrick Murphy. He says we processed some of his cattle recently."

Walsh thought for a moment but couldn't place the name. He dealt with many people and keeping them straight in his mind wasn't his strong suit. Besides, he had a secretary for that chore.

"Is he on the schedule?"

"No, sir. Want me to have him make an appointment?"

"No. Let's just do it and be done with it," Walsh groused.

The secretary looked down the hall and motioned for Murphy to come forward. She passed him half a dozen steps from Walsh's door and whispered "Tread lightly."

Murphy had never been in Jeffrey Walsh's office. Judging from the room's decor, he concluded the man had a limited life outside his work. A few small photographs and a certificate testifying to his membership in a local service club adorned the walls of his office but not much else. The paneling had been constructed using imitation wood veneer, the furniture was cheap and threadbare and the window behind his desk provided only a limited view of the loading dock behind the building. If this was the man's life work, it had to have been a disappointment of the first order.

"Mr. Murphy," Walsh said somewhat testily. "What can I do for you?"

"I'm sorry to take up your time like this," Murphy began. "I thought this would be better handled face to face. I believe some of my cows your company processed may have been contaminated."

Though unsettling, it wasn't the first time a guilt-ridden farmer had come into Walsh's office and announced he'd recently off loaded tainted livestock. Usually they were infected with a virus such as herpes or hoof and mouth disease. While neither was a welcome occurrence, they weren't the insurmountable obstacle the farmers often believed them to be.

"Contaminated how?"

"Mercury."

Murphy's words hit Walsh like a blast from a shotgun. The prospect of heavy metal contamination at a slaughterhouse was every owner's worst nightmare. With limited hope of tracing the source of contamination and very real expectations of multimillion dollar legal exposure, such an occurrence had driven some plants out of business.

"Excuse me?" Walsh said. The man could feel the blood draining from his face.

"Mercury," Murphy replied. He walked to one of the chairs in front of the man's desk, and sat down.

Well, he could be wrong, Walsh thought to himself. *He'd seen mistakes made in the past. Why couldn't this be another one?*

"How do you know?"

"A few weeks ago, I sold all of my cattle to Malcolm Craig. All except one. Within a few days the animal developed some sort of illness. Couldn't walk. Moaned a lot. Drooled almost constantly. I had no idea what was happening but Ian Kellor thought it might be some brain infection. After I put the calf down, Kellor had the brain tested by the labs at the Agriculture Ministry. They told us it wasn't an infection but were concerned it might be some sort of poisoning. When Kellor told me that, I was puzzled since the calf was never exposed to anything. As it turned out, I had a few of the animal's remaining feed nuggets.

Kellor sent them to the labs and they found high levels of mercury. I learned of it yesterday."

"And the feed you gave the calf was the same provided to the rest of the herd?"

"Correct," Murphy answered.

Walsh sat in his chair slowly shaking his head. His mind was swimming with potential scenarios of the fallout, none of them good.

"I'm here to try to do the right thing. I don't know what assistance I can offer but I want to help in any way I can."

After letting his words settle in, Murphy spoke again.

"How bad is this going to be?"

"Are you kidding?" Walsh scoffed. "After I call the Agriculture Ministry and they ream me out, we'll have to trace the disposition of the animals you sent us. Then, a huge recall will take place, the plant will be shut down for at least a week while it undergoes a thorough decontamination and then, assuming anyone is willing to purchase our products, we can begin selling meat again. In short, it's going to be a catastrophe."

Murphy had little to say. He could apologize, which he did several times, but it wouldn't undo the damage. His only hope was that by being candid with Walsh things would eventually work in his favor.

"Well, I'm sorry for all the trouble this will cause. Obviously, I had no idea the feed was contaminated."

Having spoken his piece and seeing the state Walsh was in, Murphy decided to leave. He rose from his chair and began buttoning his coat.

"Where did you get the feed?"

It was a question Murphy knew he'd eventually be asked but one he dreaded hearing nonetheless.

"Sean McMillan. You know him?"

"Of course I know him!" Walsh snapped. "Have you told him about this?"

Murphy exhaled slowly. "Not yet. He's next on my list."

"When are you going to speak with him?"

"Today."

"Good. Tell him my attorney will be contacting him."

Murphy was puzzled. "Your attorney? Are you planning on suing him?"

"Of course not," Walsh snarled. "McMillan doesn't have any money. We'll need to determine the manufacturer of the feed, assuming he has that information. This catastrophe has lawsuit written all over it and I'm not going to have my business catching all the fallout. Since I doubt McMillan had anything to do with the contamination of the feed, attributing it to the manufacturer will decrease our exposure. Of course, that's all supposition but it's better to think 2 steps ahead in situations like this."

"Yes," Murphy responded. "I suppose it is."

The news of another sick patient from the drug study went through the corporate hierarchy at Omega Pharmaceuticals like a level 4 hurricane. After Leon Spangler hung up with Jennifer Maddux he walked upstairs to the company's in house counsel to tell him the bad news. Normally unflappable even in the most tense of circumstances, the man nearly came undone when told about the woman in Apalachicola. Another problem like the Rubin fiasco was something he didn't need.

Spangler was also afforded the honor of informing Gary Page of the recent events. In North Carolina pressing the flesh at several of the universities there, he seemed to take the news in stride but cancelled the remainder of his trip and flew back to Florida on the company jet. He arrived just after 7:00 P.M. and by 7:30 was in the Omega's boardroom with a select group of company executives. No one was happy to be away from their homes and families, especially not to discuss the subject at hand.

"How bad is it?" Page asked as he placed his briefcase on the massive oak table in the center of the room. Considering the stress of the situation, he appeared to be holding up passably well, something which couldn't be said for the rest of the men present. Spangler had rounded up two other vice presidents who sat on the company board, Brent DeWitt and Jerry Jordan. Also in attendance was the company attorney, Colin Maitland.

"Bad enough," Spangler answered. "I spoke again with Haverson. The woman in Apalachicola is being transferred to Shands Hospital in Gainesville. Haverson will oversee her admission and get back to me."

"Is she that sick?" Page inquired.

"Probably not. Haverson wants her there on his service so he can monitor her recovery."

"And away from the press," Maitland interjected.

Spangler looked over the edges of his reading glasses and arched his eyebrows in agreement.

"I don't wish to ask a stupid question," DeWitt said. "But, how certain are we the woman in Florida has been exposed to mercury? According to what I found on the Internet, and the one thing repeatedly emphasized about mercury poisoning is that the symptoms aren't specific."

"That's a good point," Spangler answered. "I suppose the index of suspicion is sufficient. When I talked with Haverson, he told me an internist in Apalachicola raised the possibility. When she gets to Shands, they'll do the appropriate blood work."

"It's not been done yet?" Page asked.

"Not according to Haverson. The specimen will have to be sent to a reference laboratory. Since she doesn't have insurance, it would be another expensive test the hospital in Apalachicola would have to eat. They're more than happy to let Shands take the hit on this one."

"Makes sense," Page said. "Any thoughts on how we weather the storm?"

After working with the man for 10 years, Spangler recognized a rhetorical question. Page would often let the troops have their say, allowing them to unload their pent up frustration. There was also the occasionally applicable suggestion floated. If not useful in the present, perhaps in the future. It was a trademark move of a man who was usually at his best when in the crisis mode. Few people could process as cogently as Page when the shrapnel was flying. Each time Spangler thought he'd be pushed into the panic mode, the man surprised him. Thinking about the potential ramifications of this catastrophe, however, made him wonder if the man's breaking point wasn't about to be tested. After all, this project was for all the marbles. He'd seen the figures. Omega was wagering most of its corporate soul on the botulinum patch. Win and the skies would rain money and fame. Lose, and the company would die a grisly and painful death.

"How much pull do you have on the FDA oversight committee?" Jordan asked.

"Some," Page responded.

The men around him knew better. No one ever inquired about the specifics of his relationship with the feds but considering everything Page had maneuvered through the pipeline over the years, either his connection was a near and dear fiend or someone with a particularly vile skeleton in the closet.

"Enough to make this go away?" the attorney inquired.

Page pursed his lips and slowly shook his head.

"Perhaps. Of course it depends on how much cover the elephant in the room requires. Given the current situation, it won't be easy. Clearly, we can't afford another sick patient. From <u>anything</u>."

The meeting lasted 45 more minutes before Page sent the men home. They were tired, strung out and no longer thinking clearly. Whatever suggestions made at that time of night would have been for the most part worthless. Page walked to his office, put his brief case away and poured himself a stiff drink.

He was swimming in uncharted waters and it gnawed at him mightily. Making this problem disappear quietly wouldn't be easy. He could be proactive. Contact his favorite PR agency and get them busy putting a positive spin on things. Call in a few of his Washington chits to head off trouble with the FDA. But despite his prowess at bullying and blackmail, there was only so much he could do. One study subject was dead by her own hand and that couldn't be concealed. A second problem patient, however, could be. At least temporarily.

Page began his trip home yearning for a long, hot shower and a cigar on the balcony. But one final task required his attention. He drove to Miami's western boundaries and a seedy convenience store near the city limits. After pulling his car even to a pay phone, he removed a business card from his wallet and dialed the number printed on the front.

"I have a job for you," Page said.

Mark Kovach had been dead on. When I arrived at the clinic the next afternoon there was a message Dr. Franklin had scheduled a meeting with me for 1:00 P.M. sharp. Apparently, it had been left by her secretary who made certain Julie understood I was to be excused from study duties in order to attend. No excuses were to be accepted. It wasn't really the way I wanted to begin my day but it could have been worse. I could have been in law school.

Upon my arrival I discovered the reasons for Franklin's insistence on punctuality. In her office were two Houston Police Department detectives wanting to speak with me about Helen Rubin. They mostly rehashed old material trying to get the time line straight. I had little to offer they hadn't already heard before and fortunately our interaction took only about half an hour. After they left, Dr. Franklin asked me to close the door behind them.

"I need to speak with you about something," she began. "It concerns Dr. Hart."

As much as I disliked the guy, her tone worried me. I thought she was going to tell me he'd hung himself or swallowed some pills.

"We don't know where he is."

"He's missing?"

"It appears so. As you probably know, an assault on a medical student by a member of the house staff is something not taken lightly here. Even had we wanted to keep this 'in the family' as it were, it would be pointless. Dr. Jennings and myself had no choice but to report it to the Office of Graduate Medical Education. Unlike other entities here at UT, this one moves pretty quickly, particularly when it comes to staving off legal action."

That made sense to me although I had never considered lodging a formal complaint.

"To make a long story short, the GME office notified us they were conducting a hearing but are unable to contact Dr. Hart. We have attempted to call and page him, but to no avail. He's not been in any of his clinics and none of the other residents or faculty have heard from him. I was wondering if he might have contacted you?"

"He stopped by the clinic the other day to pick up a few of his personal belongings. Aside from that, no, I haven't had any contact with him."

Franklin nodded her head as she twirled a pen in her left hand. I could tell she was tense. Having a resident disappear wasn't unheard of. When it did happen it was usually on a more high stress service such as surgery or internal medicine and then usually by someone experiencing a psychiatric break or with substance abuse problems. Often the resident would return a few days later or show up in the emergency room. Rarely would they commit suicide but there were occasions when they would disappear altogether, never to be seen or heard from again.

"Should I be concerned?" I inquired.

"Why do you ask?" Franklin answered. I hated receiving a question after I had asked one.

"It was something he said as he left the other day."

"Which was what?"

"That I should watch my back."

"I see," Franklin said softly. She stared at her hands, folded atop the desk before speaking again.

"There's something about Dr. Hart you should probably know. Something we only became privy to ourselves in the past 24 hours. It seems Dr. Hart has had some difficulties in the past which the police became aware of when they checked into his background. Specifically, he spent the better part of a year in a mental hospital. As I understand it, he had some sort of emotional breakdown during college, assaulted a grocery store clerk and barricaded himself inside the building for several hours. Since it was his first brush with the law he and his family were allowed to have him treated in a private facility outside Chicago. Obviously we knew nothing about this when we took him into the residency."

"I'd say that's considerably more substantive than a 'difficulty', Dr. Franklin," I responded.

The tone of my voice was more harsh than I had intended but considering the matter at hand, I didn't care. I was willing to overlook a great many things in securing a residency position, however, there were limits. Franklin and Jennings had placed me in the workplace with someone with a criminal record. Whether they knew that at the time was, in my opinion, irrelevant. It was their job to have known and they had failed to live up to their responsibilities. Franklin seemed to take my accusatory tone in stride.

"Well, what's done is done. We're working on damage control at this point and trying to keep the study running."

I shouldn't have been shocked that Franklin's primary concern was the health and well being of the drug study. She did, after all, have a skewed sense of priority.

"In Dr. Hart's absence," Franklin continued, "I've assigned another resident to cover the study clinic. Carla Huntington, one of the third year residents has agreed to relinquish some of her elective time. I suspect she's already over there so you should probably go lend her hand. She'll need some assistance from you and Julie in getting up to speed."

I could tell when the discussions with Dr. Franklin were over and this was one of those moments. I rose from my chair, picked up my backpack and left without saying goodbye. If Franklin could tell I was upset, she didn't let on. Just so the project kept going.

Gary Page wasn't comfortable with his surroundings. He was unaccustomed to being in sketchy parts of Miami, preferring instead to spend his time near the restaurants and marinas in the better areas of town. But desperate times call for desperate measures, he told himself, and things were getting out of hand. On the other end of the phone was someone who specialized in taking care of troublesome matters.

"I need someone taken care of," Page said as he looked over his shoulder.

"Long time, no hear."

"Yeah, can't say I've missed it much."

"Ouch."

"You still in the business?"

"Of course. You still have the number for my account in the Cayman Islands?"

"I do."

"Then let's talk."

"There's a woman in the hospital in Apalachicola I need dispatched."

"Nasty business taking someone out in a hospital. Lots of witnesses. Not recommended, my friend."

"She won't be in the hospital," Page continued. "She's due to be transferred to Shands Hospital in Gainesville. I don't just need her dead, I need her incinerated."

"Why?"

"Why is my business. Can you do the job?"

"What's the time frame?"

"Tomorrow morning."

"Tomorrow morning?" the man said incredulously. "Couldn't you have waited until the last minute?"

"This came up in the past 24 hours. Again, can you do the job?"

"Not much time for preparation. Could get messy."

The man was angling for an increased fee, something Page found annoying.

By the front doors of the convenience store two questionable characters were arguing over a bottle of malt liquor. Page hoped they didn't notice the make of his car sitting in the parking lot. He was anxious to conclude the phone call and get out of there.

"Yeah, yeah. It's last minute. What's the word"

"I think something can be arranged. I'll have to call in additional help and considering this is last minute, it's going to be expensive."

"How much?"

"Five hundred K," the man said flatly.

Page winced at the figure. He knew the cost would be high but he hadn't planned on it being that much. Still, he was in no position to bargain.

"Done."

"Now by incinerated, what exactly do you mean?"

"You are familiar with the term, aren't you?" Page responded testily.

The men at the convenience store were looking at his car and pointing.

"Temper, temper. How much incineration are we talking about?"

"Complete. Turning her to dust would be preferable."

The men were staggering toward Page's car.

"Nothing left suitable for an autopsy."

"Correct."

"I have just the tool in mind."

"The hit will have to be while she's riding in the ambulance."

"Makes sense. Any preference as to where?"

"Some place along the highway between Apalachicola and Gainesville."

"Collateral damage?"

Page understood the man's meaning.

"Irrelevant."

The drunks were within 20 feet of the car and closing.

"That will be fine. Consider it taken care of."

"Good. I'll expect to read about it on the news. Remember, incinerated."

"Got it," the man responded before hanging up.

Page quickly replaced the phone receiver. His visitors were less than five feet from the car and yelling something inaudible. He ripped the car into drive and sped out of the parking lot. In his rear view mirror he could see the men flailing their arms and stomping the ground. *Some other time fellas.*

* * *

"Terrific," McMillan said sarcastically. "Just what I needed. Some hoard of mental midgets scrutinizing my affairs with a fine tooth comb."

"I'm sorry, Sean," Murphy said. He had known his conversation with McMillan wasn't going to be pleasant but he was glad to be getting it over with. Most of his friend's ensuing trouble would result from doing a favor for a colleague in need. But the man was right. The authorities from the Agriculture Ministry would be a royal pain to work with. In all probability, he'd get off with a fine and a slap on the wrist. The publicity could be an additional burden, but that wouldn't bother McMillan. He rarely cared what anyone said or thought about him anyway.

"What is it they say about no good deed going unpunished?" McMillan snorted. He shook his head back and forth, his arms spread out wide and resting on the countertop.

Murphy stood with his hands in his pockets and shuffled his feet.

"Still, this isn't all your fault," McMillan conceded. "There's the miscreant who tampered with the feed in the first place and then there's my contribution for selling it to you. I should have just shipped it back after the recall notice came through. But I thought it was all a big fuss about nothing. Just figured the bureaucratic weenies were overreacting."

"Are you going to contact those attorneys who were in here the other day?"

"I guess so," McMillan answered. "I doubt this was the sort of thing they were looking for but perhaps they can help shield me from some of the fallout. If nothing else, at least they'll have the opportunity to stick it to the manufacturers responsible for this mess."

The ambulance that would carry Emma Truett backed up to the emergency room doors at 7:30 A.M. For the two men transporting the patient, it was just another day at the office. They had ferried people all around the area at one time or another. Patients too sick for care in Apalachicola were usually transported up the road to Tallahassee. A trip to Gainesville, however, wasn't unusual. Driving there and back would take the better part of the day and the two paramedics looked forward to what promised to be an uneventful road trip and the chance for a drive time nap.

Emma Truett had calmed considerably during her short stay, largely due to the steady doses of tranquilizers dripping into her arm. Her attending physician had ordered a final injection to keep her sedated during the journey. While her agitation had subsided she remained unable or unwilling to reveal much about herself. In the accompanying paperwork was a note from the doctor outlining the results of her workup. She had undergone a CT scan of her head and neck, a spinal tap and a slew of blood work. Aside from some anemia and mild liver inflammation, nothing revealing had been discovered. She was still no closer to having her condition clarified than when she had arrived. The working diagnosis was 'psychosis of unknown origin', a wastebasket term invoked when someone went over the edge for no known reason.

After signing a few release papers and loading the woman into the back of the bus, the two men were on their way. They had called ahead to Shands Hospital to confirm the transfer. Following a quick stop at Burger King for some breakfast biscuits, the three resumed their trip down state road 98 towards highway 319 which would take them to Interstate 10 and eastward out of the panhandle.

The trip began uneventfully. The weather was in its typical cycle prevalent during the warmer months. Clear skies in the morning followed by a buildup of tall cumulus clouds which would eventually unleash torrents of rain for a few minutes in the afternoon. The sun was a welcome site, however, as they had tired of the overcast skies during what passed for "winter" in the Sunshine State. The men spoke of baseball and the league standings. The Florida Marlins and Tampa Bay Rays had made a few off season trades which provided fodder for discussion. After an hour or so, with Emma Truett snoozing peacefully in the back, the passenger decided to "rest his eyes". The father of a 6 month old, his night time responsibilities often left him sleep deprived and tired.

As with most ambulances, the one bore a state registration number on the doors, back panels and roof. This numerical system allowed for tracking the vehicle in the event it was lost or fell victim to some type of crime. As the ambulance left the Apalachicola Hospital parking lot, a late model Chevy Tahoe sat idling in the parking lot of a Sam's Club store. The woman seated behind the steering wheel used a small set of binoculars to note the registration number and typed it into the body of an email she had been composing. When the vehicle was out of sight, she clicked the "Send" button on the computer screen. Seconds later the email was opened by another man several hours away sitting in a small boat, his laptop computer resting on his knees. As the day progressed, more such emails would be forthcoming, each to a different website domain in a unique name and by a different driver. With a rotational system in place, as one car peeled off the interstate and out of surveillance, another would take its place, providing the man in the boat with frequent updates on their location and estimated time of arrival at a fixed point of his choosing. Things would have worked just as easily using Global Position Satellite (GPS) imaging but that potentially left a footprint of activity, something he always avoided. The emails were a primitive means of communication but essentially untraceable.

The final email transmission was sent and received 5 minutes before the ambulance reached ground zero. By then, their recipient was sitting in a small collection of pine trees adjacent to Interstate 10 a mile west of the Sewanee river. Despite the limited amount of time he had been given to prepare for the job he had researched the area sufficiently for the task at hand. He was a professional and as with those in other occupations, he knew what worked and what didn't.

This section of the Interstate was flat and allowed for a long look at traffic coming from the east. A vehicle traveling at 70 miles an hour would take 80 seconds to cover the visible area allowed for by the foliage. It was more than enough time. When the final email arrived the man knew exactly how long it would be before the ambulance came into sight. He used the remaining time to assemble an RPG-7 grenade launcher he had transported through the swampy terrain and load a modified PG-7N grenade to its front tip. Despite the longevity of the anti-tank weapon, it had a well documented history of effectiveness. Initially designed and built in the former Soviet Union, these grenade launchers had been manufactured in numerous other countries as well. His particular model had been obtained from an associate who dealt in such contraband and who preferred weapons from Bulgaria. Different types of grenades could be used depending on the target in question. For this job, the man had selected one with the capacity to pierce metal and a highly flammable component containing phosphorus.

Scanning the road in front of him with binoculars, the man soon spotted the vehicle in question. After assuring himself that the numbers on the ambulance corresponded to those he had been given, he set the binoculars to his side, picked up the RPG-7 and nestled it into his shoulder.

The driver of the ambulance had been alone with his thoughts for some time. His partner had drifted off to sleep and their passenger hadn't made a sound since leaving Apalachicola. Bored, the driver began scanning the radio dial. After finding a sports radio talk show, he settled into his seat content to cover the miles to Gainesville and finish out his day.

Crouched within the foliage lining the highway and well concealed with his camouflage cover, there was little chance of the man being spotted. He had done this before and knew that the element of overwhelming surprise would serve to both successfully complete the job and assure his unnoticed departure from the scene. He centered the sighting mechanism on the ambulance, mentally calculated the amount of lead time required for the grenade to reach the target and nudged the weapon an appropriate distance to his right. Satisfied with the trajectory, he switched the safety off and gently squeezed the trigger. The weapon emitted a burst of propellant as the missile began its flight towards the ambulance. A white trail hovered in the air marking the ordinance's path. Covering the distance of 300 yards took less than 3 seconds during which the vehicle had traveled 250 feet. Its forward momentum would carry it less than half that.

The grenade's impact into the vehicle's structure was minimal compared to what followed. As a munition designed to penetrate as far as possible into thick armor, piercing the ambulance chassis was child's play. The grenade lodged near the back of the engine block and detonated. The exploding grenade detonated the flammable liquid in the fuel lines and gas tank with devastating force. A fireball shot 40 feet in every direction as the ambulance disintegrated. The vehicle's remains veered off the asphalt into a nearby ditch. Cars and trucks swerved to avoid the inferno, some losing control and ending up on the side of the road. Within a few seconds people began retrieving their cell phones and dialing 911. The missile's phosphorus component ensured the ambulance's remains would stay white hot for several hours evaporating all forms of human tissue.

The man in the woods watched without emotion. Satisfied he had done his job sufficiently, he replaced his materials into a large duffel bag and retreated into the thick woods. Several minutes later, as the sounds of approaching emergency vehicles pierced the air, he reached the small boat he had fastened to a nearby tree, untied the rope and began his journey down the river. When he was well away from the area he removed his cell phone and called in a status report.

Ewan Calcote arrived at the Agriculture Ministry for Northern Ireland. Situated in downtown Dublin, it had long since exceeded its capacity to house the ministry but fiscal realities being what they are, the government had decided to make do and simply squeeze its occupants into smaller and smaller confines. Calcote's office was situated on the third floor. Given his seniority with the ministry, he had been afforded one of the better ones, meaning his contained a window with a panoramic view of an adjacent elementary school playground. From his vantage point he could watch the children at play, often wishing he could trade places with them and experience their oblivion to what was happening in the world around them.

The previous evening, Calcote had been contacted at home by one of the ministry's undersecretaries informing him of the contaminated feed. Learning the details of the mishap would fall to him. Adulterated animal products were a subject with which he had experience. Spongiform bovine encephalopathy, or mad cow disease as it was referred to in the press, was a matter he was intimately familiar with. In fact, it had become almost his sole preoccupation in the previous 3 years. With the European Union anxious to expand its agricultural exports, the presence of tainted meat was an intolerable situation. Stringent testing and destruction of entire animal herds had sufficiently suppressed the outbreak with no reported cases in the previous

18 months. The production of beef and beef products had nearly regained its pre-epidemic footing suggesting the industry was poised to regain its market share. A crisis such as the one looming could hardly have come at a worse time. The undersecretary made it clear in no uncertain terms that getting to the bottom of the problem and correcting it was of paramount importance.

While Calcote had investigated a occasional contamination cases in his career, he had little experience with those involving heavy metals. Certainly nothing approaching this degree of adulteration. The laboratory report on his desk suggested a large quantity of mercury had been involved. His first order of business would be to determine how such an event occurred. One of the ministry's secretaries had obtained the phone number of Surrey Manufacturing Associates in Cardiff, Wales. Calcote took off his coat, hung it on a small rack in the corner of the room and picked up the telephone receiver.

In less than 20 seconds he was transferred to Arthur Graham, the man in charge of plant operations.

"I was expecting your call," Graham said. "What can I do to help?"

Calcote was relieved to find the man cooperative. Some of his previous experiences had been confrontational, a situation he was always eager to avoid.

"I'm sorry to have to call you, particularly on such a matter as this. Surrey has always enjoyed a favorable status with the ministry and we value your service to the industry. As you know, our laboratory evaluated the brains of a dead calf and found evidence of mercury poisoning. Its feed was traced to a lot manufactured at your plant."

"Correct. Lot number ZM23765. Manufactured January 3, 2003."

"Before we delve into the business of tracking the feed's dispensation," Calcote said, "I was wondering if you had any thoughts on how this could have happened. To be honest, I don't know a great deal about mercury and its current role in 21st century industry but I'm assuming it's fairly negligible in the animal feed trade."

"Again, correct," Graham responded. "To my knowledge, there is no place for its use in our line of work. Pesticides in the past have contained mercury but they were outlawed over 25 years ago and, of course, wouldn't have anything to do with the manufacturing of animal foodstuffs. We don't permit heavy metals in our plants at any phase of production. All of the invoices for raw materials have been reviewed, twice now, and none bear any mention whatsoever about mercury."

"What about with the machinery you use?"

"I've checked on that as well. None of the equipment in our plant have mercury as any sort of metal alloy. It wouldn't make much sense anyway since it's quite a soft element. I considered whether it might be used as a lubricant or cleaning material and evaluated that angle as well. Again, nothing."

Calcote was writing notes to himself on a legal pad as the men talked.

"So, do you have any idea as to how this might have happened?"

"All I can think of is that the raw materials were tampered with intentionally."

"Some sort of industrial espionage?"

"I suppose that's not out of the question, however we're on good terms with competing manufacturers of agricultural products. As you know, the number of firms engaging in our type of work isn't large. In the past 2 decades there have been no new startup companies. At least not in the UK. It's a small club. We all know each other and get along reasonably well. Behavior like this from a competitor is highly unlikely. A rogue group would be another matter."

"By 'rogue group' I assume you are referring to some element of the animal rights movement?"

"Certainly. It's possible a disgruntled employee could have been responsible, but usually such malcontents wouldn't be sufficiently sophisticated to design and carry out something of this magnitude."

Graham paused for a moment to sip his coffee. When he continued, the tone of his voice was darker.

"The animal rights fringe. Now that's another matter. We've dealt with them for years. Tricky little insects. Always looking for some chink in the armor and with no short supply of free time to exploit it."

"I take it they've targeted your business before," Calcote mused.

"Of sorts. They've protested at the front gates occasionally, fortunately less so in our case as we're one of the smaller operations. This sort of attack has their name written all over it."

"Is it possible they made their way into the plant and deposited the mercury into the meal themselves?"

"Possible? I suppose anything is possible, but quite unlikely. We've spent considerable time and money training our security staff about these groups. Most of their operatives are known to our people from photographs we've distributed. Whether they could have encouraged someone on our workforce to do their dirty work, that's another matter."

"I assume you're looking into that?" Calcote asked.

"Absolutely. We've hired a top flight security consultant to examine our employee records for someone capable of such an act but of course, that's all in the preliminary stages at this point."

Calcote made a few more notations on his legal pad. They spoke briefly about the measures being enacted to test the products currently distributed and the ensuing recall. Surrey seemed to have things under control, at least as well as could be expected. The tainting of their cattle feed was certain to cost them a considerable sum but it couldn't be argued they weren't doing everything possible to address the situation.

Working with Dr. Huntington was decidedly more pleasant than with Galen Hart. In addition to being a hard worker, she was kind and liberal with her compliments about the efforts Julie, Lisa and I were making. I had worried she might resent being pulled from other clinic duties to oversee the drug study but if she harbored any ill will about the turn of events, she kept it to herself.

I hadn't heard a peep from or about Hart during the week, which was fine with me. His final words kept playing over in my head like a worn out record. I had taken his warning to heart, looking over my shoulder more often and straining to spot his ugly mug wherever I went. The week had gone by so smoothly I was beginning to think things were approaching some degree of normalcy. That was about to change.

Late on Thursday afternoon I received a page to a telephone number I didn't recognize. From the first three digits I knew it originated in the hospital, I just didn't know where. Those sorts of pages always made me nervous. I considered ignoring it but curiosity got the better of me. I picked up a nearby phone and dialed the number.

"Is this Justin Douglas?" the voice asked.

"It is," I answered.

"Justin, this is Mark Kovach. Have I called at a bad time? I know you're probably in clinic."

"Not really. We're just finishing. What's up?"

"I wanted to show you something. Think you can drop by the psych resident's offices on your way out?"

"Sure. What's this all about?"

"I'd rather discuss it in private. It won't take long, I promise."

I told him I would be there within the hour. Julie gave me a quizzical look after I hung up the phone but I decided not to tell her or Lisa anything. At least not until I found out what Kovach had to say.

Locating the psychiatry residents' room wasn't difficult. Situated a few doors down the hall from the department offices I was comforted to find the place abandoned aside from Dr. Kovach sitting in his cubicle typing on his computer. When I opened the door he looked up and waved me in.

"Thanks for coming," he said. "I have something you might want to see."

Turning to his side, he picked up a single piece of paper and handed it to me. It was a fax from a reference laboratory in Syracuse, New York. At the top was the name of the patient, Helen Rubin.

The document outlined a list of tissue samples from Mrs. Rubin with a corresponding measurement of the mercury they contained. Kovach had highlighted those from her skin biopsies. All demonstrated grossly elevated levels above the norm but one in particular was off the charts. The one taken from her forehead.

I didn't know what to say. The calculations suggested a massive exposure to mercury and far higher in the skin than any other organs evaluated. I decided to let Kovach tell me what I already suspected.

"So what does all this mean?"

"It means," the resident began, "that in all likelihood, the point of entry for the mercury was through the skin on her forehead."

I sat down in a nearby chair. I believed Mrs. Rubin's death was probably connected to the study, though I didn't know exactly how. The most obvious scenario, that the botulinum toxin had induced a psychotic break and precipitated her suicide, had been all but abandoned. The use of adulterated materials, supplied by the manufacturer no less, had never crossed my mind. Worse, if this had happened to her, how many other study participants were at risk?

"It was the patches," I whispered under my breath.

"Certainly looks like it," Kovach responded. "This one is going to get messy."

I couldn't put the paper aside, instead repeatedly scrutinizing the values printed on the page.

"Is there any chance these values are inaccurate?" I asked.

Kovach gave me a strange look. "I suppose. But that far out of bounds?" he asked. "Not very likely."

My mind was racing with every conceivable scenario bouncing around my brain at the same time.

"Have you told anyone else about this?" I asked.

"Nope. Just you."

"Not your attending?"

Kovach managed a wry smile. "Out of town at the Neuropsychiatric World Congress in Seattle. He'll be back tomorrow. I thought you might like to be the first to know."

"That was kind of you," I responded. "So what will he do when he sees this?"

"I'm assuming he'll call Dr. Franklin and/or Dr. Jennings. An emergency Pow-Wow will ensue where they put their heads together and come up with something. They'll require a viable scenario to keep the press from getting wind of the story while the drug company warms up the paper shredder. Goes on all the time."

I realized I was still wet behind the ears, but Kovach's prediction of future events was disturbing. For one thing, it made little sense. If there was any suggestion of espionage or criminal activity, the legal authorities wouldn't let it be swept under the rug. Secondly, it didn't seem realistic to legitimately expect any affected participants from finding out and seeking legal redress.

"Oh, I doubt they'd be capable of something like that," I responded.

Kovach looked over the top of his glasses. "Don't think so?" His tone made me feel about 2 feet tall.

"A frat buddy of mine from college just made partner at a law firm in Chicago. This practice has an entire section dedicated solely to helping training institutions and pharmaceutical companies to prevent and defend exactly these sorts of legal challenges. If even half the stories he tells are true, the amount of subterfuge and skullduggery taking place is mind boggling. Trust me, it'll get cleaned up. This institution and whatever drug companies involved can't afford for it to be otherwise."

As much as I didn't want to admit it, I knew Kovach was probably right. Particularly, his final point. If there were more sick patients like Mrs. Rubin out there, the exposure of the parties involved would be unacceptably large. Something would have to be done.

"How far can I go up the food chain in terms of revealing this information?" I asked.

"As far as you want. Like I said, my attending should be getting back tonight and will be in his office in the morning. I'll be telling him about it then so he'll be prepared to deal with the specifics. Besides, it will make you look like the hero. Lowly medical student solves the great mystery of Mrs. Rubin's death."

Frankly, I could have done just as well without the headlines.

It wasn't so much a matter of the law enforcement assigned to the case being incompetent as just inexperienced. They were more than capable of dealing with smugglers of drugs and human cargo, gang bangers taking pot shots at one another on the freeway or some idiot racing his friend home from college break. Terrorist activity, however, was another matter. The local officers and highway patrol personnel assigned to this central stretch of Interstate 10 had been given additional training on national security matters, particularly in light of September 11. But it had largely been of an interdictory nature. Crime scene investigation was another matter and this one exceeded their comfort zone.

In addition to the violence of the assault, the explosion had created a 5 foot hole in the pavement, there was evidence that military weaponry had been used. The investigating officers quickly realized if they weren't already in over their heads, they soon would be. They radioed their shift captain who in turn contacted the appropriate federal agencies. Within 90 minutes an FBI team was on the scene.

The agents initially scoured the nearby woods. It didn't take long to find evidence of the assassin's presence. He hadn't bothered to cover his tracks since his efforts would have been both futile and time consuming. There was no practical way for anyone to follow him. A full scale investigation was underway within hours, the general assumption being an act of terrorism had taken place.

One of the highway patrol officers informed the hospital in Apalachicola about the deaths of their employees and patient. The staff were shocked but cooperative. With the identity of the patient still uncertain they were unable to contact any family, instead calling Dr. Haverson in Gainesville to inform him of the incident. When told of the patient's murder, he thanked the hospital for their efforts, extended his sympathies for the men killed in the explosion and informed the nurse on the phone he would take care of things from his end.

The biochemical supply business is comprised of a relatively small and homogenous population. Forty years ago hundreds of companies were in business providing materials for laboratories large and small throughout the world. However, following numerous mergers, many of the smaller operations had either been swallowed up by bigger ones or put out of business. As a result, the market was dominated by several large corporations each with a toehold in the field courtesy of their fiercely protected materials or protocols.

The initial botulinum patches were designed and manufactured at the Omega headquarters in Florida. Produced in small quantities, the startup materials had been obtained from a local wholesaler. After exhausting the initial supply of patches, the company had begun using those manufactured at the production plant in Ireland.

By all accounts, the site outside of Dublin had been an unqualified success. Terry MacGregor had done such excellent work, he'd been awarded several bonuses along with a trip for he and his wife to Miami to meet with Gary Page and tour the facilities. At the time no one questioned the integrity of the stock materials used in producing the botulinum toxin. No one had reason to.

At the heart of most biochemical research laboratories, particularly those employing bacterial cultures, is the protein albumin. Produced exclusively by the liver, albumin is a key constituent of the blood. Among other duties, it's responsible for controlling fluid flow from blood vessels into the surrounding tissues. Almost every mammalian species depends on its biochemical properties in one respect or another.

Importantly, albumin provides a transport system for other chemicals in the blood, including certain drugs. After absorption from the gut, these medications attach to the protein molecule and are delivered to different internal organs. Unfortunately, albumin performs this task passively, which is to say, without much discretion. Chemicals and other molecules adhere to it based on the biochemical properties of attraction between the two. If the molecule in question happens to be a sulfa drug designed to kill the bacteria responsible for a bladder infection, then so much the good. However, if the molecule is a heavy metal contaminant destined to poison cellular enzymes, so much the worse. Albumin doesn't discriminate.

When the cattle in Patrick Murphy's pen moved towards the large metal feeding trough, they only knew it was time to eat. The half dozen bags of meal purchased by their owner had been part of a single batch of food nuggets contaminated with mercury 12 weeks earlier. The Murphy's cattle pens had become ground zero for the dissemination of this metal.

When the serum from Murphy's calves arrived at the biochemical company it was processed and tested to ensure its suitability for distribution. Screening for heavy metal contamination wasn't performed. Within a few days the serum had been bottled, labeled and shipped to different wholesalers who in turn sold it to individual customers.

One such purchase was made by Omega Pharmaceuticals. Had the material been used in bacterial cultures, the mercury levels would have killed the organisms, triggering an investigation. Testing would have eventually disclosed the underlying problem. However, Omega used the tainted serum not for the growth of bacteria but in the protein rich medium required for a measured and sustained toxin release from the patches. With no impediment to its movement, the mercury traveled into the blood stream and ultimately to different internal organs, including the brain.

Small quantities of mercury are found in almost every mammalian species. Being a ubiquitous metal in the environment, excluding it from the food chain is a practical impossibility. The body will tolerate mercury in small amounts without any side effects. However, when a certain threshold is reached, particularly in the central nervous system, toxicity ensues. Skin rashes of the type suffered by Helen Rubin are common and present in the early stages of poisoning. With time, the symptoms become more sinister, specifically psychiatric changes. Depression and forgetfulness are typical initially, but with continued exposure, psychosis ensues.

I didn't know what to do after my conversation with Dr. Kovach. Obviously, his information mandated some action. The problem was, do I tell someone, and if so, who? I considered going to Drs. Franklin or Jennings, but as luck would have it, they were in Chicago for a conference. I didn't think they would appreciate having their trip interrupted with the sort of news I would be bearing. I could tell Julie, of course. Being the good soldier she was, she would probably shut the study down pronto. But if that action proved premature, it would cost the department dearly and my hopes for a residency position at UT Houston or anywhere else would be shot. Besides, closing our arm of the project wouldn't address the exposure of patients at other sites. I finally settled on talking with Jennifer Maddux. She seemed appropriately positioned on the food chain and, of course, had access to all the study participants. I needed a phone with privacy where I could speak freely.

I walked to the department library, opened the door and found the place empty. Fortunately, I was able to get through to Maddux on her cell phone. Half the time it seemed she was in an airplane or had her phone turned off in a meeting. The last thing I wanted to do was leave her a voice message.

"Jennifer Maddux," she said. Her voice sounded cheery. I didn't like the idea of ruining her day.

"Miss Maddux, this is Justin Douglas," I announced. "Do you have a minute?"

"Yeah. I'm in my car on the way to the airport. Okay if we chat on the speaker phone?"

"Sure. I just finished talking with Mark Kovach, the psychiatry resident who hospitalized Mrs. Rubin."

"Oh, right. Did her autopsy show anything? I'm hoping we got a clean bill of health."

Not hardly.

"Actually, just the opposite. The pathology service sent off tissue samples for specialized testing. All of them demonstrated toxic levels of mercury."

There was a pause on the other end of the line.

"Hello? Are you still there?"

She was.

"What are you talking about?" Maddux asked carefully

"Mercury poisoning. It all fits. The headaches. The peeling skin on her palms. The depression. All are classic signs of heavy metal toxicity."

"Well, that's certainly tragic but what does it have to do with Omega?"

"Some of the tissues evaluated were skin biopsies. Those from the arms, legs and torso showed modest mercury contamination, but those from her forehead were off the charts. They're hypothesizing the source of her exposure was from the patches."

There was an audible click on the other end of the line. At first I thought she might be recording our conversation but then I realized she had taken the phone off the speaker mode.

"There must be some sort of mistake," Maddux replied. Her voice had lost its cheerful tone. "Neither the process involved in refining the toxin or the patches themselves have any mercury in them. It simply couldn't have come from there. They'll just have to repeat the testing."

"I suppose a lab error isn't out of the question," I said, trying to sound hopeful. "But all three specimens from her forehead? I'm not a toxicologist or a statistician, but that's not a very likely scenario."

There was another uncomfortable pause in the conversation.

"Drs. Franklin and Jennings are out of town which is why I'm calling you. Until there's additional information I think it would be prudent to consider suspending the study."

I knew my suggestion bordered on arrogance and would probably be ignored but I at least wanted it on the record that I had brought it up.

"We can't do that," Maddux said flatly. "At least, I don't have the authority to make that call. I'll relay the information to the corporate office. I think the most important thing to do at this point is to keep all of this just between us."

"Shouldn't Julie know?"

"Until we have more of the facts, I think it would cause some potentially unjustified concern."

"Unjustified concern? There's credible evidence that Mrs. Rubin died of mercury poisoning!"

To my surprise, Maddux appeared to be taking the matter in stride. Either that, or she didn't comprehend the gravity of the situation. I was frustrated and asked what she *did* want to do.

"Let me handle it," she replied.

I wasn't eager to turn things over to Omega and hope they'd make the right decision. Their objectivity on the matter was an open question. After all, they did have millions of dollars invested in this project. Maddux must have sensed my reticence.

"After we hang up, I'll call the big boys at the home office and speak with them. They may be paging you in an hour or two for additional information. I'll leave emails for Franklin and Jennings before I get on the plane and phone them in the a.m. For now just go forward with the afternoon clinic, mouth closed. You have my word that everyone who needs to have this information, will."

Dr. Haverson needed to take Gary Page's phone call like he needed malaria. His schedule was already overextended as it was and the thought of a confrontational chat with the head of Omega Pharmaceuticals wasn't appealing.

"This is Gerald Haverson," he said as he picked up the receiver.

"Dr. Haverson. Gary Page. Have I caught you at a bad time?"

"Yes."

"Sorry to hear that," Page responded. "What's the story on the patient from Apalachicola?"

"You mean Emma Truett?"

"Exactly."

"She's dead."

"I'm aware of that. I wanted to know if there was any indication as to what was wrong with her."

"Not yet."

"Not yet?" Page asked with exasperation. "What sort of answer is that?"

"The honest sort."

"Do you have anything in the works?"

"Well, there's no way to do an autopsy . . ."

Page smiled to himself.

". . . with the body burned as badly as it was."

"I see."

"Later today, I'm going to speak with her admitting physician in Apalachicola. If there are any remaining blood or tissue samples available we might be able to do some toxicology screening but I'm not hopeful."

Page had already dispatched one of his minions to sleuth around the hospital searching for the same. He had been relieved to learn there weren't any.

"Well, it seems you have things well in hand. How are the other participants in the study doing?"

"They're fine, so far as I know. I had the nurse coordinator for the project contact each of them. None seem to be demonstrating any untoward effects. Most weren't pleased to hear the testing had been suspended."

"Excuse me?" Page said, sitting up straight in his chair.

"Given the magnitude of Ms. Truett's condition, surely you didn't think we would be moving forward until an investigation was completed?"

"Investigation or no, you don't have the authority to suspend anything without consulting with Omega first."

"I believe I'm well within my rights to do so and even if I'm not, there's no way I or this institution are going to have any patients near those patches until this matter is cleared up."

Page cleared his throat.

"Dr. Haverson, I would like to make this as clear as possible. This project will either be moving forward while an investigation is undertaken or you and your institution will find themselves on the ugly end of a very large lawsuit."

"I'll be here," Haverson said before hanging up.

Page was livid. The audacity of academic physicians never ceased to amaze him. Page briefly considered arranging for Haverson the same fate as Emma Truett but quickly put it out of his mind. Things were beginning to unravel and he needed his intellectual energies for more constructive purposes. When things had settled down, Haverson would be dealt with.

He poured himself a drink and leaned back in his chair, looking out the plate glass window behind him. When he had regained his composure, he picked the phone up and placed an overseas call.

He woke Terry MacGregor in the middle of the night and explained the situation. The Scotsman was both shocked and confused. He'd never had any reason to consider the possibility of heavy metal contamination in his production facilities. Now completely awake and in a full panic, MacGregor drove to the laboratory and began the arduous task of preparing for a top to bottom review.

Page ordered the assembly laboratory on Omega's Florida campus shut down. Employees reporting for work the following morning were given a vague story about an overnight hazardous leak requiring a thorough cleaning of the equipment and materials. The workforce would continue to be paid but no additional production would take place until further notice. It was now largely a matter of damage control, something Gary Page had experience with.

My efforts in the clinic the next afternoon were half hearted at best. I wouldn't be able to speak to Jennings and Franklin until the next day. I wondered if Jennifer Maddux might try to make contact. It would take a load off of my shoulders. I didn't want to be the bearer of bad news.

I began scrutinizing each patient more thoroughly, probing for any subtle neurologic or psychiatric symptoms. The previous night I had scanned several dermatology textbooks regarding mercury poisoning and their skin manifestations. To my relief, no subjects in our study came to mind, or at least none I could recall. By the end of the day I was hoping Mrs. Rubin's case had been an isolated event.

Lisa and I were getting along well. She told me her father had completed his workup for Parkinson's disease. His doctors felt he was in the early stages, as she had thought, and were beginning a course of medical therapy designed to let him do as much as he was capable of for as long as the condition would allow. Lisa had encouraged him to visit the Mayo Clinic in Rochester, Minnesota for a second opinion. A team of physicians there was doing research on the disease. He might qualify for an experimental drug study or at least learn more about any newly available surgical procedures.

I mentioned I thought her father was fortunate to have a daughter with such concern for his health. She seemed to appreciate my sentiments and thanked me with a big smile. When the clinic was finished, she picked up her purse, told me good-bye and headed for the door. Halfway down the hall she stopped and began walking back.

"Forget something?" I asked.

"I think so," she replied. "Are you busy tonight?"

At first I thought she might need some help on her dermatology residency applications. All of them are submitted on line and their completion can be time consuming. As usual, I was wrong.

"I got a flyer in the mail last week for Antoine's," Lisa continued. "It's a new Italian restaurant on Holcomb Street. They have a two for one special this week and I thought if you weren't doing anything, we might give it a try. We could split the bill. Make things as cheap as possible."

She concluded her invitation with a short laugh and what appeared to be a faint blush of embarrassment.

Her question caught me off guard. As I sat there speechless, Lisa asked if I was okay.

"Oh, sure. Sure," I responded, trying to sound like I had been mentally calculating whether my jam packed social calendar could accommodate dinner with an admiring female. In reality, the thought of being on a date with Lisa was anesthetizing my brain. The only thing missing was drool on my chin.

"We can do it another night, if you like," Lisa said. From the look in her eyes, I couldn't tell if she was genuine about the rain check or just wondering if spending time with the mentally ill was a good idea after all.

"No, no," I blurted out quickly.

"Tonight would be great. Just great. Looking forward to it. Really."

I was pathetic.

Lisa narrowed her eyes and looked at me as though I was having a stroke.

"You sure?"

"Oh yeah. Absolutely. Just a little surprised, that's all."

"About what?"

"Well, I don't know I've ever had a girl ask me out for dinner before."

"And?"

"I'm assuming there has to be reason for that streak of luck."

Lisa reached across the distance between us, straightened up my tie and said,

"Cowboy up, big fella. Meet you at the restaurant at 7:30." With that, she gave me a wink and left the office.

I wasn't sure how I felt about the entire matter. Obviously, it was thrilling to think a woman like Lisa would want to spend any of her free time with a loser like me, but I couldn't exactly call tonight's dining arrangements a true date. Still, it was a positive turn of events and I decided to consider the glass half full.

I glanced at my watch. It was just after 5:00 P.M. I had plenty of time to get home, grab a shower and drive to the restaurant.

Jennifer Maddux arrived at Miami International Airport from Newark, New Jersey a few minutes ahead of schedule and with a troubled mind. Gary Page had snapped at her when she told him about the laboratory results. Like it was her fault.

Omega's car service ferried Maddux from the airport, allowing her to call and check her messages with the receptionist. She had several. Most were from BT test sites. The troops were getting nervous.

After being dropped off at the main office, Maddux took the elevator to the 5th floor, placed her belongings on her desk and asked the secretary as to the whereabouts of Mr. Page. He was in a meeting in Coral Gables and wasn't expected back for the remainder of the day. In her profession there was rarely a shortage of paperwork and Maddux decided to take the opportunity to massage a few stressed out psyches. Most of her messages regarded questionable neuropsychiatric symptoms in patients on the patch study. She immediately began phoning the primary investigators at their respective sites. After ninety minutes, she leaned back in her chair, exhausted from putting a positive spin on the matter and depressed at what she had heard.

The University of Pennsylvania, Wake-Forest University and Medical College of Ohio had at least one patient in their programs with symptoms similar to those of Helen Rubin. All were experiencing headaches with several complaining of either worsening of their depression or new onset of the disease. Two were also displaying skin findings including unusual rashes and/or peeling on their palms and soles. If a problem with the patches existed, it appeared to be systemic. It was a disaster in the making. As difficult a hurdle as glossing over the suicide and heavy metal poisoning of a study subject would pose, if there were others in the same boat, the FDA would never let it slide, regardless of how much juice Page had with the oversight board. The one saving grace was that none of the patients enrolled in the private practices had reported any symptoms.

Maddux needed an audience with her boss.

"Trouble in paradise?" the man asked as he lifted his water glass to his lips. He was seated at a single table on a large veranda overlooking the Pacific Ocean. Above him was an expansive umbrella designed to keep the sun off his balding head. He'd already survived one melanoma and had no intentions of suffering through another round of surgical misery.

Gary Page pulled his chair away from the table and sat down hard into it. The strain of the past few days had been more than he was accustomed to and he looked it. His ever present tan barely hid the circles beneath his eyes. He needed a vacation in the worst way.

"You might say that," he replied.

A young man wearing a white waiter's coat appeared with a pitcher of ice water and filled the glass in front of the visitor.

"Would you care for something to drink?" he asked.

"Not right now," Page replied.

"Bring us the salads would you, Juan."

With a respectful nod, the young man left as quickly as he had appeared.

"So, to what do I owe the honor?" the elderly man asked.

"There's been some developments with the study."

"So I hear. And not the good kind."

"No," Page replied. "Not the good kind. We have reason to believe some of the patches are contaminated. Mercury, to be exact. The scope of the problem isn't clear at the present but we now have a dead patient on our hands."

"Well, two actually," the man corrected him.

Page looked out over the ocean. On the beach perhaps a hundred yards away a family was playing in the surf. The father was lifting his young son into the air and tossing him into the oncoming waves. Intermittently, peals of laughter could be heard. Page felt a pang of jealousy.

"Right. Two."

"Haste," the old man said, adjusting his sunglasses. "The nemesis of the young."

"Okay. So, you were correct. It wasn't a judicious decision. If you knew it was going to be such a bad idea, why didn't you do more to stop me?"

The old man laughed softly.

"Not much stops you, Gary. Not when you get an idea into your head. You should listen more to the elderly, particularly when it includes problem solving. What is the catch phrase these days? 'Been there. Done that'?"

"Well, I'm here, hat in hand, asking for your help and guidance now."

"And you want me to what, exactly?"

"Damage control. Something I thought you were good at."

"I am good at it. One doesn't acquire a $9 million dollar oceanfront estate without some knowledge of how to navigate life's speedbumps."

"This is slightly more than a speedbump. It's an outright catastrophe. The cutbacks in reimbursement for chemotherapy medications are strangling the company. We're still showing a profit, but just barely. Cash flow has become a concern and the answer to our problems, the patch study, is teetering on the brink."

"Then snatch it back."

"Easier said than done."

"That depends on your outlook. How many patients are we talking about?"

"Obviously, the two you know of. From what some of the other investigators are telling me, there appear to be a handful of participants with early symptoms. Whether they have been poisoned as well remains to be seen. It could be just the tip of the iceberg. When the lab work returns . . ."

"Funny thing about lab work, you know," the man interrupted. "Something I learned early on in trying cases was that when the analysis is against you, question its accuracy. All you have to do is plant a small seed of doubt and sometimes it grows into a giant oak tree. Of course, the ultimate solution would be to have the numbers support your position."

Page sat back in his chair absorbing what the man had said. He wasn't certain he understood his point.

"But they won't support our position."

Juan had returned with their salads and his employer was busy munching on the greens in front of him. Page hadn't touched his. The man stopped eating long enough to dab some bleu cheese dressing from the corner of his mouth.

"Let me ask you something. How difficult will it be to find the source of the contamination, fix it and begin producing an unadulterated product?"

"From a practical standpoint, it's not an insurmountable problem. It will be time consuming and expensive, but that's not the issue. The issue is the patients in the study with mercury poisoning."

"Who will be determining whether a given patient has actually been contaminated?"

"The investigators at the institutions overseeing the study. Look, I don't understand what . . ."

"And where will they be getting their information?"

"They'll send off blood samples and perhaps tissue biopsies to a reference lab for evaluation."

"It won't be done at the institutions?"

"I doubt it. Analysis for heavy metal toxicity is an esoteric test. Almost no university or academic medical center receives enough requests to make it economically practical to keep the necessary equipment and reagents in house."

"So the materials will be referred to a larger laboratory?"

"Correct."

"How many places perform this testing?"

Page shrugged his shoulders. "Half a dozen, at the most."

The elderly man put down his salad fork, pushed the plate away and folded his hands on his chest.

"It would seem to me, the most expedient solution would be to have all the work performed at a single location. The results would be much easier to, how should I put it? Manage?"

Page had to hand it to his mentor. The man knew how to simplify a problem.

CHAPTER 13

Lisa's locker was on a different floor from mine. When they'd been assigned during our first year of medical school, hers had been part of a small allotment previously used by M.D./PhD candidates wanting to be closer to the laboratories in which they worked. Consequently, her locker resided on the 4th floor at the south end of the building. It was less congested at peak traffic hours but it was inconveniently out of the way.

It was now nearly 5:30 in the afternoon. Lisa was walking quickly to her locker, hoping to catch the 5:45 shuttle back to the apartment complex. Normally, her evening plans would have included running but tonight was different. Tonight, she had a date.

Well, a semi-date she told herself. When she had entered medical school, she decided her love life would have to wait until graduation. Energy and time were precious commodities. Christian values weren't abundant in modern medicine and Lisa was unwilling to associate herself romantically with anyone not meeting her standards. It wasn't clear what, if anything, was going to happen between herself and Justin Douglas, but he was sweet and had grown on her. At least she owed him a dinner out considering all he'd done for her.

Lisa walked down the hall, her footsteps echoing loudly. The lights were out, including those overhead in the hall.

Lisa passed a dark laboratory when she heard a sound over her shoulder. She was about to turn around when something flashed in front of her eyes. As soon as it had disappeared from sight, Lisa felt it at her throat, jerking her backwards. She reflexly drew her hands to her neck, her fingers palpating the coarse texture of rope. The cord was choking her as it pulled her out of the hall and into the empty room. She was off balance, the rope pressed ruthlessly against her larynx. Lisa couldn't scream, couldn't find her equilibrium and couldn't stop the attack. Just as she felt herself begin to fall the rope fell lax. At that moment, her attacker slipped something soft and fragrant over her face and mouth. Every natural impulse told her to take a deep breath, to fill her lungs to capacity and she gulped air greedily. Immediately, waves of nausea and dizziness began to wash over her. Her physical strength began to wane as if a thick, dark shroud was enveloping her body. A few seconds later, she passed out.

Lisa's assailant laid her motionless body on the floor. After securing the door, he folded her into a fetal position and bound her extremities with duct tape. Placing a strip across her mouth, he loaded her on the bottom of a metal cart and draped a white sheet overtop.

His task now complete, he donned a brown wig and surgical mask. To all appearances, he looked like any other laboratory worker pushing a cart of medical supplies or chemical reagents.

He opened the door, pulled the cart into the hall and began walking towards the service elevators.

"Contact Maitland and the rest of the brass for a 7:00 meeting in my office," Page told his secretary. "No excuses and I don't care where they are. Attendance is mandatory."

Page hung up the phone and pushed his Porsche into 4th gear as he negotiated the afternoon traffic in what had turned into a sweltering South Florida day. Twenty minutes later he was back at Omega's headquarters. He opened the door to his office to find Jennifer Maddux waiting for him.

"I need a word with you," she said.

"Not now," Page said taking off his coat and loosening his tie. He walked to the bar and poured a considerable volume of scotch into a glass.

"This can't wait," Maddux said.

Page considered arguing with the woman but decided against it. He swallowed the golden liquid in his glass with a single gulp and poured himself another round.

"Fine," he said. "Make it quick."

Maddux took a seat on one of the leather couches.

"Were you aware there are other patients in the patch study complaining of symptoms similar to Mrs. Rubin's?"

"Yes," Page responded. He glanced at his watch. "Are we done?"

Maddux was surprised at the man's lack of concern.

"Did you hear what I just said?"

"Of course I heard what you just said!" Page barked. "I'm not deaf."

"And this doesn't worry you?"

"Look, I've known about the problems at these institutions for several weeks and have been addressing the situation. I don't like our current circumstances, so we're going to be proactive. After you hear all the particulars at tonight's meeting, you'll understand the bigger picture."

Maddux nodded her head and left the room. She knew any further conversation would be pointless. Maddux couldn't imagine how Page was going to clean up this mess, but her boss had extracted himself from thorny situations before.

Page closed the door behind her and locked it. Back at his desk, he removed a cell phone from the bottom drawer. It was one he had purchased several months earlier at a convenience store for just such a purpose. As it was a "throw away", there would be no means of tracing any calls he made with it.

Page dialed the number and leaned back in his chair.

"Spectrophotometry," the voice answered.

"I need to speak to John Catchings, please."

"Speaking."

"This is Gary Page."

Catchings leaned hard against a nearby lab counter. He had known for some time this phone call would come. In some measure, he was relieved to finally be getting it behind him.

"To what do I owe the pleasure?"

Ten years earlier, Catchings had been employed by Omega Pharmaceuticals overseeing several of their clinical trials. With a PhD from the University of Chicago and a post-doctoral fellowship at Stanford University, he arrived in south Florida with impeccable credentials. His initial work had been nothing short of spectacular. His laboratory had developed a novel chemotherapy agent, useful for treating breast and colon cancer. The early clinical trials showed considerable promise and his group of investigators had been cleared by the FDA for Phase II evaluations. His private life, however, was disintegrating.

The Catchings marriage was on the rocks with both participants gradually drifting apart. Mrs. Catchings hated south Florida, wishing to relocate to her home in western Pennsylvania. Her parents were in poor health and she wished to be nearby to care for them. John refused to consider moving. His salary was far more than he could expect working in an academic center and none of the private firms in the region were involved in his field of research. Eventually, it became a divisive issue, no longer worth discussing. Mrs. Catchings began spending increasing amounts of time in Pennsylvania, often only returning to Florida for a few days before leaving again. Lonely and frustrated, Catchings began having an affair with one of the lab techs at Omega.

When Page heard about the romance, he had a private investigator follow the couple to the woman's apartment where he obtained several incriminating photographs. He showed them to Catchings a few days later. The man was devastated. By nature, Mrs. Catching was not a forgiving woman. If the pictures were shown to her, his marriage would be over and any divorce settlement would be decidedly in her favor.

Page routinely engaged in underhanded measures and considered it good business practice. Employees, particularly the higher ups, had occasionally fallen prey to various vices, typically substance abuse, gambling and pornography addiction. The CEO knew from experience, if his employees were fallible in their private lives, it could spill over into their work. Given the sensitive and propriety nature of Omega's product development, they could easily become an embarrassment or worse. Page collected files on many in his workforce with incriminating photographs, receipts and video. Once confronted with the evidence, the men and women were on the hook for whatever the man wanted. Page typically fired them on the spot, telling them the same thing he had told Catchings. Someday the debt would come due.

Page cut to the chase.

"I have a problem requiring your assistance," he replied and proceeded to give him a thumbnail sketch of the situation.

"What do you need from me?" Catchings asked suspiciously.

"Omega will be sending a large number of specimens to your lab for evaluation of mercury contamination."

"What type of specimens?"

"Transdermal patches, similar to those for pain relief and estrogen replacement, will comprise the bulk of the materials. There will also be blood samples and probably tissue specimens as well."

"That's a lot of work."

"No doubt. I need them to demonstrate uniformly negative results."

"All of them?"

"All of them."

Catchings thought for a minute, rolling the numbers around in his head.

"We have over 20 employees working in this lab. How do you propose I keep all of them out of the loop on this?"

"Do the work yourself," Page responded.

"Are you kidding me? I don't have time for a project that big."

"Make time. The materials will begin arriving within a few days. I'll expect all the results on official lab forms from your company one week after the last shipment."

Catching stared at the phone receiver, slowly shaking his head. This assignment would require working nights and weekends, the bulk of his efforts performed after regular business hours to keep things under the radar.

"Look, I don't have a problem doing the job," Catchings replied. "But, if the workload is as much as you say, I'm not sure there will be enough hours in the day. Why not just have me falsify as many records as you require and be done with it?"

"Because I need to know what each specimen actually demonstrates. I simply don't want it noted on one of your lab reports."

Catchings realized there was no point in protesting further. Page had him over a barrel and there was nothing he could do about it.

"I'll do as you ask," he said. "But this is a one time deal."

"I hardly think you're in a position to be dictating terms, Dr. Catchings."

"Could be. But I'm not going to go around for the rest of my life waiting for the other shoe to drop. I'll get you your results as well as the clean reports but in return, I want an affidavit from you stating you've destroyed the photographs."

"Or else?" Page inquired.

"Or else I go to the Feds."

Page was savvy when it came to blackmail and knew he could exert his influence only up to a point. Catchings was frightened but weary of looking over his shoulder. He wouldn't be pushed any further.

"Fair enough. You live up to your end of the bargain and I'll live up to mine. I've rented a large post office box three blocks from your office. The key for it will arrive tomorrow morning. Look for the first shipment of materials within the next 72 hours. I'll let you know when the last installment has been sent. Keep the documentation until you're finished and incinerate all the materials. You'll be informed where to send the reports when the job is complete. Are we clear?"

"Crystal," Catchings said as he hung up.

* * *

At 7:00 sharp, Colin Maitland, Brent DeWitt, Jerry Jordan, Leon Spangler and Jennifer Maddux arrived in Page's office for what promised to be a unique meeting. No minutes would be taken nor anything written down. This one was strictly off the books.

Page spent the first ten minutes bringing everyone up to speed on where things stood. He mentioned the death of the woman in the ambulance, careful to show an appropriate amount of reverence for her demise but mentioning nothing about his role in the matter. Everyone present seemed to take things well enough until he unveiled his plans for the near future.

"The FDA will want us to suspend the testing until things are straightened out to their satisfaction. We will impose a moratorium on our own. A month should be sufficient, I would think. During that time, the testing centers will return all the patches in their possession, including those currently held by the test subjects. I've arranged for a laboratory to evaluate the materials we provide them. Their report will state that no traces of mercury were discovered. After we have collected all the patches they will be incinerated and replaced with ones known to be clean. At month's end, we'll issue a press release with an affidavit from the lab declaring our product free of contaminants and we'll be back on track."

Page's words evoked no great response from the three vice-presidents present in the room but not so with the company's in house counsel. Maitland was dumbfounded.

"Have you taken total leave of your senses?" he asked.

"Not to my knowledge," Page replied calmly.

"This violates at least a half dozen laws I can think of off the top of my head. Even if your plan works, there are too many people in the loop for it to remain undetected in the long term. I would strongly discourage this. It isn't a smart move."

"I'm in agreement with Maitland," Maddux said. "It's too risky."

"Have you seen the 6 month sales figures for our other products?" Page said as he tossed a folder on top of his desk. "Let me give you the short version. They're appalling. Between competition from other companies, discounting from third party payers and generic substitutions we're getting hammered. Most are barely holding even and several are showing losses. Omega can afford delaying the marketing of the botulinum patch by a few weeks or even months but not much more. The impending release of this product is our only hope and if it tanks, the company tanks. It's as simple as that."

Spangler, DeWitt and Jordan sat quietly nodding their heads. Each was well aware of the ongoing turbulence in the pharmaceutical industry. If Omega went under, finding another position at their ages would be difficult.

"Well, I'm not in for this," Maitland announced.

"Yes, you are," Page retorted. "If you jump ship now, we all drown and I can assure you, your name is affixed to enough documents, real and otherwise, to place you in the crosshairs of any ensuing investigation. It wouldn't surprise me if more weight fell on you than any of us."

Maitland's eyes narrowed as he reflexly clenched his fists. "What is that supposed to mean?!," he thundered.

"Cool your jets, Maitland," Page said dismissively. "All I'm saying is that we need to hang together. This mess is survivable, but only if we circle the wagons."

The point wasn't lost on Maddux. Page's threats of paperwork bearing Maitland's name were probably genuine. If he had something on the company's in-house counsel, he almost certainly had something incriminating on her. She began to break out in a cold sweat.

"Anything from you, Miss Maddux?" Page asked.

Maddux slowly shook her head.

"I don't care, Page," Maitland continued as he stood to leave. "I have no intention of allowing you to blackmail me into some half baked idea to save this company. I'll take my chances with whatever forged paperwork you procure."

"Well, that's certainly your prerogative. But remember, accidents have been known to happen. Like exploding ambulances, for example."

Page's words were a bombshell. Everyone in the room sat in stunned silence, the same blank expression on their face. Until then, none of them had any reason to suspect the attack on Interstate 10 had been anything more than an isolated act of domestic terrorism. A Tampa newspaper reporter had even been contacted by an Islamic fundamentalist group claiming credit for the incident. Now, everyone knew better.

Maitland slowly sat back down, too shocked to speak.

"Well, now that we all seem to be in agreement, I've jotted down some specific assignments which will require your attention," Page said. He handed each member of the group a single sheet of paper with a short list of duties. Maitland took his and without looking, folded it and placed it in his coat pocket. The others glumly reviewed what had been given them.

"Any questions?" Page asked.

No one said anything. Everyone knew they were now captives of Omega and its CEO.

I arrived at Antoine's just before 7:00 P.M. excited at the prospect of having dinner with Lisa. Given the traffic around the medical center at that time of day, I had made good time. I scoured the parking lot for Lisa's car but didn't see it. The hostess suggested waiting in the bar. I declined. I had cleaned myself up better than usual and had no desire to smell like a used ashtray. I told the woman I'd wait outdoors on one of the benches.

Sitting outside was pleasant. The evening air was unusually cool for this time of year with the oppressive humidity normally plaguing south Texas yet to make its annual appearance. Couples steadily strolled in making me wonder if we would get a table. Antoine's didn't take reservations and even though it was a Thursday, restaurants in this part of town were typically full to overflowing no matter when you patronized them.

I found myself checking the time frequently. By 7:30 I thought I might have been stood up, a scenario which didn't seem likely. I wasn't any great catch for a dinner engagement but Lisa wasn't the type. I called her cell phone and then her apartment but got no response. At 7:45 I began to worry and just before 8:00 I left. Something wasn't right.

I drove to the apartment complex and went to Lisa's place. After knocking on the door for the third time I was satisfied she wasn't home. Peering through the windows revealed nothing. Her car was in its assigned parking space meaning she was probably still at the medical center. I returned to my truck and headed back.

The medical school garage was mostly deserted and I found a parking space close to the 3rd floor elevators. Calls to Lisa's cell phone continued to go unanswered. It was now nearly 8:30 and I was becoming frantic. I considered contacting the police but didn't know what I would tell them. They'd likely just blow me off assuming I'd been had and tell me to file a missing persons report in the morning.

My first stop was Lisa's locker. I dialed her number again but didn't hear her phone ringing behind the metal door. The only other logical place she might be was the dermatology clinic. I called Julie to see if they were working late for some reason. She was at home and said she last saw Lisa when she left the clinic around 5:00. I thought about phoning the offices but the answering machine would be on, meaning Lisa wouldn't pick up. The only thing left to do was go there myself.

Martin Goldstein was furious. He had learned about the patient in Houston who had committed suicide and assumed Karen Mahoney had as well. If Omega Pharmaceuticals had produced a defective product, her practice, and more importantly his reputation, would suffer. He had left three phone messages and two emails for Gary Page but had yet to hear back from him. Goldstein assumed the man was being evasive, making him all the more angry. Finally, he tracked down Jennifer Maddux who gave him Page's cell phone number.

"Why haven't you returned my phone calls?" Goldstein asked pointedly.

"I didn't realize you'd called, Martin," Page responded. "My secretary must have failed to give me the messages."

Being lied to didn't improve Goldstein's mood.

"Well, I did. What is going on with the patches? My understanding is that one of the test subjects killed herself."

This is just what I need, Page thought to himself. *One patient offs herself and the brainiacs come unglued. What a pansy.*

Page took a deep breath and tried to remind himself of the bigger picture.

"Well, Martin, as you mentioned, one of the patients did indeed commit suicide. Obviously, a full scale investigation is ongoing but from the preliminary information available, it doesn't appear the patches had anything to do with her demise. She was suffering from an acute episode of psychotic depression which began prior to her entry in the study. As you know, patients are required to complete a questionnaire to ferret out those with mental instability but it appears she wasn't completely forthcoming in her answers. We should know more in the next few days."

Page paused to take a long drag on his drink. Keeping his temper in check was becoming increasingly difficult, particularly when dealing with insectile personalities such as Goldstein's. Despite his efforts, his conciliatory attitude hadn't placated the good professor.

"So what?" Goldstein retorted angrily. "The press is going to have a field day with this unless you and Omega get out in front of it. Call a media conference. Emit a stream of press releases. Get some publicity firm to put a positive spin on things. Be pro-active, for goodness sake!"

Page's patience was at an end.

"Get a grip!" he yelled. "It's not like this is the end of the world. You are being lavishly compensated for your role in this project, so do your job and let me do mine! Omega's products, *all of them*, are safe and effective. We do not have a problem with the patches. In time, that will become abundantly clear. In the interim, chill out and keep focused on the end game."

Page hung up and cursed under his breath. If Goldstein was anxious enough to call and ream him out, it stood to reason others in the study were equally nervous.

Downstairs, in the lobby of the Omega Pharmaceuticals office building, Cliff Bolton had just taken his place behind a small bank of video monitors. It was his third week on the job as a night security officer and he had long since become bored with the position. Bolton had been unemployed for 3 months after being laid off from an auto body painting shop and while he was grateful to be working, he didn't like the night shift, preferring instead to be home in his trailer watching the Game Show channel and drinking beer.

Bolton worked for a private security firm who leased his services to companies throughout south Florida. He had been assured he would receive better hours as his seniority rose. There was a lot of turnover in this business and he now understood why. His supervisor said he'd probably be on nights for at no more than 6 months. Bolton believed he was deliberately underestimating the time frame.

After relieving the attendant on the preceding shift, he'd ticked off the checklist of required duties. It was the same as the night before and would be identical for each evening to come. He adjusted the monitors' brightness, poured himself a cup of coffee from his thermos and tuned in the Florida Panther's hockey game being played that night. They were hosting the Red Wings, a team almost certain to crush them.

It was early in the first period when a middle aged man walked through the front doors. He was dressed in a wrinkled brown suit, his tie loosened and his eyes bloodshot. The man looked worn out.

"Can I help you, sir?" Bolton asked.

"I need to speak with Mr. Page," he replied.

Bolton had been on the job long enough to know which visitors were out of place.

"Hold on a second."

Bolton scanned a sheet of paper on clipboard. There was no mention of an appointment or scheduled meeting.

"I don't show anything on Mr. Page's agenda."

"Oh, right," the man said, placing his briefcase atop the reception desk. He unsnapped the latches and lifted the lid. Inside was a small black object no larger than a package of cigarettes. He thrust it quickly towards the guard.

Caught completely by surprise, there was little Bolton could do. The visitor had placed a Black Cobra Gamma stun gun directly on his chest. Despite his thick uniform, the 600,000 volts easily penetrated into man's muscles. Temporarily paralyzed, the guard's mouth opened and intermittently spasmed as he tried unsuccessfully to scream. He slumped out of his chair onto the floor. His attacker bound his wrists and ankles with nylon twine and rolled him beneath the credenza.

At this time of day, visitors weren't likely but he checked the clipboard on the wall just in case. The guard had been truthful. Page would be alone for the evening.

I don't remember it ever taking me longer to walk from the back of the medical school, across Fannin Street and into the clinic building. While it couldn't have required more than 4 minutes, my legs felt like they were encased in iron. I was scared to death but the possibility that Lisa was in danger frightened me more.

Since the clinics resided on UT property, I considered involving the medical center police. However, I didn't know what they'd do in a truly hostile situation. From what I'd observed, when things became tense, they quickly called Houston PD. I decided against it for the time being. I had my cell phone with me. If I needed to, I'd call the Metro uniforms. The worst they could do is berate me for wasting their time.

The medical school's clinic building was an eight story affair originally constructed to office physicians practicing in Hermann Hospital. It had been refurbished in the late 1980's to provide space for outpatient oriented specialties including dermatology. Unnervingly, at this time of day, it was deserted.

I took the stairs to the 4th floor and gently nudged the door open. The hallway was empty and dark, illuminated only by the overhead exit signs. I could see light escaping from beneath the dermatology office door. Either someone was working late or the cleaning crew had failed to turn off the switch before leaving.

At the end of the hall was the office's private entrance. I removed the key from my pocket making sure the others didn't jingle together and slid it quietly into the lock. Holding my breath, I gripped the doorknob firmly and slowly turned it clockwise. After a few seconds, the latch disengaged. I could hear someone's voice coming from the back but couldn't make out what they were saying.

Convinced I hadn't been detected, I carefully opened the door and slithered into the hallway. The conversation continued as before, but occasionally in whispers. The sounds seemed to be coming from the treatment room, a large area in the center of the clinic used for surgery and cosmetic procedures. When I was about 5 feet from its doorway, I recognized the speaker. It was Galen Hart.

I was relieved. At least it wasn't a break-in by some low life looking for drugs. Remaining in the hall and eavesdropping on his conversation held a measure of appeal but I wasn't there to see him. I was looking for Lisa. Even though we'd had a rocky past, I assumed Hart would be considerate enough to tell me if he'd seen her.

I was about to stand up and knock on the door when he began speaking again.

"Rejection is something I've never been fond of. This pitiful program in general, and you in specific, should learn to be more appreciative when someone of my caliber comes along. You holy rollers get on my nerves. Your piety quickly wears thin."

Hart still had no audible partner in his conversation. Between sentences I could hear tearing sounds.

Lying on the floor, I stretched out until my eye was even with the space at the bottom of the door. From this vantage point, I couldn't see much more than Hart's feet shuffling around on the tile floor.

Hart disappeared from view but returned a few seconds later pushing one of the clinic lasers, maneuvering it next to the treatment table. After unwinding the power cord, he guided the plug into the wall socket and hit the "on" switch. It began emitting a soft, high pitched whine as the computer hardware sprung to life.

I could see the resident pressing on the machine's foot pedal. Bursts of light bounced around the room as Hart squeezed the trigger like a teenage boy playing an arcade game. The scene was interrupted when something hit the floor and began rolling toward me. It was a spool of duct tape. Instinctively, I backed away.

Hart cursed and began walking towards the door. He picked up the roll and returned to the table, apparently not having detected my presence.

The time for surveillance had passed. Rising to my feet, I straightened my shoulders and opened the door. What I saw chilled me instantly.

On the examining table lay Lisa, restrained with multiple bands of duct tape, including one strip across her mouth. She didn't appear to be moving and at first I thought she was dead.

Standing over her was Galen Hart, wearing space age looking sunglasses and holding the laser hand piece. When I saw Lisa's eyes were uncovered, I realized Hart's intentions. He was going to use the laser to blind her. Firing the device onto her unprotected retinas would fry them.

"What are you doing here?" Hart growled. "Shouldn't you be off somewhere holding a Bible study?"

I was terrified Hart would quickly place the handpiece over Lisa's eyes and begin engaging the laser. He pushed his foot down on the activating pedal but to my surprise turned towards me. A rapid succession of light flashes began bouncing around the room, most of them in my direction. As the treatment room took on the aura of a 70's disco bar, I secured my left hand firmly to my forehead, squinted my eyes and looked towards the floor.

Hart was tethered to the laser by the plastic cord and its handpiece. He couldn't maneuver much. But with my vision obscured, I couldn't see what he was doing either. He could be using the laser to distract me while getting a pistol for all I knew. Worse, at some point he might realize the futility of discharging the laser in my direction and return to his original objective, blinding Lisa.

"Not much fun being on the other side, is it?"

Hart seemed to be enjoying himself. Rationally, he should have known he couldn't complete his plan and get away with it. Even if he did manage to dispatch me and blind Lisa, there was too much evidence of his involvement. He would quickly become the prime suspect. The frightening part was he behaved as if he had nothing to lose. I didn't know what I could do to slow him down but I had been able to get under his skin in the past. If I could needle him again, I might be able to distract him long enough to subdue him.

"Forget our Prozac this morning, did we?" I asked. "You seem more psychotic than normal."

Hart took little notice. I knew he had heard me but whatever demons controlling his mind apparently weren't offended at questioning his sanity. He continued to fire away with the laser. I kept my eyes shielded and began slowly moving towards him.

"I don't recall anyone sending you an invitation for tonight's get together," Hart said. "Oh that's right. I almost forgot. You and Miss Pennington have some sort of romance blossoming."

"You know, after they cart you off to Shady Acres, maybe you can set up a dermatology spa on the grounds. Could be a real niche for you."

Hart scoffed but continued engaging the laser.

"I was on the fast track to setting up practice in Chicago until you and Star Bright here took it upon yourselves to ruin me. However, I'll persevere. We Harts always do."

"Thought about how you'll get out of here when you're done, Slick?" I asked as I shuffled forward. The flashes of light were bouncing all around the room. "But I guess you've been down that road before. The grocery store fiasco must have been a real learning experience."

The light flashes stopped.

"How do you know about that?!" Hart screamed.

I had hit a nerve. As long as his attention was directed towards me it wasn't on Lisa. Time to exploit my advantage.

"How did all that end again? Oh, yeah. The cops trotted some social worker down there and she convinced you it wasn't your fault. Strong work. Maybe you and daddy's lawyers can work a deal with the DA's office here in Houston? That is how it works with you trust fund pansies, isn't it?"

"I was sick! It **wasn't** my fault!"

"Oh, please. Very original. Something else made me do it. What was it Galen? Mommy living for her bottles of scotch? Drying out just long enough to cavort with the tennis pro? Daddy never at home? No one there to read you bedtime stories? Poor baby. I feel your pain."

Since the light flashes had stopped, I lifted my hand to assess the situation and spotted a brown blur coming towards my head. I tried to duck, but it was too late. A chemical bottle hit me just above my stitches and I staggered back a few steps. The impact opened my head wound which until then had been healing nicely. Dr. Robbins wouldn't like knowing all his careful suturing had been for naught. The bleeding began almost immediately. Within a few seconds I could feel the steady flow of warmth trickling down my forehead and onto the floor.

Hart seemed as surprised by the accuracy of his shot as I was. I had closed the distance between us, but Hart was still 15 feet away and reaching for the laser again. I wasn't close enough to charge him. My hand went back up to shield my eyes.

"Impressive throw, Galen. I bet you played sports in college, didn't you? Would that have been before or after you got back from Happy Hollow? The girls must have been all over you. Or was it the boys? Which did you decide on, by the way?"

Pay dirt. From beneath my palm I saw the laser handpiece fall to the floor.

Hart was emitting a primeval-like scream as he ran towards me. I pulled my hand away from my face at the last minute just before he put his shoulder into my chest and tried to wrap his arms around my torso.

The impact lifted me off my feet. When I returned to earth I had to back peddle to avoid losing my balance. It reminded me of the endless football drills we practiced when I was on the high school team.

I twisted to disrupt his equilibrium trying to gain an advantage. It worked. Hart's back slammed into the door frame. I could feel his breath leave his lungs in a burst. Propping him up with my left hand I gave him a few quick shots to the face opening his nose and giving him a cut under the left eye. He screamed like a girl but began thrashing his arms such that I couldn't pop him again.

The blood flow from my forehead had made the floor slippery. Traction became a problem. Hart managed to separate himself from my grasp but lost his balance when his foot hit a patch of blood. Seeing an advantage I closed in, grabbed his shirt and hit him a square shot in the nose. I could feel the cartilage and bone give way. He went down like a sack of potatoes and hit his head hard on the edge of a nearby countertop. Hart was breathing heavily but appeared to be unconscious or nearly so. I wasn't sure if our battle had come to an end but I took advantage of the break to check on Lisa.

Hart had done a credible job binding his captive. She had been secured to the examination table with more reams of duct tape than I could count. I would have to cut her free. Her mouth was taped shut but not her eyes. She appeared to be sleeping and I had no idea what kind of sedative Hart had given her. I removed the strip of tape from her mouth while calling out her name. After a few seconds and some light slaps to her cheeks, she began to come around.

"Lisa. Lisa!"

"Uuuhhhh . . ." was the only sound she made. Her head began to move slowly back and forth but her eyes remained closed.

"Can you hear me?"

"Yeah. I hear you," she replied in a whispered voice.

"Are you hurt anywhere?"

"I don't think so. Where am I?"

"You're in the dermatology clinic. Do you remember . . ."

I heard the thud of the blow and felt its impact on my ribcage before the pain registered with my brain. Hart had found a metal intravenous pole in the corner of the room and was bludgeoning me with it.

I moved away from Lisa and clutched my side cursing like a sailor. I assumed she would be willing forgive my language.

Hart pulled the metal pole back and swung it at me. This time, he aimed at my head. I ducked out of the way at the last second and rolled to my left. I had just regained my balance when Hart swung again. This one didn't have as much torque but it still stung when it smacked into my arm. Between the crazed look in his eyes and the blood streaking down his face, Hart looked like a character in a mad slasher movie.

"I know your kind," he said. "White trailer trash. Useful for little else aside from construction projects and military service."

He was brandishing the metal pole like a baseball bat and slowly moving in a circle around me. From what I could tell by feeling my arm and chest, I didn't think I had any broken bones.

"So what was the plan, Mary?" I asked. "Blind the girl?"

The longer I had him trying to think and hit me at the same time the better my chances were for getting the pole away from him.

Hart smiled. His teeth were various shades of red and pink. "Very perceptive."

Hart poked the end of the pole at me. I hadn't been expecting it and missed an opportunity to wrest it away from him.

"What did she ever do to you? Or was this just something your gimped out brain came up with between Star Wars conventions?"

Hart swung the pole half heartedly. I moved out of its way easily. He was testing me. Trying to ascertain how much damage his previous blows had inflicted.

"I tried to give her the benefit of my superior clinical experience," Hart replied. "Despite doing such pitiful work, she had no interest. I could have taught her quite a lot but eventually she told me my advice was no longer welcome."

"I would think you'd be used to rejection by now."

Hart and I continued circling around one another, his eyes rarely making contact with mine. He was looking for an opportunity to strike, the way a predator sizes up his quarry. I tried to stay in the center of the room, allowing me space to maneuver and keeping him away from Lisa.

Hart drew back his weapon and whipped it through the air so hard it made a whistling sound. He had placed his plant foot on a small patch of blood and his shifting weight produced a momentary loss of balance. There wouldn't be a better opportunity. I rushed him, grabbed the pole with my right hand and hit him as hard as I could with my left fist in the neck. Bulls eye. Right in the voicebox. He went to the ground clutching his throat and gasping for air. This time, I was taking no chances. I kicked him solidly in the ribs, the blow eliciting a cracking sound upon impact. With Hart out of action, I grabbed the roll of duct tape, tore off a few lengths and wrapped them tightly around his ankles. Moaning and cursing as best his voice would allow, I turned him over on his face, wrenched one arm free and then the other before binding his hands behind his back.

When I stood to admire my work, the pain in my ribs was excruciating. I returned to Lisa's side walking like the Hunchback of Notre Dame. She was still pretty out of it.

"Did you get him?" she asked sleepily.

"Yeah," I replied. "I got him. He's tied up on the floor."

Using a scalpel from a nearby drawer, I cut Lisa loose from her bindings.

"What did Hart give you?"

"He held a towel over my face with some funny smelling liquid on it."

"You mean like chloroform?"

"I guess so. Next thing I knew my head was spinning and I must have blacked out. Good thing you found me."

"When you didn't show at the restaurant, I knew something wasn't right."

"Our date!" Lisa said, her eyes fluttering open and adjusting to the light. "I suppose this means next time's on me."

CHAPTER 14

The man in Omega's offices was unaccustomed to espionage and looked it. He was more comfortable crunching numbers for a year end P & L statement than skulking around the halls of an office building. But he was here for a reason and after assaulting the guard in the lobby, there was no going back. When he came to the door in the stairwell with a large "5" on it, he pushed it open and walked into the hall.

The corridor was aglow from the banks of overhead fluorescent lighting. The man had only gone a short ways before Jennifer Maddux stepped into the hallway from the ladies bathroom. She was drying her hands with paper towels when she spotted the visitor ambling along the carpet.

Maddux approached him cautiously. It had been a day full of surprises and she didn't need any more.

"May I help you?" she asked.

"Oh, yes," the man answered without missing a beat.

The stun gun was out and on Maddux's chest before she could react. Her assailant quickly engaged the device which made an audible buzzing sound as it released the voltage into her body. Maddux's eyes opened widely and fluttered for a moment before she fell in a heap to the floor. The man returned the stun gun to his pocket and continued his search. Thirty seconds later, he found what he had been seeking.

Gary Page was lost in thought as he stared out the large picture window behind his desk. It had been one of the longest days he could recall since taking over the company and it couldn't be over soon enough. His soul searching was interrupted by the sound of his office door opening.

"Forget about it," Page growled without turning around. "Whatever it is, it will have to keep until tomorrow."

"I don't think so," the visitor said. "This is sort of important."

Page didn't recognize the voice but wasn't in the mood for insubordination. He whirled his chair 180 degrees to see a disheveled man standing in front of his now closed door.

"Who are you?"

"My name is Harold Rubin and I don't have an appointment."

"As I said before, whatever you're here for will have to wait."

Rubin chuckled softly and shook his head.

"Does the name Helen Rubin mean anything to you?"

"I'm not in the mood for guessing games."

"The woman in your patch study in Houston who killed herself? Her name was Helen Rubin and she was my wife."

"I see," Page said in a flat tone. "We were very sorry to learn of your loss. I trust you received the flowers we sent."

Page was lying. There had been no flowers. It might have been viewed as an admission of guilt and Colin Maitland had quashed the idea.

"No. No flowers or card. No one from your company attended her funeral. It was as if she never existed."

Page was becoming annoyed. He was at the end of a long, bad day and he had no energy left to hold some widower's hand. The man's wife had involved herself in a medical device study and things hadn't worked out. It happens. Deal with it and move on.

"I take it you never met my wife," Rubin said.

"No," Page responded impatiently. "Look, you'll need to make an appointment with my secretary . . ."

"I thought as much," Rubin interrupted. "Helen and I had three children. Our youngest died of leukemia 10 years ago. Time was when Helen couldn't stand doctor's offices. Too many bad memories. To be honest, I was thrilled she had worked through it enough to be a part of your research. Perhaps all that unpleasantness was behind her. But apparently not far enough."

Page stood to begin escorting his visitor towards the office door. It was late and the man was boring. He'd expressed his sympathies. What more did he want?

"This conversation's over," Page said. He placed his hand around the man's arm, nudging him forward.

"I don't think you've been listening to me," Rubin said. He retrieved the stun gun from his coat pocket, glanced at its settings and discharged it into Page's chest. The man screamed in pain as he collapsed on the floor. Rubin walked back to the office door and locked it. When he returned, his host was spitting profanities and struggling to sit up.

"Do I have your attention now?" Rubin asked.

"What do you want?" Page growled through gritted teeth.

"Your attention. I think I just mentioned that."

The muscles in Page's chest were going in and out of spasms. The voltage of the shock, although less than that given to the guard or Jennifer Maddux, was enough to provoke considerable pain.

"Fine! You have my attention!!"

"Good," Rubin said as he sat down on a nearby couch. "Gather your thoughts and then we'll get to work."

Page rolled around on the floor for a few more minutes, the torment in his muscles gradually subsiding. He lay almost motionless, his face an ashen color and dripping with sweat. As he tried to sit up, Rubin produced a small revolver from his briefcase and pointed it at his head. Page's eyes widened.

"Look, there's no need for bloodshed," he pleaded as he tried to push himself away on the carpet. "I'm sure we can come to some sort of arrangement."

"I agree. It involves money."

"Doesn't it always?" Page said with an air of relief. "How much were you thinking about? $50,000? $100,000? I can cut you a check tonight. Or we can go to the bank in the morning and get it in cash."

"It's not for me."

"It's not?"

"No, it's not."

"Who then?"

"Let's see," Rubin said, removing a small sheet of paper from his briefcase. "I've taken the liberty of jotting down some suggested charities and amounts. These are just rough figures, you understand. The Esther Project needs a new wing on their building. $100,000 should do. One of the YMCAs in the Bronx has a broken water pump on their outdoor pool. They need $60,000 to repair it. A Baptist church in Tucson is constructing a hospital in rural Honduras. For $250,000 they can construct an outfit complete with . . ."

"Are you out of your mind?!"

"Probably."

"And you're suggesting I fund all of these projects?" Page asked incredulously.

"Well, not suggesting."

"Cut to the chase. How much, all totaled."

"Let's see." Rubin said looking at the paper. "Three point six million dollars."

"Oh, is that all? Just 3.6 million. Why not make it an even 4?!"

"That can be arranged. I have a supplemental list of additional worthy causes."

Page's temper flared. With everything falling apart around him, the thought of being robbed in his own office galled him.

"Forget it! I'm not caving in to this extortion! If you think you can just march into my office, zap me with some laser thing . . ."

Rubin swung the barrel of the gun around and squeezed off a round. The bullet pierced the carpet six inches from Page's head who spontaneously recoiled in terror and began screaming.

"The next one won't miss," Rubin said calmly

"Allright!! Alright!!"

"Very wise of you. I knew we could reach an agreement. Since all of these institutions were kind enough to provide me with their bank account numbers so transferring the money should be easy. Let's get up off the floor . . ."

Rubin lifted the barrel of the gun several times indicating his directive for Page to stand up. The man did so reluctantly.

". . . and make our way to the computer."

Page shuffled slowly to his desk before slumping into his chair. Stalling wouldn't do him any good and he knew it. Although he was sure Rubin wasn't going to kill him, he knew he wouldn't have a problem wounding him.

With a few strokes of the computer keyboard, the funds flowed into the appropriate accounts. Rubin stood behind Page making certain things were done correctly, occasionally tapping the gun barrel on the back of the CEO's chair. The transactions took less than 30 minutes. When they were complete, Rubin walked back to the couch.

"Now, that wasn't too painful was it?" he said as he picked up his briefcase.

"Not for you," Page responded. "What makes you so certain I won't retrieve the money?"

"You won't."

"Why not?"

"Because it's not in your best interest."

Page laughed sarcastically. "Am I supposed to be afraid of you?"

"Of course not. I'm nothing more than a middle age bean counter. The only reason you cooperated tonight was because I surprised you."

"You got that right."

"This was a one time affair."

Page swallowed hard. "So I won't be hearing from you again?"

"Oh, you'll most definitely be hearing from me again," Rubin said calmly. "However, our future contacts will be via third parties. I'm betting Omega will begin a 'scorched earth' policy. At least, that's what I would do in your situation. Get rid of the evidence and try to finesse the feds. I don't know much about the FDA but I'm guessing you have your hooks into one or more of them so Omega should be able to come out on the winning side in this one."

Page was perplexed. If Rubin was so perceptive, why didn't he worry about recriminations? It didn't make sense.

"I always thought it was odd," Rubin continued, "that Omega wanted the patches returned and in their original boxes. Do you think all of them were inspected?"

"I assumed they were."

"Perhaps you should have made certain. Someone might have placed, say, a folded supermarket flyer in one and passed it off as returned materials. In so doing, they would be in possession of the original patches."

Page's face blanched. He opened his mouth to speak but couldn't form any words.

"Your silence speaks volumes. I have several patches. They're in safe, protected places with people watching over them. In the event something happens to me, these folks will retrieve the patches and, with much public fanfare, make certain they arrive in the hands of the nearest states attorney. As long as I'm doing passably well, the patches will never see the light of day. For your sake, let's hope I live a good, long time."

"You son of a . . ."

"As unusual as it may sound, I don't blame you for my wife's death," Rubin said pausing at Page's office door. "It wouldn't make sense for you to knowingly market a product that endangered the public's health. It's almost certain this whole matter was an unforeseeable mistake. However, you **are** the CEO of Omega and as such, you will be held to account for its actions. The coroner estimated it took my wife half an hour to bleed to death in a hospital room shower stall. Your bleeding will continue for much longer."

Page slumped back into his chair. He could see the writing on wall.

"I suppose I could go to the police," Rubin continued. "You might or might not be given jail time. But what good would that do? Helen would still be dead. No, you can benefit society much more by funding the charities I'll be contacting you about. I think my wife would be pleased."

EPILOGUE

Lillian Franklin

An oversight committee with the University of Texas Medical School at Houston reviewed Dr. Franklin's direction of the botulinum patch study. A letter of reprimand was issued citing, among other infractions, her "cavalier attitude towards day to day patient interaction and safety." A copy was also sent to the National Institutes of Health, the federal agency holding most of the paper on her research projects. None of her grants have been renewed.

Alfred Jennings

Following the collapse of the patch study, an internal audit of the dermatology department's finances was undertaken. While short of alleging embezzlement, the final report did suggest poor fiscal management by its chairman. Jennings resigned his chairmanship and retired. He currently lives in Ohio working part time in the dermatology practice of a former resident.

Galen Hart

Arrested and charged with aggravated kidnapping and assault, Hart's father arranged for his representation by a prominent Chicago criminal defense attorney. Eventually diagnosed as suffering from bipolar disorder, charges against him were dropped after he agreed to commit himself to indefinite inpatient therapy. He remains at an exclusive treatment center in Idaho with no set date for release.

Julie Bergstrom

Julie resigned her position with the dermatology department shortly after the Omega clinical trial closed. She was heavily recruited by other practices in south Texas wishing to expand their clinical research efforts. Despite receiving numerous lucrative offers, she undertook a 3 month sabbatical in rural Guatemala working with indigenous Indian tribes. She has yet to return.

Jennifer Maddux

Jennifer Maddux left Omega Pharmaceuticals two days following her attack. She returned to Houston and within a year had married a prominent cardiothoracic surgeon. Maddux currently works for a national company producing infomercials.

Lisa Penning

After an extended leave of absence, Lisa Penning finished medical school near the top of her graduating class. She obtained a dermatology residency at the University of Nebraska and upon its completion plans to remain on faculty there.

Justin Douglas

Lauded as a hero for his role in rescuing a fellow medical student, Douglas was pursued for television and print interviews. He spoke with the Houston Chronicle but quickly tired of the notoriety and refused all others. Fox Television proposed a made for TV movie version of his experiences however, Douglas declined. His application for residency in dermatology was well received and he was ultimately offered a position in Houston by the new chairman. His relationship with Lisa blossomed to the point where, at the Italian restaurant they were to have dined in the night she was abducted, he proposed marriage. His proposal was accepted.

Gary Page

Despite his best efforts, keeping the news of the tainted botulinum patches from public and federal scrutiny proved impossible. With only a fragmented paper trail in place, he managed to avoid incarceration but was forced to sell the patent on the product to a competitor. The funds kept Omega Pharmaceuticals solvent allowing it to continue manufacturing its chemotherapy products.

Harold Rubin

With the contaminated patch secure, Rubin returned to Houston. He never spoke with Gary Page or anyone at Omega Pharmaceuticals again. Two years later he became a grandfather and devotes his time to his extended family. He did not remarry.

Sean McMillan

Engulfed in a whirlwind of publicity surrounding the town and its livestock feed retailer, McMillan maintained a low profile and refused all requests for interviews. He did not participate in any of the ensuing product liability lawsuits and continues to ply his trade in the small town where he grew up.

Patrick Murphy

Murphy also remained unscathed by the litigation which ensued. Unlike Sean McMillan, he allowed a single interview with the London Daily Mirror. He was paid enough for his story to subsidize the upcoming potato crop. The next two years were successful allowing him to return to full time work on his land.

ABOUT THE AUTHOR

ALAN S. BOYD is Professor in the Departments of Dermatology and Pathology at Vanderbilt University Medical Center in Nashville, Tennessee.

www.ingramcontent.com/pod-product-compliance
Lightning Source LLC
Chambersburg PA
CBHW032221050726
47591CB00001B/212